James Aiello

JAMES AIELLO PRODUCTIONS, INC.

I0583347

# Forbidden Child
# II

## Secrets Revealed

**By: James Aiello**
**6/10/2015**

Cover Design: Graphic Art Designer, Leonardo Rabathaly
Cover Revised by: Graphic Art Designer, Tyler J. Gillespie

ISBN- 978-0-578-16533-2

James Aiello Productions, Inc.
Vero Beach, FL32962
CEO- James Aiello
Jimgil99@yahoo.com

# DEDICATION

This novel is dedicated to the memory of Michael James Gillespie 4/16/48-2/8/13 You will never be forgotten.

I also want to say thank you to some very special people who have touched my heart, my life and helped me to fulfilling my dream of being a world renowned author,

Frank Rossi
Roger Collins
Ken Carpenter
Michael Wilson
Tyler Gillespie
Charles Michael Gillespie

I love and thank you all, your friend, James Aiello

# CHAPTER 1

Like I said, it was just the beginning. My mind and body were totally numb when Michael and Jimmy, helped me walk out of that Las Vegas County Court room on June 27, 1989. As Michael pushed our way through the midst of the frantic pace of the police and emergency medical crews, all I could think of was Kathy and the horrible way she had just died. Then like a slap across the face, we walked right into the press with their cameras and a million questions, and I couldn't utter a word. But, as stunned as I was from my emotional trauma, when we reached the madness of the cheering crowds out in front of that courthouse, I still walked out a vindicated woman and a national hero. That afternoon I was on the front page of every newspaper in the world, and for the next two weeks I had top billing on every news broadcast in the country.

The headlines read, "***Christina Powers*, found innocent in the most dramatic court trial in history!**"

As for the response of my fans to my personal triumph and tragedy, it was overwhelming. Once again I received millions upon millions of cards and letters from all over the world, all sharing their love and support.

Within two days of the trial, I received requests from every single woman's association in existence, all asking me to address women's groups on how a woman can achieve corporate success in a man's world. I was also the main topic in every coffee shop, hair salon, gin mill, and grocery story in the nation. The court trial turned out to be a publicity agent's wet dream, as my record sales and requests for personal appearances soared. But, with the way I was feeling, I couldn't have cared less. I went into a state of depression immediately after Kathy Brown's funeral. The service was held three days after her death on June 30th in her hometown of Kittery, Maine.

You see, Kathy Brown's funeral turned out to be quite an emotional and awakening experience for me. It was 11:00am when I stood beside Barbara on a rainy Maine day at the cemetery where Kathy was being laid to rest, I found out her war with me ended many years ago, when she apologized to me after our fight.

As we stood there in the rain listening to the eulogy, Barbara inconspicuously turned to me and whispered, "Christina, I know you're here because of what happened in the courtroom, otherwise you wouldn't be here."

I thought for a moment about what Barbara had just said to me, looked at her honestly and said, "You're absolutely right; I have hated Kathy for sixteen years, but when she stood up in that courtroom and said what she did, I truly forgave her for all of it."

Barbara took my hand squeezed it and replied, "I'm glad to hear you say that Christina, because there is a lot more about Kathy you don't know."

I looked at her with questioning eyes as I said, "Now that came from out of the blue! So what are you trying to say?"

Barbara tilted her head even closer to mine and in almost a whisper, "Kathy never wanted you to know, but she was the one who kept saving your ass from Frank."

My eyes grew large as I said, "Why would she risk her neck like that for me, and not tell me about it?"

Barbara gave me a look of disbelief as she answered, "Come on Christina don't tell me you really don't know?"

I was baffled and annoyed by her response to my question and it showed on my face as I snapped at her in a tone just above a whisper, "I really don't know what you're talking about Barbara, so if you have something to say to me, then for God's sake girl, spit it out. I'm not up to your guessing games today."

She let go of my hand and sarcastically snapped her reply back as everyone was beginning to take notice of us, "For just one reason Christina, she didn't trust you any more than she ever really trusted Frank. You know, sometimes I can't believe someone as intelligent as you can be so dense." Her voice level went up an octave, "Christina, because I love you, I'm going to be honest with you. Don't you see over the years you have become just as vindictive as Frank was? So please, for your own good, wise up and start looking at how you have been treating people. Then reflect a moment on Frank and how he dealt with people, you may surprise yourself."

With that, Barbara turned to walk away and just as she did, Kathy's Mother caught us both off guard by appearing right in front of us. She just stood there for a moment looking at us both with disgust in her eyes. She cleared her cracking voice until she could finally say, "What kind of people are you two, arguing at my daughter's funeral? Don't either one of you have any respect for the dead at all?" At that she placed her hands to her face and began to cry. With compassion, I reached out for her and with all her might she slapped me right across the face and said, "You are just as evil as Reverend Timmy Swinebert says you are. Now take your wickedness with you and let my daughter rest in peace. Because I rebuke you! You demon from hell!" Then she began crying hysterically.

I stood there stunned, looking at her for a moment. Then I held my head up high as I turned, and trampled through the mud past Kathy's angry and grieving family. When I reached the limo, I climbed in and said as I started to cry, "James, get me the hell out of here!"

On the road back home I was wishing Michael had come with me. I had decided I wanted to attend the funeral alone, so I asked Michael not to come. I also told him, I wanted to take the ride by myself, but he insisted James take me in the limo. After my encounters with Barbara and Mrs. Brown, I was glad he did, because there was no way I would have been able to drive back home. I was feeling so miserable after the two good blows I had just taken to my self-esteem that I would have never made it, and my tears showed it.

As we headed west on the Massachusetts Turnpike, I was reliving the drama which took place at Kathy's funeral, over and over again in my mind. I wondered to myself, if I was as bad as they seemed to think I was. With these thoughts racing through my mind, I brought down the partition between James who was driving, and myself in the back seat. When the partition was completely down, I said, "James, may I ask you something?"

James gazed at me through the rearview mirror and said, "Of course, Christina."

I looked into his eyes through the mirror and with a sincere tone asked, "James, what do you think of me as a person?"

James smiled warmly, "Christina, I think you're the most incredible person I have ever met. That's what I think about you as a person."

I managed half a smile, "Thank you James, but I sure don't feel incredible, I feel like a horrible person right now."

With a sympathetic tone he replied, "Christina, I saw and heard what Mrs. Brown did and said to you, so I do understand why you are feeling like you do, but it's not true. I have known you for a long time now Christina, and all I can say is Carman and I love you. There happens to be a reason for that, and it has nothing to do with the overwhelming salary you pay us either." He shook his head as if to say, 'you should know this', "Christina, it's because of who you are as a person, and how you treat us as people. I guess what I'm trying to say is, you're real Christina. Carman and I have worked for other important people before, but not one of them was ever genuine. Not one ever truly cared how either one of us might be feeling from day to day. But not you, you treat us like family, not like servants. If there was ever any one person who I believed deserved to be treated like royalty, it's you. But instead, you treat us with the kind of respect there should be between a child and a parent, and we love you like one of our own daughters because of it."

My eyes began to tear from James' kind words, "Thank you again James, I only wish I felt the same about myself." My tears began to roll off my cheeks as I added, "Right now, I feel like the kind of person who just caused the **'deaths of three people'**. James, may God forgive me, because I have allowed my desire for revenge to take over my every thought, until I not only destroyed Frank financially, but I took his life as well. I chose to build my life around my desire to have revenge on Frank, and what did it get me? Nothing but sixteen pain fought years, which ended up with just another trip to a cemetery, because I refused to forgive. James, how can I take pride in achieving something which no one will even care about, because none of it matters anymore?"

James handed me a tissue, "Christina, the whole world has stood up and taken notice to what you have accomplished in the past sixteen years, and believe me, it does matter to every person whose life has been touched by the good you've done. So please stop condemning yourself for something you had no control over, and let yourself live again."

I used the tissue when James finished speaking and said, "I only wish it were that simple James, but it's not. Somehow I am going to have to find a way to make up for all the hurt I've caused or I will never get past this moment in time."

With a reassuring tone James replied, "Christina, I don't know how to help you, but I do know you will come through this tragedy just as you have in the past."

Sincerely I said, "James, thank you for answering my question, now if you'll excuse me, I think I'll rest until we arrive home." Then I closed the partition along with my weary eyes.

It was 4:10pm and still raining when we pulled into the underground garage of our home on the grounds of the Corporate Headquarters of Powers Incorporated. As soon as I entered the house, I called Michael who was at the office and told him I was home. I explained to him some of what transpired at the funeral, and mentioned I was going to try to keep my 5:00pm appointment with my new gynecologist, a Doctor Steven Hart. His office was in Poughkeepsie, so I had to run, but I'd tell him more later that evening. When we finished our conversation, I grabbed the keys to Jimmy's favorite white 1987 town-car, and left for my doctor's appointment.

I inconspicuously entered Doctor Hart's reception room and signed in. When the receptionist read my name, she immediately took me to Steven's private office and told me the doctor would be in shortly. As soon as Doctor Hart entered the room, he reached out his hand to shake mine, and as I stood up from my seat he said, "Christina, it's so good to see you again. I've received your records from Doctor Sonne yesterday and I went over them all last night. So let's sit for a minute and I'll tell you what I know."

As we sat down, I said, "Steven, all I really want to know is what I can do to become pregnant again?"

He lifted his eyebrows discontentedly and said, "Christina, from what I could see from your files and from what Doctor Sonne has told me personally, I don't think you will ever be able to conceive a child again." I knew he could see from the expression on my face I was not pleased. Then he slapped his hands together and added, "But I won't know for sure, until I look myself. So why don't we do the examination first, then we'll talk more."

I tried to smile as I said, "Oh well! At least that gives me something to hope for."

After the examination Steven said, "Christina, I must be up front with you. From what I could see, I would recommend a hysterectomy as soon as possible, just to make sure you don't accidentally become impregnated. Your uterus is so fragile; it would be life threatening for you to try to carry a full term pregnancy. It would tear your uterus apart. So until you decide when to have the surgery, I'm putting you on oral contraceptives and I want you to take them."

With that cheerful news, I took a deep breath and said with utter frustration, "Oh well! I guess that's that, then. There will be no more children for *Christina Powers*. It looks like Frank will indeed have the last laugh."

Steven looked at me strangely then said, "This doesn't mean you will never be able to have a child again Christina, there is still adoption."

Sadly I stood up and said, "Thank you Steven, I know you're right. I'm just not having a very good day today, so I think I'll go home for now and figure this one out tomorrow." I shook his hand and left his office with my heart breaking again.

After dinner that evening Michael, Jimmy, and I, went out on the back porch with our cocktails to watch the rain splashing on the surface of the river. As the three of us sat on lawn chairs watching the rain, I was sitting between the two of them, and sadly began to tell them what happened at Kathy's funeral. In an even sadder voice, I told them what Doctor Hart had said. Then with tears in my eyes, I looked at Michael and added, "Michael, I will never be able to bear your child."

Michael reached over and took my hand, "I love you Punkie, and I can live without having a child of my own. Why don't we try to adopt?"

I squeezed his hand as I sadly answered, "I know we can adopt, but that's not the point. I wanted to give you a child from your seed."

Jimmy took my other hand and said, "If you really want Michael's biological child that badly, then why don't you look into finding a surrogate mother?"

As soon as Jimmy finished talking, Carman came out onto the porch with the cordless phone and said, "Excuse me Christina, but Barbara is on the line for you. Would you like to speak to her?"

I reached for the phone, "Yes I would, thank you, Carman." Carman handed me the phone and left as I said, "Hi Barbara, how are you?"

"Not too good Christina," she replied. "But, I still wanted to call you and tell you I'm very sorry for what I said to you this morning."

I brushed my hand through my hair and said with concern, "Barbara, I forgive you and I'm also sorry, but as for my reaction it was because I was shocked. You came out of nowhere this morning and I had no idea what you were talking about. Why in the world would you pick Kathy's funeral to start telling me how she helped me?"

I could hear Barbara's voice begin to breakup, "Christina, what you don't know is that I've been in a lot of pain since Kathy's death. Although you and I have been the best of friends for years' now, I have not been totally honest with you about myself." Starting to cry harder she continued, "You see Christina, Kathy and I had been secret lovers since the night you took Tony away from her at the Governor's Ball in Hawaii. So I not only lost my best friend, I lost my lover too."

I could feel her pain and my heart went out for her as I spoke with compassion, "Oh God! Barbara, I'm so sorry. Why didn't you tell me? You could have trusted me Barbara. You should have known that."

Quickly she replied, "I know Christina, but I was honoring Kathy's wishes. You must be able to understand that?"

Sympathetically I answered, "I do understand Barbara, and once again I'm sorry, girlfriend. I only wish I'd known."

She stopped crying and said, "I'm sorry I never told you Christina, but I wanted to tell you before I leave the states tomorrow."

With a surprised tone I replied, "I didn't know you were leaving the country. Where are you going?"

Sadly she answered, "I'm heading for Israel in the morning to begin shooting the new screenplay Kathy and I wrote together."

With curiosity I asked, "Where are you now, Barbara?"

"I'm at my Manhattan penthouse. I'm leaving from Kennedy at 11:00am. So I think I'll say goodbye for now Christina, because I'm really beat."

Not knowing what to say, I simply replied, "All right girlfriend, take care of yourself and remember I love you."

"I love you too Christina, goodbye." She replied with a saddened tone.

When I hung up the phone, I thought to myself, 'I wish I could be there for her right now, I think she could use my company.'

I was in that state of mind for about a minute before Michael snapped me out of it by saying, "What's going on Christina, is Barbara all right?"

I placed the phone on my lap and answered, "She is still very upset over Kathy's death. I didn't know it, but they were best friends."

Michael leaned over, kissed my cheek and said, "Come on Punkie, let's go to bed."

He stood up, took my hand, and pulled my tired body out of the chair. We both said good night to Jimmy and headed for our bedroom. When we entered the bedroom, we undressed and climbed right into bed together. I was really very tired and not feeling romantic at all when Michael kissed my cheek, and gently began to stroke my nude body with his strong right hand. As he began to stir my passion, I stopped him, "Michael, honey, I really don't feel up to making love tonight."

He kissed me tenderly, "I understand, Punkie. Why don't we look at the calendar, and set a new date before we go to sleep?"

I looked at him strangely, "What date are you talking about?"

He lifted his eyebrows like, 'Duh' and said, "What date! Our wedding date! Remember? We missed it, you were in prison."

I shook my head in disbelief and replied, "Oh God! Honey, I can't think about a wedding date now. I just lived through hell, came out of it to discover I can't even have your child, and you want me to start smiling and plan a happy wedding. Well I can't work like that Michael, I need to sort through my feeling's some first. Then maybe we can reset our date, so please don't start with me about it okay."

His face showed his surprise at my statement as he said, "I didn't mean to upset you, Christina. All I wanted to do was get you thinking about something pleasant. But it sounds like I may have made a bigger mistake than I thought when I heard you say, 'maybe we can reset the date'." Then he turned his back to me and flicked off the light. I immediately flicked on my reading light, hopped out of the bed and began to get dressed.

Michael quickly turned back toward me and asked, "What are you putting your clothes on for?"

I turned to him and with anger in my voice, "You know what Michael, I can't handle this bullshit right now, so I'm going for a ride."

Michael hopped out of the bed, "Going out! It's 11:00pm and its pouring out there, and you think you're going for a ride?"

I looked at him as I tied my sneaker, "Michael, I don't think I'm going for a ride, I'm going for a ride."

Michael began to slip on his pants as he said, "Well, I don't want you going for a ride."

I finished tying my other sneaker, stood up and said, "Right now Michael, I don't care if you want me going for a ride or not. I'm going for a ride anyway. I love you Michael, but you're really pissing me off right now. Just who do you think you are, my boss? Well, I think it's time you get off your power trip, because you're trying to run my every move, and I'm getting sick of it." Then I headed out of the room with Michael in hot pursuit.

When I reached the garage door, Michael grabbed my hand, "Christina, please I'm telling you not to go out there as angry as you are, and leave me here alone to worry about you."

I pulled my hand out of his and sharply said, "Michael, don't do this to me. Don't tell me what to do, because I'm going for a ride for my own mental well-being so now please excuse me." Then I walked back to Jimmy's Towncar, and drove away.

Ten minutes after leaving the house, I found myself on Route 87, heading south toward Manhattan. When I reached the Harriman exit, I picked up the car phone and dialed our private bedroom number.

Michael picked the phone up on the first ring and anxiously said, "Christina, are you alright!?"

"No not really Michael. I've calmed down some and I just wanted to say I love you." I started to cry as I added, "Michael, I'm just feeling really bad right now. I didn't mean all those things I said, I was just taking my frustrations out on you baby, that's all, and I'm sorry."

Tenderly he replied, "Don't cry Punkie, I love you too.  Where are you?"

"I'm on the Thruway heading south."

"Why don't you come home Punkie, and let me hold you," he answered anxiously. "I feel so empty without you being here, and I miss the hell out of you already."

"Michael, I miss you too, but I want to go spend a few hours with Barbara before she leaves tomorrow.  So I'll see you in the morning all right?"

Sadly he replied, "Okay Punkie, if that's what you want.  I love you and I'll see you tomorrow, just drive carefully."

"I will, and I love you too, Michael."  Then I broke the connection with Michael, and dialed Barbara's private number.

## CHAPTER 2

She picked up on the tenth ring and sounded slightly incoherent when she said, "Hiii, who a, who is thisss?"

I answered with concern, "It's me Barbara, Christina. Why are you slurring your words?"

"I'm, I'm a little tired Christina, that's all. What *a a a*, time *isss* it anyway?"

"It's midnight and I'll be pulling into your parking garage in two minutes. So wake up and call the security office, and tell them to let me in. Then put on some coffee and I'll see you in ten minutes." I waited a few seconds for a response from Barbara, but none came so I shouted, "Barbara! Can you hear me?"

A groggy voice answered, "Yes, I hear you." Then she hung up the phone.

When I pulled into the garage of her building, I drove up to the security guard at the gate and said with a smile, "Hi, I'm Barbara's guest, and I'm hoping she just called to inform you to expect me?"

He smiled back, "Yes Ms. Powers, she just called. You can leave your car here and we'll park it for you."

When Barbara finally answered the door, she reeked of alcohol and looked like hell. I walked in past her as she held onto the door for balance. I grabbed her, held her up with one hand, and closed the door with the other. I hugged her and with compassion said, "I know girlfriend, losing someone you love is the worst hurt in the world."

I walked her toward the kitchen, turned on the dim stove light and sat her on a chair at the table. Barbara sat there with her head buried in her curled up arms on the kitchen table, as I proceeded to put on a pot of coffee. As the coffee brewed, I took a seat beside Barbara, gently rubbed her back and said, "What did you mix with the booze, Barbara?"

She rolled her head toward me, "I've been snorting coke and gulping gin since 2:00pm this afternoon, and I feel like I'm dying."

I chuckled, "Well, you look like you're not far from it. So we're going to pump you up with some coffee and have a heart to heart chat."

I got up and fixed us both the first of many cups of coffee that night. We talked about our lives, our loves and where we hoped our futures would go. Then I'll never forget it, it was around 1:15am when Barbara grabbed my hand and said, "Christina I have something of yours and I need to talk to you about it." Then she got up and went into her bedroom. When she returned she had an envelope in her hand, handed it to me and said, "I have had this for years, but I could not give it to you until now. Your real mother gave this to me two weeks before her death. I knew your real mother and father. Your mother was my best friend. When she gave me this envelope she said, "If anything should ever happen to me, please look out for my sweet little angel. And don't give this to her until you know she will be safe.'

I opened the envelope and inside was the original copy of my birth certificate. It read, "Mother: Norma Jean Montensel. Father: John Fitzgerald Kenny. Child: Christina Kenny." I was shocked as I read it and thought, 'Oh my God! It's true! I am her daughter and he is my father!' Then I got angry and asked, "Why did you take so long to tell me this!?"

She took my hand softly, "Baby, your mother asked me not to tell you until I thought you'd be safe with this information."

I pulled my hand from hers angrily, "Why would she leave me with someone like Frank?"

Barbara Replied swiftly, "She left you with Frank because she was being watched by the FBI from the moment she first met your father. When you were born, she was afraid that if the Kenny family discovered that you were John's child they would have made you disappear. When your mother gave me this envelope I didn't even know you existed. Marilyn told me that in 1953 when you were born Frank was her best friend and she trusted him. At that time she knew he was the only one who had the power to keep you safe from the Kenny family. Christina, I was afraid to give this to you as long as Frank was alive. Your mother told me that after she sang happy birthday to your father on national TV, Frank became furious with her. When she returned to Frank's to see you, he asked her to marry him. When she refused, she told him that she was taking you and starting a new life. She told me that Frank went crazy as soon as she said it and wrapped his hands around her throat and nearly choked the life from her. When she came to, Frank told her she would never see you again if she refused to marry him. She escaped from his grasp and ran away from him as fast as she could. That's when she came to me. That's when she gave me this envelope and left and I never saw your mother alive again after that night. What she did Christina was save your life." Then she took my hand and added, "Look in the envelope again."

I started to tremble as I noticed a hand written note with a photo of Marylyn Monrow and myself as a small child smiling at a child's tea party. I could hardly breathe as I opened the note and began to read my mother's words,

*"My beautiful Christina, I instructed Barbara, my longtime friend, to give you this letter in the event of my death. You see my darling daughter, I am your real mother and have spent all these many years watching you grow up, but afraid to approach you for fear that your father and his family would endanger your safety in some way. I met your Dad at a dinner party and we were immediately attracted to one another. In time we began a secret affair because your father was already married. He led me to believe he would leave the marriage for me. Only we discovered that his family and his father's political ambitions for your dad would not permit that to happen. I had just discovered that I was carrying you, when your father stated that we could never be together and our affair would have to remain a secret, he said, "The world can never know." At that moment, I became afraid to tell him about you. You see your father was a United States Senator and came from a very rich and powerful family. I knew they were capable of taking any action to protect their son's political aspirations and I had to keep you safe.*

*I know the world will say that I was just another dumb blonde sex-symbol, but I am far from that my sweet Christina. I didn't tell anyone that you were born because I was afraid for your safety. That is why I asked Frank to raise you. I turned to Frank who was my friend because he was rich and powerful. I entrusted him with you swearing him to secrecy. I knew that he could protect you and also give you a beautiful home with anything that you wanted until I could come and take you away with me. Then, your dad ran for the office of President of the United States and won. All those years I never stopped loving him and when he became President, I knew I could never tell him about you or how much I still loved him. Even though I married several times, no one replaced him in my heart. When I finally reestablished a relationship with your dad, I thought he was going to walk away from everything for me; only I discovered that was not true. It was then that the FBI began to watch my every move and I became even more paranoid about your safety. When I turned to Frank he betrayed me and I learned that he was more interested in having me as his trophy wife then being your surrogate father. When he proposed to me I was horrified and refused him. He became very angry and tried to hurt me. I ran from his house and was more determined than ever to make enough money with my next movie, so you and I could just disappear. Once again, I learned the hard way that the only person I could depend on was myself. All those people in my life who I thought really loved me, did not. They would leave me like my dad or were unable to love me like my mother who was sick and all the rest just used me.*

*I want you to know a little about me. All I ever really longed for was to be loved and wanted. I never knew my dad, and my mom was too sick to take care of me. I went from foster home to foster home until one day my mom came back for me. We were happy in our own little house, only not for long, because mom was once again hospitalized. I ended up in an orphanage until a couple came and brought me to live with them. They were very strict and mean to me. Many nights I cried myself to sleep, because I just wanted my mom back.*

*If you are reading this letter my sweet darling, then you know that something terrible has happened to me. I may not be able to tell you what, but I can tell you why. I am a threat not only to the Kenney family whose son is your father and the United States President, but now to Frank as well, who continues to harbor a great deal of resentment toward me, for refusing his marriage proposal.*

*Please know my beautiful baby girl, that you have always been the most important thing in my life. I love you with all my heart and soul. I know in my heart, that if you had the opportunity to know me, you would love me just as much as I love you. Not a moment has gone by without my wondering what you are thinking and doing. I have lots of photos of you growing up and I keep them in a secret place. Every night I take them all out and study each one carefully. I know every hair on your head, your laughing eyes, your little adorable nose and those beautiful little pink lips. How I long to hold you, how I long to kiss you, how I long to show you how much I love you. No matter what happens to me, please know that I never stopped loving you and will always be with you. I pray for you to have a far better life than I had; wherein, people will love, adore and shower you with tons of attention. One more thing my sweet angel, I beseech you not to ever reveal to the world whose daughter you really are. I fear they will come after you as well. Good bye my sweet darling,*

*All my love, your Mommy"*

In total shock I looked into Barbra's tear filled eyes and with my heart pounding said, "That bastard Frank stole everything from my mother and from me!" I started to cry, "He stole me from my mother and my beautiful Joy from me; and now I'm being told I will never have a baby again! He kept me from my Johnny as the Kenny family withheld their Johnny from my mother! May God forgive me, but I am glad I was the one who finally stopped that evil monster! My mom was right, the world's perception of my mother was indeed that of a dumb blond sex symbol, but she was actually one of the most incredible women to have ever lived. I finally know the truth and I'm proud to be her daughter." I grabbed Barbara's hand, "Thank you Barbara, I finally understand myself, because I am so much like my mother. I now know there is truly a higher purpose for my life and I am more determined than ever to fulfill my destiny whatever that may be."

Barbara took me in her arms and we cried together until there were no more tears to shed. Exhausted and emotionally drained, we finally headed for bed around 4:00am that morning. I helped Barbara into her bedroom, switched off the light, kissed her forehead and said, "Now, let's try to get some real sleep and I'll wake you up around 9:00am, okay?"

She grabbed my hand and sadly said, "Christina, please lay with me? I don't want to lay here alone to night."

Lovingly I looked into her sad tearing eyes, "Sure move over."

I climbed into the bed, put my arm around her, and beckoned her to lay her head on my shoulder. As she did, she kissed my cheek and as she softly snuggled up to me she said, "Thank you Christina, you really are my best friend and I love you." Then she passed out. Even with everything I just discovered, I don't think it was five minutes later that I passed out and we fell asleep in each other's arms.

I think it was the sound of the rain hitting the patio doors which made me stir, and when I opened my eyes I shouted, "Oh shit! Barbara, wake up! It's 10:00am!" We both flew out of the bed and I said, "Go shower quick and I'll call your driver and have him come pick up the bags."

All at once Barbara shouted, "Oh shit!" as she stubbed her toe on the dresser and began to jump up and down shouting, "Ouch that hurts! Fuck me! What a way to wake up!" She hopped toward the bathroom and said as I laughed at her, "Stop fucking laughing you asshole and make me a cup of coffee to go, would you please?"

I shouted back, "Sure, sure, you're just like a man! Sleep with them once and they think they can start telling you what to do."

As soon as the coffee started to perk, I called Barbara's driver and had him come up and take down her luggage. I called Michael at the office. His secretary answered and told me he left at 9:45am. I tried him at home and the answering machine picked up. Then I tried his car phone and I heard Michael say, "Hello!"

When he answered the phone, I said, "Hi, honey it's me. Where are you?"

"Hi Punkie, since I didn't hear from you I thought I'd take the day off too, so I'm on my way to my Mother's. Where are you?"

"I'm still at Barbara's, but I'll be heading home in about an hour. What time do you think you'll be home?"

He hesitated for a moment, "I'm not sure Christina. I think I need some time to put my thoughts together before I see you. I have been thinking all night about the things you said last night, and if you resent my right as your lover to have a say in what you decide to do, then I think we may be coming to an impasse in our relationship. Christina, if we get married then we are saying we belong to one another. What that means to me is you and I are one, so I can't and won't do anything without considering you first. I'm feeling marriage and oneness doesn't have the same meaning to you as it does to me, and I don't think I can live with the way you think it should be."

With that I took a deep breath and said, "Michael, if you think my marrying you means I must surrender my free will to your approval, then you're right, we do have a problem. Because I'll tell you right now, you're talking to *Christina Powers* and if you can't see by now that I don't do anything for anyone unless I want to, then you will never truly understand me. Michael, no matter how much I love you, no one, not even you, will tell me, what to do! So maybe we both need to rethink this relationship."

With a surprised and saddened tone he said, "That sounds like a good idea to me, so let's meet at home around dinner and we'll talk."

With a disgusted tone I said, "That's if I come home! Goodbye, Michael."

I heard him yell, "Christina, wait! Don't hang up! What do you mean, if you come home? Aren't you coming home?"

Sarcastically I answered, "Well you sound like you need some time, so I'm giving it to you."

Then for the first time since I met him, Michael raised his voice to me, "If you don't come home to me tonight, then I won't be there tomorrow."

All I heard at that moment was the pitch of his voice and I shouted, "Don't you ever use that tone on me. Oh shit! Forget it! I have to go now Michael, goodbye." I hung up the phone, poured myself a cup of coffee, sat at the kitchen table and started to quietly cry as I thought, 'What the fuck is it all about, and why do I bother trying anyway?'

As I sat there crying, Barbara came running into the kitchen shouting, "Where's my coffee, girlfriend?" When she realized I was crying, she came to me, put her hands on my back, nestled her head next to mine and said, "Christina, what's the matter?"

I turned to hug her and said, "I think Michael and I may have just broken up."

She looked at me as if to say 'what are you crazy' and exclaimed, "Come on, the two of you are made for each other. I don't know what the problem is, nor do I have the time to find out." She kissed my cheek and added, "Go to him and straighten it out whatever it is. Don't lose this one, Christina. Michael is a good man and he loves you. Now I have to go, so just lock up when you leave and I'll call you as soon as I can." She grabbed herself a mug of coffee, kissed me goodbye, and as she ran out the door she shouted, "Next time we have to do dinner, girlfriend!" Then she was gone.

After Barbara left, I sat there thinking over what she had just said about Michael. I was trying to prioritize my life in my mind and I realized Barbara was right about Michael. So I got up, walked over to the sink, rinsed my cup, grabbed my purse off the table and headed out the door.

Once I hit the car, I climbed in and I was on my way home. When I pulled out of the garage the rain slowly stopped and the sun was beginning to peek through the clouds. By the time I reached the Thruway, the sun had broken through the clouds in several places in the sky. Its beautiful golden rays were painting the sky over the mountains on the horizon ten different glorious shades of blue and pink. The sight of it was breathtaking, and it somehow helped me realize my going home to Michael was the right thing to do. The closer I got to the Poughkeepsie exit, the more my heart began to pound with the anticipation of a school girl with just the thought of seeing him.

From out of the blue, I had a flash back and my emotions were filled with fear as I thought to myself, 'Oh my, God! I feel the exact same desperate feelings I felt the night I went racing to Johnny's home and found him in bed with Kathy.' I really started to sweat as I put my foot to the floor with the gas pedal under it and all I could think was, 'Would Michael do that to me? Would he cheat on me?' I shook my head and thought, 'No! Don't play this game with yourself Christina. I will choose to believe Michael's love is still stronger than that. If I can't trust him, then we don't have anything and I need to trust him.' So I let up on the gas and continued home at a legal speed.

It was 2:15pm when I pulled into our garage and I almost started to cry when I didn't see Michael's car. I parked and ran into the house hoping to find a note or a message, but there was neither. I began to pace the floor for a few minutes, until I thought of Tess. I headed for my address book and dialed Michael's mother's number. I let the phone ring twenty times before I decided no one was home. Then I thought of Michael's townhouse in Poughkeepsie and I began to dial the number. When the answering machine picked up, I started to cry as I said, "Michael, I know I'm a stubborn fool sometimes, but honey, I love you. Please if you're there, pick up and tell me you still love me. Please Michael, it's you I adore baby. You're the one I live for Michael, and I forgot that baby." I got so scared I lost him that I started to sob, "Please I'm begging you Michael, pick up the phone baby, I can't live without you."

I started crying so hard I couldn't speak and I heard, "I love you too, Punkie." I turned around and leaped into Michael's open arms.

He held me as I cried, and with tears filling his eyes he said, "Oh, baby! I'm sorry I hurt you. I love you more than life itself and I will never chase you away from me again." He picked me up, carried me into the bedroom, and proceeded to gently take me to heaven in a whirlwind of love, fire, and passion.

After our lovemaking I gently said, "Michael, I know how strong willed I can be, so I'll try my best to learn to be completely open minded to whatever you say in the future." I kissed his lips, looked at him cross eyed, and added, "Oh yes, by the way Michael, I also want to get married and bare your child more than anything in this world."

He laughed at the face I was making, kissed my nose and said, "Punkie, I love you, and I want that just as much as you do, but you know what the doctor said. How can you still want to have my child?"

I looked seriously into his eyes, "Honey, we can do what Jimmy said. I'm sure there must be some decent woman out there who would bare our child for us."

His eyes opened wide as he replied, "You mean a surrogate mother?"

"Yes!" I answered with excitement.

"But if we do that, then the child will only be mine biologically, and I would rather adopt than to have a child that you're not the biological mother of."

Kissing him all over his face I said, "I love you honey, and that is exactly what I'm talking about. I have read where doctors at U.C.L.A. have taken the egg from one woman, fertilized it, and implanted it in the womb of another woman. So don't you see? The child would still be biologically ours. I can call Tom Davies tomorrow and talk to him about finding a suitable surrogate for us, if you agree?"

Michael's eyes lit up, "Well let's do it!" He kissed me again, "Why don't we go out for dinner tonight to celebrate? We can invite Jimmy to come with us if you like?"

"That sounds great to me honey, but I have got to hop in the shower before I go anywhere."

Michael kissed me again, "Okay, I'll see if Jimmy's home yet, while you get ready." Then I headed for the bathroom, as Michael headed for Jimmy's room.

# CHAPTER 3

Over our seafood dinner at a quaint Country Inn called the Lobster Pond, in Wallkill, New York, we told Jimmy of our decision to have a child.

As we talked, a little girl no older than ten came up to our table and said, "Excuse me, but are you *Christina Powers*?"

I smiled and answered, "Yes I am, can I help you?"

Her eyes lit up as she smiled at me, turned to her parents and said, "I told you it was her." She turned back toward me and asked, "May I have your autograph?"

I smiled at her, as I pulled a 5-x 7 photo of myself out of my purse, signed it and said, "What's your name, sweety?"

"Kathy," she answered.

Still smiling warmly I said, "Then I will write 'To Kathy, Love *Christina Powers!*' You know what Kathy; you're the first person to recognize me in public, in more than ten years. How did you know it was me?"

She gave me a great big smile and said, "Your smile." Then she thanked me and left. Not two minutes later, I was saying 'hi' to everyone in this small country restaurant and before we knew it, we were in the middle of a family style dinner. Everyone in the place began talking to one another as if we all knew each other for years, and it turned out to be a delightful dining experience. The place is right off Route 44/55, if you're in the neighborhood stop by, you'll love it. Tell them I sent you.

As Michael drove us home that night, I thought of the little girl at the restaurant named Kathy. Then I realized how much she reminded me of Kathy Brown and I thought, 'Kathy, wherever you are I want to thank you for saving my life. I'll never forget the lesson you taught me on forgiveness.'

I was deep in my thoughts when Jimmy brought me back to the living, by saying, "I didn't have the chance to say it in the restaurant, but I'm really very happy the two of you have decided to find a surrogate. I think it's a wonderful idea, and I can't wait to have a baby around again." He began to rub my shoulders from behind me in the backseat and continued, "I also have some news of my own. I met someone about three months ago and we have fallen in love."

I turned around in my seat, hugged him and smiled as I exclaimed, "Finally! Jimmy! I thought you gave up on love. Who is he?"

He kissed my cheek and said in a way I once heard a long time ago, when he first told me about Bobby, "Christina, his name is Richard Green and I adore him."

When he said the name, I thought for a moment, then said, "Gee Jimmy, that name sounds familiar. Do I know him?"

He smiled mischievously, "No, you never met him. But, believe it or not, I actually met him because of you."

I looked at him strangely, "You did, how?"

"You had set up a personal tour of the recording studios for Richard and his fifth grade class just before Easter. Since you were involved in the trial, I decided to give the tour for you, much to the disappointment of the class, but Richard and I hit it off great and we have been dating since."

I kissed him again, "I'm so happy for you, Jimmy. Now, when do we meet him?"

With an excited tone he replied, "How about tonight, I can have him come over for coffee?"

"That sounds great; do you want to use the car phone to call him now?"

Jimmy lifted his eyebrows, "No, I'll call from home. I need to talk to the both of you first, and then I'll call him."

This time I lifted my eyebrows, "Now that was an opening for sure, and you know me Jimmy, I never pass up an opening. Now start talking, what's wrong with him?"

He gave me half a smile, "There is nothing wrong with him

Christina, it's me."

"You, what do you mean?" I said with a concerned tone.

Shaking his head he replied, "We want to get married Christina, then we want to take a year off and go to Africa together. The problem is I can't do that while I'm trying to reorganize and head operations of companies I never even heard of until we took them over."

I instantly slapped him in the back of the head and said, "Africa! What are you nuts!? Why the hell do you want to spend a year of your life in a backwards third world country that condemns your lifestyle?"

He looked at me like I had two heads, sat back in his seat in a huff and said, "For just that reason." And that's all he said.

I looked at him as if he had five heads, "You're not making any sense Jimmy, I can understand getting married; but going to Africa, that's crazy."

Michael snuck in a word, "Punkie, you're not even listening to Jimmy. Why don't you calm down and let him finish what he's trying to say?"

Jimmy pulled himself back up toward the front seat, "Thank you, Michael." Turning to me he added, "Now will you please listen to me Christina?"

"Okay, okay, I'm listening. So start talking and please make some sense this time."

He calmly began, "It's simple Christina, it's what we want to do! There are hundreds of thousands of people suffering and dying from AIDS every day, just because no one is adequately educating them about the disease. Not only that, but because of what is happening with the AIDS epidemic the fundamental Christians our getting the whole continent to turn against all homosexuals. They are actually putting them to death. Christina, I feel like I am being called to do this. You of all people should understand that."

I looked at him with frustration on my face and said as I let out a deep breath accompanied by a sigh, "I guess I can't argue with that, now can I, Jimmy? But you know I'm going to miss the hell out of you while you're gone. Now tell me, when are you planning to do this?"

His eyes lit up, "We are going to be married on July 4th and then leave on the 10th."

Shocked, I replied, "This July10th! Jimmy, I haven't been in the office since we took over three major corporations! How in the world do you think I'm going to figure out everything you've done in only ten days?"

Michael grabbed my hand and said, "Christina, I'm right on top of it all with Jimmy, we can handle it and you can learn it."

I looked at them both as we pulled into the garage and said, "Well it sounds to me like you two have this all planned out already. So who am I to try to stop you, I love you Jimmy, and I give you my blessing. Now go call Richard, I want to meet my soon to be new brother in-law."

Within a half hour of Jimmy's call, Michael and I were meeting his new love, Richard Green. Richard was a quiet, attractive, well dressed, forty-five-year-old, six foot tall man, with brown hair which showed just a touch of a receding hair line. After my first glimpse at Richard, I winked to Jimmy in a way which indicated to him I was impressed with his choice. Over our coffee Richard was overwhelmingly polite, friendly, intelligent, and cordial. He seemed like the perfect man for Jimmy, but by the end of our splendid two hour get together, I realized there was one thing which concerned me about Richard, he seemed to have a slight tendency to be obsessive toward Jimmy. I noticed it with the little things. Since it didn't seem to bother Jimmy, I figured to myself, 'Who am I to judge, as long as Jimmy's happy. Besides, maybe that's what Jimmy needs in his life, someone to dote over him for a change.'

The next morning it was time to go back to work, and Michael insisted we have James take the three of us to work in the limo. So we did, and when we arrived James pulled up to the main building of our complex and as we climbed out, Michael handed me a long scarf and said, "Here, put this on over your eyes, Punkie."

I took it, looked at him like he was nuts and said, "What the hell do you want me to do that for?"

Jimmy jumped in laughing, "Oh just shut up and put it on. We remodeled the lobby to surprise you. So humor us a little, would you please!?"

I started laughing, "Okay, I'll do it. But Michael, you better not be going along with another one of Jimmy's stupid jokes, because I'll slap you both." Then I put on the blindfold, and let them lead me to the main lobby.

When we entered through the large electronic front doors, Michael shouted, "Okay!" as he took off the blindfold to reveal my entire staff applauding me. Sitting in the middle of the lobby was a great big cake, and written on it was, *"We love you, Christina! And welcome home!"* I was shocked by it all. They had really pulled it off, because I never expected it. It felt wonderful to be welcomed home by all my friends like that.

After our morning welcome home celebration, it was back to work. I mean heavy duty work, the kind I really didn't care for, but was very good at. There was no time for doing what I loved best, entertaining, and writing. Not this time! This time all my attentions were directed toward finding out what had been accomplished by all my staff under the close direction of Michael and Jimmy without my close supervision and direction.

Finally, after a six month delay due to a murder, it was now time to truly turn my corporate holdings, into a mega conglomerate. Not only did we jump into the corporate world feet first, but Michael and I also went full steam ahead with a very discreet nationwide girl hunt to find the perfect surrogate Mother.

# CHAPTER 4

It was on July 27, 1989, two weeks after the newlyweds left for Africa, that Michael and I had an interview with our first prospective surrogate mother. The interview was held at Tom Davies' office in Manhattan. Tom had researched every detail of the lives and backgrounds of twenty-five women, which he had personally chosen over hundreds of possible candidates.

Tom told us he felt one of these twenty-five women would make a suitable surrogate. The arrangements of our contract were to be kept strictly confidential at my request. I felt the world knew enough about me as it was, and for some reason, I didn't want my fans to know I could no longer conceive a child.

The terms of our contract would be as follows: Upon successful in-vitro fertilization, the surrogate mother would receive one-hundred-thousand-dollars cash, with nine-hundred-thousand-dollars to follow after the birth. Tom Davies tried to convince me one-million-dollars was an exorbitant amount to pay for a surrogate mother, but I insisted I wanted the best money could buy for our child. The surrogate would also have to live on the premises with Michael and me; so, we could monitor every aspect of the surrogate's life during the pregnancy from her meals to her sleeping habits.

So, when Miss Joanne Naccarato entered the office with Tom where Michael and I were waiting, we already knew everything there was to know about her, without actually being inside her mind. She was a beautiful twenty-six-year-old law graduate, who had just passed the Bar Exam. She was from a respectable Italian-American family and she had a higher than above average intelligence.

In response to one of the questions on the questionnaire Miss Naccorato stated, *"My decision to become a surrogate mother was made out of my empathy for couples who are unable to bear children of their own, and being a surrogate 'for me', is an act of love and generosity."*

She also wrote her initial decision to become a surrogate mother was truly first motivated by a desire to help, then followed by her own need for financial compensation. On another question she stated she intended to use the compensation for her services to pay off her student loans, and to help establish a law office of her own. We liked her responses to the questionnaire from all the rest, which made her our first choice on paper. Now it was time to see if she remained so in person.

Miss Naccorato was aware of the requirements of the contract for her services, but she was not aware of who was setting the requirements until she entered the room where Michael and I were waiting. Her face showed her surprise and shock when she recognized me. When she reached us Michael and I stood up to greet her with a warm embrace. She hugged Michael, then me as she said with a big smile, "Oh my God, *Christina Powers*! I can't believe it's you! I was so nervous when Mr. Davies opened the door, but now that I see it's you, I feel so much more relaxed. I have got to be your biggest fan! I can't believe it's really you. Oh please forgive me for rambling on. I'm just so thrilled to think I might have the opportunity to be a surrogate for someone like you, Ms. Powers." Excitedly, she hugged me again and continued, "May I also say I would be honored to help a couple with your stature and reputation for helping others, to have a child of your own. Now I'll try to control my excitement and answer your questions to the best of my ability, under the circumstances."

Michael and I looked at each other and we both knew this was our girl. We fell in love with her sweet, jovial, disposition immediately. As we said our hellos, Michael indicated to me with his eyes, his approval. I knew Michael was right so I said, "Joanne, are there any questions you would like to ask us?"

She smiled again as we took our seats and said, "I know all I have to know about both of you, and like I said, I would be honored to carry your child for you, Ms. Powers."

I reached over, took her hand in mine and said, "When would you like to sign the contracts and get started?"

She shook my hand wildly with happy excitement, "Right now Ms. Powers, right now!"

Ten minutes later we had our surrogate mother and I was now more than ready to get the baby show on the road. For some strange reason, I felt an overwhelmingly desperate desire, as if it were planted within my soul from a higher power to have Michael's child, and I was determined to fulfill that desire as soon as humanly possible.

On Monday, August 16th at 11:00pm, Joanne Naccorato moved in with us for a one week trial. We decided to take this time in order to give the three of us the opportunity to make sure; we still wanted to proceed with the implantation. We were hoping in one week's time, we would know for sure whether she was truly ready to take on this tremendous, nine-month commitment for us.

As soon as we unpacked Joanne's belongings from her car, we took them straight up to her new bedroom. After we dropped off her suitcases, I took her on a tour of our Hudson River mansion. As we toured the mansion, I explained she was welcome to use any room she would like in the house, except the master bedroom of course. Then I said, "Joanne, I hope you realize what the terms of our contract truly mean. I want to make sure you are totally aware you can come and go as you please, but once you conceive, you will have two security guards assigned to you whenever you leave the mansion. I hope you also realize you will not be allowed to have even one sexual encounter during the pregnancy. Nor will you be able to take overnight outings without one of us being present."

As we arrived back at Joanne's room, she shook her head in agreement with what I was saying as she said, "I am completely aware of the terms of the contract, Christina. I also want you to know I understand and agree with the need for the stringent terms completely."

I smiled at her response, "I'm glad to hear that Joanne, because I know the terms of our contract are strict, but that is one of the reasons why your compensation is one-million-dollars." As I walked to the door I added, "Now why don't you take a few minutes to settle in before lunch, and I'll meet you in the family kitchen, in say twenty minutes?"

She sat on the soft bed, bounced a few times, then said with a smile, "That sounds good to me. I only have a few things to unpack and that will probably take me twenty minutes to do, if I don't get lost in the size of those bedroom closets first."

I smiled with half a giggle at her sweet attempt to be humorous then said, "I think you can handle it." I turned, closed the door behind me, and headed toward the kitchen to see if Carman had found the new house menu I left for her. As I walked down the hall, I thought to myself, 'Oh, Dear God! I pray we're not making a mistake.' As I thought this I felt a cold chill go up my spine and I thought, 'All I ask you God is that you please let Joanne be the right one to carry our child for us!'

Over lunch I explained to Joanne the diet she would have to be on during the entire pregnancy. Then I said, "Joanne, I hope I'm not making you uncomfortable by asking you all these questions. I only want to show you that yes, this is going to be a wonderful experience for all of us, but at the same time I also want you to understand this is not going to be all peaches and cream either. I want to remind you there will be no smoking, no drinking, and absolutely no drugs unless they're prescribed. Like I said Joanne, I just want you to realize when you sign this contract; you will be actually surrendering your rights for many things to me totally until you've given birth."

Joanne took a sip of her milk, smiled and said, "Let me try to put your mind at ease, Christina. I have read the entire contract and I am more than aware of the stipulations, and once again, I can live with them. After all, you are paying me one-million-dollars aren't you?"

I didn't particularly care for her little dig and I expressed it by saying, "Good! Now that I know, that you know, where I'm coming from, I will feel much more at ease placing my unborn child's life in your hands."

She looked at me very seriously and said, "I never looked at it in that light before." Taking my hand she added, "Christina, I will give my life for your child if need be, so please try to dismiss any fears you may have over your child's safety with me. I know the losses you have suffered with your children in the past, and I would never willingly endanger your child's life."

With tears in my eyes, I reached over the table to hug her and said,

"Thank you Joanne, you truly are a remarkable person." I stood up as I added, "Would you like to take a walk with me?"

She returned my hug with tears beginning to well up in her eyes, and said, "I'd love to take a walk with you."

It was a beautiful, sunny, afternoon, and the river glistened like a rippling sea of shiny pennies from the sun's reflection, as we strolled along its bank together. When we reached the boat docks I said, "I feel like taking the motor boat out for a while, won't you please come with me?"

She jumped in the boat before I did, "You don't have to ask me twice, let's go!"

I laughed as I untied the boat, hopped in and said, "Ha! Ha! You're a girl after my own heart." Then I started it up and off we went.

As we cruised smoothly up the river toward Kingston, Joanne turned to me and asked, "Christina, may I be candid with you?"

"Of course Joanne, I would expect no less," I answered sincerely.

She smiled mischievously and said, "I think you must be an absolute genius to have pulled off the most incredible, tri-corporate takeover in history. I have to tell you, I researched every move Wall Street took that day for my thesis, and I could not figure out how you could have pulled it off without some kind of advanced knowledge of what was going to transpire during that day. Won't you please give me just a clue as to how you did it?"

I started to laugh as I rode the wave off a passing boat, then said, "That will be the question of the decade for everyone on Wall Street and all I can say Joanne, is you're right. I am a genius."

She smiled at my answer, "When I look at all you've accomplished, I have to wonder. How did you get to where you are now without a college education?"

"Joanne, I'm surprised at you. This is America and throughout history most of your successful business entrepreneurs had no more than a high school education. What made them stand out was what they had to sell, and how they sold it. I just happen to have a talent the world loves, so that is what I used to help me arrive where I am today. But everyone, no matter who they may be, has the ability to tap into their own genius whether they have a formal education or not."

With a concerned tone Joanne asked, "Are you advocating

continued education is not needed?"

I looked at her with a surprised expression, "No, not at all. I believe whole heartedly in higher education. All I'm saying is in my case, for me to reach my career goals; I didn't need a college education."

She shook her head, "Well then, how can you explain your business success?"

We had reached Kingston and as I began to swing the boat around I replied, "Well, as for my business skills, they came from many hours of on the job training and a whole lot of personal intuition."

She put her hand on my shoulder and said, "Christina, I would love to put an application in with your company after the baby is born. I would relish the opportunity to practice business law, under the direction of the 'Queen of Wall Street' herself."

I smiled, "Joanne, I'm sure we could use a woman with your skills on our team, and I can tell you right now the position will be there for you." Then I thought for a second, scratched my head and said with a surprised tone, "Guess what! It just so happens I have a staff and board of directors meeting tomorrow evening in Denver. I'm going to be addressing one of the subsidiaries I recently acquired. Would you like to join me for some hands on action?"

Her eyebrows lifted with excitement as she answered, "I wouldn't miss it for one-million-dollars."

I laughed at her eager response as I said, "Great! It's a date then."

We didn't say too much more on the way back, because we were both caught up in enjoying the beauty of the river. When we arrived back to the mansion, we docked the boat and headed straight for the house.

Joanne and I were sitting on the balcony chatting, as a Hudson River Tour Boat passed by, and I noticed a group of passengers had draped a sign over the side of the boat which read, **"We love you, Christina!"** When I saw the sign I stood up, walked over to the edge of the balcony and began to wave. As soon as I did, you could hear the river come alive with shouts and whistles. The Captain sounded the ship's horn, so I blew him a kiss.

Joanne walked over to me and said, "It must be an incredible feeling to know you're loved and respected by so many people!"

I turned my head toward her as I leaned on the railing and

answered, "You're right!  It is a wonderful feeling, but it can also be an enormous responsibility."

Just then Michael walked out and said, "Yes it is my sweet, but you handle it with such finesse."

We embraced and I said with surprise, "Michael!  You're home. We were having such a wonderful afternoon together I totally forgot the time."

He kissed me then said with a snicker, "Yeah!  Yeah!  Out of sight, out of mind, I know."  He turned to Joanne, "Welcome to our home, Joanne.  I apologize for not being here to welcome you when you arrived, but somebody has to work around here."

She smiled at Michael, "Thank you, and there is no need to apologize.  I've been in good hands."

Michael kissed me again and said, "Well if you ladies will excuse me, I'll go change."

I took his arm in mine and with my Mae West impression said, "Come on, big boy!  I'll help you change into something more comfortable."  Laughing I added as I dragged Michael away, "Make yourself at home Joanne, and we'll see you at dinner."

When we arrived at our bedroom, I immediately began to tell Michael what transpired between Joanne and me during the day.  As I lovingly began to help him undress I said, "Honey, I really think she is the perfect one to carry our child for us, but I don't want to influence your decision either. I just hope by the end of this week we both make the right choice."

Michael led me by the hand to the bed, where we laid down together.  He kissed me tenderly and said, "Punkie, I love you and if you feel comfortable with Joanne, then so do I."

I kissed him back as I replied, "Michael, I want you to come to a decision based on your own feelings, not mine. Honey, I have to tell you as much as I want this to work, I'm still nervous about it. I don't know if I can handle losing another child."

He looked at me very seriously, "I know how you feel Punkie, I lost a child too, remember?  I promise you I am taking this just as seriously as you are."

"I'm sorry Michael," I said with compassion. "I never really asked how you felt about losing our child."

He kissed me and said, "It hurt a lot, Punkie. The only thing that saved me was you coming back to me." He gave me a sexy smile, as he put his finger to my lips and added, "Shh, let's continue this conversation later." He passionately kissed me and we melted into one another's embrace.

# CHAPTER 5

Our dinner together that evening was lovely and as for Joanne, she was simply charming. She seemed to win Michael's heart over within minutes as she shared some of her childhood stories with us. When we finished dinner, we headed for the family room to continue our conversation.

As we got to know one another a little better that night, it turned out Joanne and Michael had many common interests. So much so that at one point they went into a ten minute discussion over skiing, which I knew nothing about. I didn't mind being left out. I was just pleased to see Michael and Joanne getting along so well together.

As we talked, Carman entered the room with the phone in hand and said, "Excuse me Christina, Jimmy is on the line."

I thanked her, as I took the phone and with an excited tone exclaimed, "Jimmy! I have been waiting two weeks to hear from you. How the hell are you guys? Never mind that, where the hell are you guys?"

"Hi girlfriend," he answered in a not so cheerful tone. "I'm sorry I haven't called sooner, but we're in Ghana, and let me tell you, it's crazy here. Christina, you cannot believe what we are dealing with. There are hospitals full of people dying of full-blown AIDS and no one can do anything to help."

I didn't understand what Jimmy was saying so I asked, "Jimmy, if you're there to help, then how can no one be helping?"

With a disgusted tone he answered, "It's not that no one is trying

Christina, there just happens to be a civil war going on here. It appears the warring factions are not letting medical and food supplies through to the needed areas."

When Jimmy said these things, I became even more concerned over his safety. So I said, "It sounds dangerous Jimmy, are you sure you're doing the right thing by staying there?"

With a tone of pure compassion he answered, "I know I am Christina, but Richard and I can't do it alone. We need your help."

With a surprised tone I said, "My help, how can I help?"

His reply sounded more like a plea, "Just by making the world aware of the travesty which is taking place here. Somehow we have got to get the warring factions to allow the supplies through. From what I gather, it's actually the national government which is stopping the supplies, so I think if you could pressure Congress into threatening to cut aid to the Ghana Government, then maybe they will let the supplies through."

I answered reassuringly, "I'll tell you what Jimmy, you send me positive proof of what is going on there and I'll do everything I can to help from here."

"Thanks', Christina. I knew I could count on you." Relaxing his tone he continued, "So tell me, have you found a surrogate yet?"

I chuckled then said, "Why don't you give me a number where I can reach you. I'll call you back later and tell you all about it."

"I don't have one," he answered. "But if you have to go, I'll call you back tomorrow."

"That sounds good Jimmy," I answered. Then I continued with a tone of concern, "And for God Sake's, please take care of yourself! I love you and I would be devastated if something were to happen to you."

"I love you too Christina and I'll talk to you tomorrow night." I hung up and rejoined Michael and Joanne's conversation.

Later that evening after Michael and I retired to our room, I told him what Jimmy had said. Then we climbed into bed together where Michael took me into his arms, kissed me, smiled and said, "Punkie! I don't think we could find a better surrogate then Joanne, if we looked for twenty years. So as for my vote, she's got it."

I hugged him with excitement and said, "Oh God, Michael! I love you, and I can't wait to have our baby in my arms."

Michael climbed on top of me, looked deep into my eyes and passionately said, "The only thing that could make my heart happier right now is for us to set our wedding date."

I smiled and lovingly replied, "Why don't we call your mom and ask her to set everything up for us again? Tell her to set the date for Thanksgiving Day. I think we have a lot to be thankful for."

He kissed me passionately and said, "Christina, I love you Punkie, and I have never felt happier or more complete then I do at this very moment."

I returned the kiss and we lovingly indulged in one another's anticipation and excitement for our future family.

# CHAPTER 6

The next morning, Joanne was accompanying Michael and me, to Denver on a trip that was strictly business. On the plane to Denver Joanne sat quietly beside me as Michael, my staff, and I, all worked on a last minute review of our proposal. As I read through the pamphlet Michael had prepared to hand out to all the staff of Salerno Sodas, I turned to him and said, "Michael, we state in here we have the financial records for Salerno Sodas for the past ten years and we compare them to the five-year financial records of Catskill Mountain Soft Drinks, so where are the figures?"

He grabbed the handout from me as he answered, "I had them on a separate sheet which was to be included in the pamphlet. Don't tell me they're not there? I shook my head as I said, "You can look for yourself honey, but it's not there."

He looked for Terry Baggatta my senior secretary, who was on the other end of the cabin working on the pamphlets and shouted, "Terry! Would you come here, please?"

She walked over to us, "What's up?"

Michael looked up at her and asked, "How come the sheets with the financial figures are not in the handout?"

She smiled and said, "Don't worry about it; I'm on top of it right now. The printing room accidentally left them out, so we're inserting them by hand."

Michael smiled, "Great job Terry, I'm glad you caught it."

I smiled and said, "Well in that case gang, I think we're all set."

40

My entourage and I arrived at the headquarters of Salerno Sodas at 10:00am, where we went straight into a prearranged board meeting. After Michael, Tom Davies, Joanne, and I, were introduced to everyone by the current president of the company Paul Barer, we took our seats.

Paul stood up and said, "Ladies and gentleman of the board, now I would like to formally turn this meeting over to the new owner and top shareholder of Salerno Sodas, *Ms. Christina Powers.*"

Everyone in the large conference room applauded as I took the mike and said, "Good morning and once again I would like to thank you for your kind welcome. Now the first thing I would like to say is that the final proposal which most of us in this room agreed upon concerning the future of this company, has been drawn up in a pamphlet form. Right now my people are distributing copies to all the staff in the plant. I want to make sure everyone involved is totally aware of our plans before putting it to a vote this evening.

Now if anyone has any questions, this is the time to ask." After answering several questions I continued, "Now if there are no more questions, I would like to take a walk through the plant to meet the staff before I address them this afternoon."

We left the board room at 11:00am and went straight into the heart of the two-thousand employee, soda producing and distributing plant. Once there, I began to personally introduce myself to every employee I could. As I shook their hands, I offered a copy of our pamphlet to those who had not yet received one and said, "All I ask is you please read and come to a complete understanding of my proposal before you make your decision for this evening's vote."

After a two-hour tour of the plant, it was off for a 1:30pm luncheon with the head union representatives, which led right into a 3:00pm meeting with the entire union membership.

I was scheduled to address the meeting at 4:40pm, which was shortly after the opponents of our proposal addressed the assembly. The union representatives present included all the members in the main plant, along with seventy truck drivers and the three-hundred employees, who manned the thirty distributing centers based throughout the West Coast.

Finally, my turn came to speak, and I was introduced to the members by Paul Barer. When I took the podium, I was welcomed by a hardy round of applause. After the crowd settled down, I smiled and said, "I thank you all for your warm welcome, I also thank you for giving me this opportunity to address the issues before this evening's crucial vote. Now, I would like to come straight to the heart of why I am here today, which is to try to save a dying company. My hope is after you have read our proposal on eliminating the production of Salerno Sodas, as well as overhauling and modifying the entire plant, so it can be smoothly transformed into the West Coast branch of Catskill Mountain Soft Drinks, you will see that our proposal is the proper business decision to be taken under the circumstances. When I'm finished speaking here tonight, my hope is to have convinced you all, our terms are generous so that you will all vote yes on our proposal. The reason I am making these proposals is because, since Powers Inc., acquired Salerno Inc., we have discovered Salerno Sodas has been steadily losing profits during the past five fiscal years. As you can see by the figures, we have in our handout, if left to its present management course, Salerno Sodas will be filing chapter eleven within two years. Now if you take a look at the profit figures shown for the past five years of Catskill Mountain Soft Drinks, you will see there is quite a difference. Our intent is to combine the two companies into one major soft drink company, which will truly be able to compete with the big guys. We plan to have the transformation of Salerno Sodas, into Catskill Mountain Soft Drinks, completed by the end of the first year. This will be stage one in a three-stage plan to turn this company around in only two years. As you can see by the figures, this transformation will cost an initial investment from Catskill Mountain Soft Drinks, of thirty-six-million-dollars. Now as for stage two of our proposal, it's true that during this time our proposal calls for a two-year salary freeze, accompanied by a two year hiring freeze. But, I give you my word right now, if you agree to tough it out with us, then at the end of the two years this company will be in the position to give a 30% across the board salary increase, to every employee! We also promise the company will provide a comprehensive health care plan, which will include full dental coverage to every fulltime employee. As for stage three of our proposal 65% of the top management responsibilities will be transferred to our New York office; thus, saving eighteen-million-dollars a year in top management salaries."

Someone from the audience shouted, "How can you be so sure you can deliver after only two years?"

I looked in the direction the question came from as I said, "Very good question, and I was just about to come to that. What makes me sure we can turn this company over in such a short time, is because even though Salerno Soda is losing revenue, it still has a firm hold in the Central and Western corridors of the country. This fact, accompanied with its distribution centers, trucking, and Salerno Soda's shelf space availability, all make the company worth salvaging under a new label. On the other hand, Catskill Mountain Soft Drinks is basically an East Coast phenomenon at this time. But, if we can pull that East Coast success into the Central and Western markets where Salerno Soda is now losing business, then I believe we can combine the two companies, into one mega profit making, soft drink, powerhouse. I also feel if we take this path together, then by the end of the two years we will be ready to carry it to the International Markets."

I stopped to take a sip from my soda cup and added, "Now that I've summed up our proposal for you, I encourage everyone here for the benefit of us all to vote yes. Oh yes! I think I should mention one more thing, and that is concerning my opponent's proposal, which was submitted by the current management. I hope everyone here can recognize a pipe dream when they see it." With that I gave them all the thumbs up and added, "Now that I've said my piece, I would like to thank you all again for your time." Then I turned the platform back to Paul Barer, who was looking visibly frustrated by my remarks to his proposal, as I returned to my seat in the midst of another round of cheers.

After my address, thank God, we were finally served our lunch. We mingled with the members as we impatiently waited for the results of the vote. By the time the eight o'clock hour rolled around, the final vote was tallied and our proposal had received a 92% approval.

When the winning proposal was announced I once again took the platform and said, "I just want to thank everyone for their vote. Now together, we can swing our plans into action for a brighter financial future for us all." I waved goodbye to them all as I shouted, "Great job, guys! And may God bless us all."

Later that night on the flight home, Joanne took a seat beside me and said, "Christina, I have got to tell you, you were amazing today. That was the most exciting business experience I have ever had." She shook her head in astonishment and added, "The way you handled that crowd, with such confidence and finesse was incredible. Do you realize you would make an excellent political candidate? Have you ever considered running for a public office?"

I looked at her and started to gently chuckle as I said, "With my life history being an open book, who would vote for me?"

She put her hand on my shoulder as she replied, "I'm serious Christina, I think you would make an excellent senatorial candidate and most of all, I think you could win."

Michael who was sitting on my other side, jumped into the conversation rather quickly by saying, "Please! Don't give her any more ideas; we have enough to do as it is."

Joanne took her hand off my shoulder and said, "Oops, I'm sorry! It was just a thought. Just the same, I had a wonderful time today and I learned a lot. I must admit the pace of this learning experience itself, was what I truly enjoyed most about the day."

I replied with a smile, "Well if you're still with us next week, then you will be more than welcome to accompany us to the West Coast for a few days. We have three more corporate meetings which will be quite similar to todays. In addition, I am hosting two AIDS benefits next week; one in L.A. on Thursday night, the other in San Francisco on Friday night. If you really enjoyed today's pace, then I think you're going to love next week's." I smiled, patted her hand and added, "The only reason things are not so hectic this week is because of your stay with us."

She sat up in her seat, looked at us both very seriously and bluntly asked, "If your lives are so busy all the time, then how do you plan to find the time to properly raise a child?"

I smiled at Michael, then I turned to Joanne and answered, "That is a very responsible question and I'm glad you asked it. It shows me you truly care about the welfare of the child you might carry." I took Michael's hand and added, "It's because we have a plan Joanne, which includes our wedding this coming Thanksgiving Day. Our plan places us on a strict time schedule for the next eight months. If things do go as planned, by the time our baby arrives we will have completely overhauled every company acquired from our corporate takeovers. By then our other partner will have returned from his hiatus, to take over my duties and assist Michael, while I stay home to raise our child."

She smiled and said, "I'm sure the two of you are going to make excellent parents and I hope I'm the one to help."

I smiled back at her with warm sincerity, "I hope so too, Joanne."

# CHAPTER 7

By the time Friday had arrived, the three of us had made our final decision.  So at 9:00am that morning we entered Tom Davies' office in Manhattan, and we were more than ready to officially and legally sign our surrogate contract. After signing, it was straight to Poughkeepsie for a 1:00pm appointment with Doctor Hart for our first attempt at in-vitro fertilization. Doctor Hart told us if all went well, we would know in six to eight weeks what sex our child would be.  Then he added, "But we must be realistic, there's always the risk Joanne could abort at any time between the implantation and the first three months."

Joanne had to remain in a supine position for two hours after the procedure; so, by the time we finished everything, we didn't end up arriving back home that evening until after 6:00pm

We were so excited over our experience when we entered the family room talking; none of us noticed the 12 X 12 inch package addressed to me, which was sitting on the coffee table right in front of us. Carman entered the room and said, "Excuse me, but dinner will be ready in ten minutes. Oh by the way, there's a package for you on the coffee table, Christina."

I looked down, laughed and said, "Thanks Carman, if it had teeth it could have bitten me." I picked it up and added, "It's from Jimmy. That was quick. Let's eat first and I'll open it after dinner."

After dinner the three of us went back to the family room with our coffee, where once again I picked up the package from Jimmy.  Michael and Joanne were still speaking as I proceeded to open the package to find a video tape, with a note taped to it. I carefully removed the tape from the note which read, *"Christina, this tape has all the proof you will need to back up everything I told you over the phone. As you will see for yourself, the government troops are clearly ambushing convoys of food and medical supplies shortly before they reach the refugee camps, which are in the rebel held areas of the northeastern hill country. The government justifies their raids by saying the convoys are carrying weapons to the rebel outlaws, which are held up in the jungle. Christina, this tape proves without a doubt, there were no weapons found during this raid and the troops still destroyed everything the convoy was carrying. Hold on to your seat girlfriend when you watch this, because three innocent Red Cross Workers lost their lives in this ambush. Please, do what you can and I'll call you soon. Love you guys, Jimmy and Richard."*

After reading this note to myself, I read it to Michael and Joanne. Then I plugged the tape into the VCR, and we proceeded to watch in horror as all the atrocities Jimmy spoke of, graphically appeared in front of our eyes.

As soon as I caught my breath I turned to Michael and said, "Honey, would you please make two copies of this tape for me and I'll be right back? I have to make a phone call."

I then went to my in-house office and proceeded to place a direct call to President George Rush on the private number, which he gave to me personally. The phone was answered by a recording which instructed me to leave my name and number, so I did. Not ten minutes later I received a return call from the President himself. When I answered the phone, I heard, "Hello am I speaking with Christina Powers?"

I quickly answered, "Yes George, it's me. Thank you for returning my call so quickly."

He answered in a sweet soft voice, "You're welcome, Christina. Your calling is a pleasant surprise. It's nice to hear from you. So is this a personal call or business?"

I cleared my voice and proceeded, "I wish it were personal George, but it's not. I really need to speak with you in private as soon as possible. Is there a possibility that it can be arranged?"

This time **he** cleared his voice then said, "I think it can be arranged, but first let me ask you something. Does this have anything to do with the matter we once discussed?"

"No George, nothing at all," I answered reassuringly. "This is more of a human rights issue which I believe you should be made aware of before I go public."

Then I proceeded to inform him of what I had discovered and that I had a video tape which proved what I was saying. By the time we finished speaking, we had arranged for a 1:00pm luncheon date for the following afternoon. George wanted me to meet with him at Camp David. He said he would arrange for my transportation by the U.S. Air Force from Stewart International Airport, in Newburgh, New York.

When I hung up the phone, I sat there for a moment and thought with curiosity, 'Why would he still be so concerned over the information I had on Lee Bradford? I know Lee had scammed the government for billions of dollars, but without knowing what was on the original computer disk, which by the way was still in my possession, I had no idea how he did it. Better yet, what's the real reason George is still so concerned about covering up this crime?' I turned my head to gaze at the small flag I kept in my office and I wondered, 'How can allowing a financial crime against our nation go unpunished, be in the best interest of our national security?'

With that thought, I put my finger to my lips and said in a soft voice, "Hmm, I think it's time to do some investigating of my own." So I called Tom Davies and arranged for a dinner date for that following evening at 7:00pm. We agreed to meet incognito at the Mariners Harbor Restaurant, in Highland, New York.

After my conversation with Tom, I rose from my seat, turned off the light and returned to Michael and Joanne, who were still in the family room. When I entered the room, Michael handed me the copies of the tape he made and said, "Was that 'The President' returning your call?"

"Yes," I replied. "I'm having lunch with him tomorrow."

Michael shook his head in amazement as he smiled at me and said, "You're not kidding, are you?" He kissed me and continued, "Why don't we call it a night and you can tell me all about it upstairs."

I returned his kiss then said, "That sounds good to me, because I'm going to have a busy day tomorrow." We said our goodnights to Joanne and retired for the evening.

After Michael and I snuggled comfortably together in our bed, I kissed him and proceeded to inform him of all I had scheduled for the following day, including my dinner date with Tom. I told Michael I wanted to speak with Tom after meeting with the President. The only thing I didn't tell him was the real reason I wanted to meet with Tom. I felt the less he knew about what I knew, the safer he would remain if something went wrong. When I finished telling him about my conversation with the President, I said, "Honey, I hate to leave you alone tomorrow, especially since we planned to spend the day with Joanne, but you saw the film. I have to do something."

He gently kissed me and reassuringly said, "I understand, Punkie. I just don't know what I'm going to do to entertain Joanne all day tomorrow. I was counting on you for that."

I smiled and said, "Oh, I think you'll be able to come up with something."

He began to playfully kiss my nose as he asked, "What time do you think you will be getting home tomorrow?"

I started to feel myself becoming distracted by his kisses as I answered, "Probably not until after 10:00pm." I kissed him passionately and added, "Now shut up and make love to me," and that was all I had to say.

# CHAPTER 8

At 12:45pm, on Saturday, August 21$^{st}$, I exited an Air Force helicopter at Camp David, and I thought, 'Would you look at this, I'm really at Camp David.' As I was escorted to a private luncheon with President Rush himself.

The first five minutes of our conversation was quite casual. Then I got straight to the point when I said, "George, I hate to jump right into the reason I'm here, but I must." I handed him a copy of Jimmy's tape and continued, "This tape shows Ghana Government troops destroying medical and food supplies."

I reached across our small table, took his hand in mine as I looked him straight in his eyes and with anger in my voice added, "George, this tape also graphically shows the brutal execution style murders of three innocent Ghana Red Cross workers. What is taking place there George is horrendous and the fact America is supporting this government is an atrocity." Releasing his hand I continued, "I'm sorry I don't mean to be so dramatic. It's just that when I think of what is taking place over there it angers me and breaks my heart at the same time."

This time George took my hand in his as he comfortingly replied, "There's no need to apologize for caring, Christina. Sometimes it's incomprehensible the human race can be so vicious. When I witness human behavior like this, I wonder how we've made it this far."

As he spoke, I pulled my hand from his, took a sip of water and said, "Well, now that you know what is going on my first question is, how can we stop it?"

He put his hand to his chin, rubbed it a few times as if in thought, then said, "This is going to have to be handled through diplomatic channels. I'll arrange for a personal conversation with the Prime Minister of Ghana this afternoon, and I promise you the supplies will get through." Then he momentarily squinted his eyes precariously as he looked at me and added, "Christina, you mentioned something over the phone about taking this information public. I don't believe that would be a wise thing to do at this time. So I'm going to ask you not to go public with this information." I was surprised and bewildered by his request and I knew it showed on my face. When he realized by my expression, I disagreed with him, he looked very seriously into my eyes and added, "The only reason I'm making this request of you is because if this information becomes public, it could jeopardize American security interests in the region."

I shook my head in disbelief, "Don't you think that if our security interests bring us to the point of allowing human rights atrocities to take place, then it's time to rethink our foreign policies?"

He was visibly taken aback by my sharp response to his reasoning as he said, "It's not as simple as all that, Christina. There are regional conflicts taking place throughout Africa, and we can't stop them all."

I slightly shook my head in amazement by his statement as I said, "That may be true George, but that doesn't mean we cover up murder and allow the perpetrators to go free, because we can't stop them all. You and I both know, if you stand by idly watching as injustices take place throughout the world and do nothing to expose and stop them, than we are no better than those committing these crimes."

The expression on his face showed his frustration with my rebuttal when he said, "Christina, I can't stop you from going public with this tape if you insist. So, I will be blunt with you and tell you something which must be kept strictly confidential. I want you to realize what the most likely outcome of going public will be." With a look of firmness he sternly added, "If you go public then Congress will be forced to cut American funding to the current Ghana government. If that happens, then the American backed Ghana Government will be toppled by the Communist Party of the Republic of China. China happens to be secretly backing the rebel outlaws who are trying to overthrow the Ghana Government. America can't afford to allow the Communist Party of the

Chinese Government to get a foothold in the region, and this is why the information you have **must be kept from the public**."

I was once again surprised by his statement and I showed it by saying, "My God, George, this is becoming more unbelievable every time you tell me something. The last I heard America had good relations with China, and now you tell me they're trying to undermine our stability on the African continent." I gave him a look of total amazement and added, "I'll just assume the Chinese have expansionism on their minds and that's why you want me to sit on this."

He sighed with a sense of relief as he smiled at me and said, "I'm glad you understand the delicacy of the situation."

I almost laughed at him, but I managed to stop at a smile as I said, "I understand where you're coming from totally now George, but I respectfully disagree with you." I shook my head as I continued, "Furthermore, I'm afraid I can't put a lid on this one; it's already out of my control. The tape is now in the hands of the top brass at CBS and to top that, I will be appearing on the Barbara Water's National News Program this Monday night to show the tape to the country."

His face turned white as I finished speaking and with a disappointed tone he said, "I wish you hadn't done that before speaking with me."

In an attempt to be comforting, I once again took his hand in mine and said, "George, I'm truly sorry I jumped the gun on this one." I shook my head with disgust, looked him straight in his eyes and added, "When will the leaders of the world stop playing all these top secret international games of deceit with one another, and start working together to make the world a safer place to live?"

He smiled with sincerity as he gently squeezed my hand and said, "Only God has the answer to that question, Christina."

My reply was adamant, "That may be so, but I believe if one nation truly stood up for freedom, truth, and justice for all, then perhaps it could be accomplished."

He grinned almost to the point of laughter as he said, "Christina, I would never have believed you to be so naive on international matters. I only wish it could happen that easily."

I felt a slight sense of indignation by his assumption at my beliefs, which he obviously saw as unrealistic, and somehow naive. I quickly calmed my gut response to rebuke him and said, "George, if there is one thing I've learned in my life it is that with hard work and determination anything is possible."

He gave me a surprised look and said, "That's a very noble concept Christina, I only wish it were true." Then he gazed at the time and added, "Christina, you are a lovely woman and even when we disagree, I always enjoy our chats. But now I'm afraid I must end our visit." Smiling he continued, "I have some damage control to get underway, thanks to you."

I smiled and said, "Well at least I think I can help you out with the domestic end of the damage control."

He looked at me with interest as he asked, "And just how do you propose to do that?"

I smiled deviously and replied, "If you arrange for me to address a Senate Hearing with my evidence before I break the story on Monday night; then, it will look as though I have your backing. It would also save face for our foreign policy and your administration."

He thought about it for a minute then said, "You know, it just might work." With a deep sigh of relief he added, "Be prepared to address Congress the first thing Monday morning, and I'll take care of the rest." With that, we said our goodbyes and it was back to the helicopter.

It was 6:00pm, when I climbed from the helicopter back at Stewart Airport. Just before I entered the terminal buildings, I deliberately turned back and sensually waved goodbye to the seven very charming and attractive members of my wonderful, military escort. When the valet driver brought my car, I climbed in and decided that due to the time I would head directly for my dinner date with Tom Davies. As soon as I pulled away from the curve, I picked up the car phone and placed a direct call to a personal friend of mine, Steven Bock who just happened to be the President of CBS. You see, I had to arrange to be on the Barbara Water's show for that coming Monday evening, before George discovered my on-the-spot bluff. After hearing as much of the details I carefully chose to share with Steven, he was more than willing to cover my back. He told me he would have Barbara call me personally later that evening, to go over all the arrangements for the interview. After I thanked him, I cut our connection and thought, 'Why you sly fox, you! You just pulled one over on the President. I can't believe I actually did that and with such finesse.' I laughed out loud as my thoughts continued, 'Maybe I was Mata-Hari in a past life.'

Tom and I sat at a very secluded table in the back of the restaurant where we could speak privately. While we ate, I said, "Tom, first I want to thank you for meeting me here on such short notice. As you know, I would not have asked you to drive up here if it weren't important."

He gazed across the table at me with admiring eyes and said, "Christina, you don't have to thank me, I'm more than happy to help whenever you need me." Smiling he continued, "Besides, that's one of the reasons you keep me on such a hefty retainer isn't it?"

I smiled and said, "No Tom, it's actually because you're such a brilliant sweetheart. That's why I keep you hanging around." I reached across the table and gently patted his hand as I said, "Tom, the reason I asked you here happens to be very serious. I'm asking for your help because you're the only person I trust to handle this very delicate situation."

The excitement grew on his face as I spoke and he looked at me with a gleam of anticipation in his eyes as he said, "I just love when you give me these interesting assignments, they always turn out to be quite challenging and I never know for sure where we're going to end up when we're finished."

I smiled devilishly as I said, "I do come up with some doosies though, don't I? And I think this one has the potential to top them all. Now let's get serious. I want you to find some pieces of a puzzle for me and I don't want you to let anyone catch onto what you're trying to do. I know somewhere there is a connection to be found between Lee Bradford, George Rush, NASA, and The Challenger Disaster, and I want to know what that connection is."

His eyes almost popped out of his head, as he took a deep breath and said, "You don't think the two of them actually had something to do with The Challenger Disaster, do you?"

I looked at him very seriously and replied, "If you say that too loudly you might get us both killed and no, that's not what I'm saying. All I want you to do is find me the connecting pieces and I'll put the puzzle together."

He shook his head in disbelief and said, "You got it, boss."

We had time for one quick drink after dinner, then I was finally on my way home to Michael. I walked in the door at 9:45pm and had just enough time to say hi and kiss Michael before taking a phone call from Barbara Waters. Barbara and I went over the details of the interview until midnight. When we finally had the outline for the interview completed, she said, "You know Christina, I have been trying to get an exclusive interview with you for years." With a conniving tone in her voice she continued, "Steven seems to think you're between a rock and a hard place on this one, and that you may be willing to consent to a candid interview with us, as a way of showing your appreciation to the network."

When I finished laughing, I said, "You sure have a way of saying what's on your mind Barbara, and I guess that's more than fair."

As soon as I hung up, the phone rang again and I was back on it talking with Jimmy. And as soon as I heard Jimmy's voice, I said in our joking tone, "You know I have to tell you, you're some piece-of-work girlfriend. You leave me here running around the country like a chicken without a head, trying to organize a mishmash of corporate mumbo jumbo, then you have the gall to ask me to do you a little favor in Ghana."

We both started to laugh, as he said, "I gather you've received my list of demands."

After I stopped laughing, I filled him in on the day's events; then, I said, "Jimmy, I wish you were home. You can't imagine how much I miss you. I haven't crashed on the sofa with buttered popcorn since you left."

With a sad tone to his voice he replied, "I miss you too girlfriend, but I couldn't come home now no matter how much I might want to. Christina, someone has to do something on this end, because you're not going to believe what I've discovered this time." He proceeded to tell me with a tone of anger just how the Ghana government was spending the American Foreign Aid it was receiving. By the time we finished our conversation it was 3:12am and I headed straight for the bedroom. Michael was sound asleep when I climbed into the warm bed with him. I was so tired when my body hit the mattress that I kissed Michael's bare back and passed out.

The next morning I was awakened at 7:00am by a call from the President. After the call I headed for the kitchen and a much needed cup of coffee. Over breakfast I told Michael and Joanne what transpired between the President and me at our meeting. Then I continued to fill them in on my new schedule for that afternoon and the following day; beginning with a 2:00pm meeting this afternoon with the Speaker of the House, in Washington, D.C. After which, with a sympathetic tone I added, "I'm sorry about this guys, but I have to do something to help stop this madness." I looked at them optimistically and added, "Maybe we can find the time to do something fun together while we're on the West Coast this week."

Joanne perked up and said, "Well, our day wasn't quite as exciting as yours, but we did have fun. We took the boat all the way to Albany, and that was the first time I ever saw the New York State Capital from the viewpoint of the river. I've got to tell you, it's even more of a beautiful city from the water." She reached across the table to where Michael was sitting, gently took his hand in hers and continued, "I also have to thank you for asking Michael to take me. Your husband is a gracious tour guide."

I smiled sweetly as she talked, because I realized I was consciously timing how long she held Michael's hand.

When she finished speaking, Michael nonchalantly pulled his hand from hers and said, "I'm glad you had a nice day Joanne, I did too." He looked at me as he said, "What time are you leaving today?"

I lifted my eyebrows in dismay and said, "As soon as I clean up and change, honey."

With that, I finished eating and went to take a shower. As I washed, I was sure Michael was going to be coming in any second now to make passionate love to me, but he never did. When I was ready to leave, I came down to say goodbye and I couldn't find them anywhere. I looked out the opened back patio doors, to find the two of them splashing in the pool together. I walked over to them, gave Michael a kiss goodbye as he climbed out to meet me, then waved to Joanne who waved goodbye from the pool, and it was off to the airport.

# CHAPTER 9

When I arrived in Washington, I went straight to my 2:00pm appointment with The Speaker of the House, Senator Edward Kenny. The appointment was at his downtown office, and I felt quite uncomfortable to say the least. After all, I did steal one of the family companies from him. Not to mention, humiliating him in front of the entire country. So when I opened the door to his office, you can understand why I was slightly perspiring. He rose from his seat like a true gentleman as I entered his office and very calmly approached him. When I reached him, I stretched out my hand to shake his as I said with a friendly tone, "Edward! It's nice to see you." I lifted my eyebrows to help flatter him and continued, "You're looking well. I'm pleased to see you've recovered so nicely after our unforeseen corporate collision."

I could feel his masked hostility toward me as we shook hands, and when we released our handshake he graciously said, "Christina, it's wonderful to see you as well, and thank you for your thoughtful concern over my welfare." He gestured to me to take a seat as he added, "Please make yourself comfortable, this is going to be a long night."

As I sat down, I thought, 'Well that wasn't too bad, I've experienced worse.'

After we exchanged a few more casual comments Edward said, "Well, I think we should get down to business before the committee arrives. I need to explain to you the procedures involved in addressing Congress. A six-member Senatorial Committee including myself has been chosen by the President to head the hearing of your case tomorrow morning. That committee and I will be questioning you this afternoon so we may decide ahead of time, which way to lead the questioning at tomorrow's Congressional Hearing."

I looked at him and sighed as I said, "I knew I had to prepare for this, but I didn't realize it was going to take all night."

When I finished speaking, four Republican Senators entered the room and I had had a run-in with each one of them over some human rights issue in the past. Then to add insult to injury, I was almost visibly shocked when I saw Lee Bradford enter the room. At that moment, I realized everyone in that room had a personal vendetta against me for one reason or another. I smiled as I thought, 'Touché, George Rush! You knew this payback was going to be a bitch.' I slightly shrugged my left shoulder as I thought, 'Aaa, I'm a big girl, I can handle it. Yeah! As long as no one tries to shoot me that is.'

As soon as everyone sat down it was straight to work. My grueling hours of answering questions finally came to an end around 9:30 that evening. As everyone got up to leave the office, Lee stood up, turned and walked away from me without even saying goodbye, and he hadn't even said hello. As a matter of fact, the only time he acknowledged me at all was when he had no choice. As I watched him leaving, I felt compelled to say, "Lee, are you really going to walk out that door without even acknowledging me?" He didn't even look back and I thought, 'How could I have loved that man for all those years and never truly knew what kind of man he really was?' Then I brought up the rear as we left, and headed for my waiting limo.

The moment I entered my suite at the Hilton, I phoned room service and heard a masculine voice say, "Good evening, Ms. Powers. This is Pierre Collins, head of in-house accommodations. How may I be of service to you this evening?"

I was impressed by his sense of accountability to the customer; so, in a very commanding, yet provocative tone I replied, "By accomplishing two tasks for me Pierre, as swiftly as possible. First, I would like a large serving of linguine with white clam sauce, accompanied by toasted garlic bread, tossed salad with Italian dressing, grated Parmesan cheese and a chilled bottle of Chianti. Second, I would like a Sudanese language study guide. The language guide I want you to deliver to me personally no matter what time, even if you have to wake me, I want it tonight!" Then I hung up the phone and started to laugh as I thought, 'If this guy pulls this off on a Sunday night at 10:00pm I'm stealing him from this place.'

After I stopped laughing, I figured it was time to call home. I dialed our bedroom phone first and when Michael didn't answer I called the house phone. When Carman answered the phone, we exchanged greetings, and then I asked for Michael. She said, "Hold on Christina, I have to bring the phone out to them."

With curiosity I said, "Where are they anyway?"

From between the sounds of scuffling shoes and heavy breathing I heard her say, "In the pool." When she reached the pool, I could hear Michael and Joanne laughing between the sounds of splashing water.

When Michael answered the phone, he said, "Hi, Punkie! How are things going down there?"

I was tired and irritated by his good natured greeting, so I answered with an air of irritation, "Not as smoothly as it sounds like it is there. I can't believe you're still in the pool."

He laughed as if I were making a joke and said, "We haven't been in the pool all day. We only just came back from the camp house in the mountains. Now stop fooling and tell me how you made out."

I sighed and said, "I'm too tired honey, I just wanted to tell you I love you, and miss you, before I call it a night."

Michael replied with a loving tone, "Okay Punkie, I love you too. Now I want you to get some rest, and know I'll be with you in spirit tomorrow."

After I hung up the phone, I headed straight for the shower. Ten minutes after my shower there was a knock at my door. When I answered it, there was a very attractive young man standing behind a room service, meal cart and he said, "Good evening, Ms. Powers. Here is the meal you requested, as well as the Sudanese Language Study Guide you asked for."

I took the guide out of his hand to examine it. When I confirmed its authenticity, I smiled and said, "Pierre Collins, I'm truly impressed. That's why I would like to offer you a position as one of my personal secretaries starting at three times your current salary." Needless to say, he accepted my offer on the spot.

The next morning, I was dressed like a female business tycoon should be, when I entered the Halls of Congress. Promptly at 9:00am, I formally introduced myself to the members and proceeded to address the U.S. Congress in a Congressional Hearing. At one point in the midst of my five-hour address, after the viewing of the tape, I began to condemn the Ghana Government for allowing their troops to commit such monstrous, human rights violations. As soon as I knew I had everyone's attention I said, "I believe the citizens of the United States must call upon the United Nations to take swift action in investigating the murders of these three International Red Cross Workers."

Then I began to answer their questions, right up till we broke for a one hour lunch break at noon. The moment I stepped out of the door, I was swamped by reporters, who became quite disappointed when I said, "Sorry gang, but I promised 'Waters' the exclusive on this one."

As soon as we returned from lunch I proceeded to condemn the Ghana Government for their disgraceful mismanagement of the American Foreign Aid they were receiving, and then said, "I am at this very moment gathering further evidence which will show just how wealthy the Ghana Government Officials are, while their citizens live in deplorable conditions. It's no wonder the people of Ghana are joining the Rebel Movement to overthrow the government." At that point I took a sip from my water glass, because the place was getting hot. I knew I was now treading in dangerously forbidden waters, so I cautiously continued by saying, "Ladies and gentleman of Congress, please don't misunderstand me, I'm not advocating abandoning the Ghana Government completely. All I'm saying is that America, as the leader of the world in foreign aid grants to Third World Countries, should have in place a much better monitoring system. I believe if a nation agrees to accept aide from America, then that country should be held accountable to the American people on how they spend that aid."

With that, Senator Elm stood up and said, "Ms. Powers, that sounds like a wonderful suggestion, but how in the world do you expect America to monitor all the nations who receive grants from the U.S.?"

I looked at him confidently and replied, "Senator Elm, I'm surprised at you. All we have to do is establish an international financial investigating committee, and then send them traveling the globe doing just that. And I couldn't think of a better place to get them started than in Ghana. I believe if we make an example of Ghana; then, we just might begin to curb this type of activity throughout the world."

I'm pleased to say the Senator had no rebuttal, and by the time my address was completed, I had convinced 72% of the members to openly condemn the Ghana Government and to call for an investigation of our financial dealings with them. When I left the hearing that afternoon, I left to a round of applause; and it was straight to the airport by 3:30pm, where I boarded my corporate jet and headed for New York City.

During my 9:00pm nationally televised interview with Barbara Waters, I showed the world the tape that Jimmy had sent to me. I answered some questions which led me right into telling the world just how I believed the situation should be handled. Not ten minutes after the interview and before I could even leave the CBS Studios, I received a call from Jean Fitzpeters, the American Ambassador to the United Nations. She called to invite me to address the U.N. Assembly, at 11:00am the next morning, and I graciously accepted.

When I hung up the phone, I handed it to Pierre Collins, who was standing behind me waiting for something to do and said, "Here Pierre, for your first assignment book me a suite at the Plaza, we're staying in town tonight." He anxiously took the phone from me and went right to work.

As soon as we arrived at the Plaza, I called home to inform Michael of my change in plans and that I would be home just in time to leave for our business trip to the West Coast. After we finished our conversation, I talked with Pierre for around an hour about his expected duties. After which I showered, changed and began to study the Sudanese Language of Ghana before calling it a night. I found the language to be very similar to the Bantu dialect used in the Union of South Africa, which I studied only two years' prior. So my studies that night turned out to be less strenuous then I had expected, and I was glad. I had enough to do without trying to learn a totally new language in a few weeks, because for some reason I knew I was going to need to know this language.

The next morning at precisely 11:00am, I found myself addressing the United Nations Assembly. When I took the podium I said, "I truly thank you all from the bottom of my heart for inviting me to speak here this morning especially since the reason I'm here is to ask for your international assistance. I believe that the United Nations has truly become the international symbol of peace and cooperation throughout the world that its founders intended it to be. That is why I find myself here, because this is the only organization on the planet with the power, to truly influence the world's governments into giving all people the dignity of basic human rights. These rights which we cherish must belong to every child born on the face of the earth, or no nation will ever experience true peace. This is why we cannot sit idly by, as dictatorship style governments brutally massacre thousands of their citizens and force hundreds of thousands more to flee into refugee camps, where they are left to starve because the government is cutting off all supplies from international assistance. I am asking the World Community to say no to Ghana. We must send in an international peace keeping force, accompanied by an international committee to investigate all human rights violations." At that point, I looked around at the reaction I was getting and added in a very serious tone, "If we don't act now, then millions of innocent people will die. Please don't let that happen! Not when it's in our power to do something to stop it, before we see any more atrocities such as the horrible ones we've witnessed on the video tape I've shown the world." I received a round of applause.

When everyone quieted down the lead speaker of the U.N. Assembly stood up, and said, "Ms. Powers, I would like to thank you from the World Community for so graciously addressing the assembly on such a delicate matter. Right now Ms. Powers, I promise you and the citizens of the United States, the International Community will not stand by and watch as these atrocities continue. Furthermore, let me also say we will put your suggestion to a vote this afternoon. Ms. Powers, on behalf of the International Community, I would like to make a counter request of you, which is if we agree to follow your suggestions, would you consider heading the International Human Rights Committee on behalf of your country?"

I was on the spot and I knew it. In that moment I thought, 'Oh my God! I don't have time to go running off to Ghana to do this now' Then I got angry and I thought, 'Why you, bastard! I'm standing here in front of the whole world, how can I say no?' Knowing everyone was waiting for my response, I smiled as I stood up tall and said, "Sir, I would be honored to serve the World Community in such a distinguished capacity." When I finished accepting the position, I received a standing ovation. I swallowed hard as I took my seat and thought, 'Shit, Jimmy! Six-thousand miles away, and you're still pulling me into these things! You just wait till I get my hands on you.'

Not ten minutes later, the resolution to send an International Peace Keeping Force, along with an International Human Rights Committee, headed by 'yours truly' to Ghana, was voted on and passed with 96% of the vote. I was thrilled and horrified at the same time over the vote, but I only showed my enthusiasm to the world.

By the time I arrived home, I only had one hour to pick up Michael and Joanne and get back to the airport. So when I entered the family living room at 7:00 that Tuesday evening, and found Joanne lying on the sofa with a low grade fever, 'you know me,' I became a little concerned to say the least.

When I asked her where Michael was she said, "He went to the drug store to pick up some Tylenol."

The moment she finished speaking, Michael walked in and said, "Here I am now." He came to me, kissed my cheek and continued, "Hi Punkie, I've missed you. Joanne's not feeling well and we were out of Tylenol, so I went out for some."

He opened the bottle, handed it to Joanne, and I said, "You can't take that. If you're running a fever your body could be rejecting the baby." I picked up the phone as I said, "I think we'd better call Dr. Hart before we do anything."

As soon as I got him on the phone and filled him in on our situation he said, "Listen, I'm just leaving the office now, so why don't I stop in and check on Joanne at the house."

I thanked him, hung up the phone and said, "Dr. Hart will be here in a few minutes."

After Dr. Hart's examination he said, "I can't say for sure what's causing the fever, but it may be a sign your body is rejecting the fetus. I would suggest you stay off your feet for a few days. Make sure you get plenty of rest, drink plenty of fluids, and only Tylenol for the fever. I want you to call me immediately if you have any discharge, or if the fever goes past 101."

I had ten minutes before I had to leave, when Dr. Hart left, so I took Michael's hand and said, "Honey, I think it might behoove us to have you stay home with Joanne, and I'll take this trip by myself."

He agreed with me then said, "I don't know when we're ever going to spend some time together."

I shook my head, "You haven't heard anything yet."
He looked at me strangely, "What happened now?"

I kissed him, waved goodbye to Joanne and said, "I'll call you and tell you all about it later, because I have got to leave." Looking at them both I added, "Take good care of our baby, okay guys, and you'll be in my prayers, Joanne." I kissed Michael once more, turned and headed for the airport.

After my intense four day business trip, combined with two charity dinner fund raising benefits, I returned home exhausted, only to discover I would be taking the next four weeks of planned business trips by myself as well. Not five minutes before I arrived home, Dr. Hart had decided to put Joanne on complete bed rest. So, I spent one loving night with Michael and the next morning I began a four-week business trip, which started on September 1$^{st}$, in Miami, Florida.

My personal staff and I had already completed our corporate studies on all the companies we had acquired and arranged to meet with on that trip. I wanted to personally introduce myself to all the staff and assure them I had every intention of keeping and modernizing their companies. I told them if we worked together, we could all move into the twenty-first-century as leaders in a world market.

On October 1$^{st}$, which was two days before I was to return home, I received a call from the Secretary General of the United Nations. He informed me I would need to be ready to leave for Ghana to join the International Human Rights Committee on October 6$^{th}$. Two days later, I had the glorious opportunity to spend several days helping Michael cater to Joanne's every whim before taking off for Ghana, even though Michael had arranged for her to have around the clock nursing coverage. I swear in the month I was gone, I think Joanne forgot every word in the English language except 'Michael'. If Michael and I had six hours alone before I left, it was a lot.

Then at 6:00pm, on October 6$^{th}$, Michael took me to the airport for my 7:00pm flight to Ghana, and I didn't plan on returning home until November 18th, which would be only one week before our wedding day.

Just before I boarded my corporate jet, Michael took me in his arms and said, "I don't know how in the world, you talked me into allowing you to go into a war-torn country."

I smiled, kissed him and said, "It's because you love me and you know in your heart I'm doing the right thing."

He shook his head and with a look of concern replied, "I do know you're doing right by going, I just can't stand letting you go alone."

I lovingly gazed into his warm sad blue eyes and said, "I love you honey, but we both know you have to stay with Joanne and try to keep on top of the corporate monster we have created. Besides, I won't be alone I'll have my staff with me. You already know I've arranged for the jet to be kept at the airport, so if you need me I will be able to leave right away."

He gently hugged me and said, "I know all that Punkie, I'm more worried about you being alone so far away, without me being there to protect you."

I kissed him and tried to comfort him by saying, "Honey, please try not to worry, I'll be fine. Jimmy will be meeting me at the airport with the American Ambassador. How dangerous can it be?"

Tears came to his eyes as he said, "Christina, I don't know what lies ahead for you over there and that scares me. But I do know somehow God's hand is on your life. So wherever God is leading you, keep trusting in your Guardian Angels to guide your steps." As both our tears began to fall, he kissed me passionately and softly whispered in my ear, "You're my precious Punkie, and I will keep my thoughts on you every second we're apart."

As we embraced Julie, my flight attendant interrupted us, "Excuse me Ms. Powers, but the captain has said we must leave now."

I felt an empty feeling come over me as I pulled away from Michael's embrace. I wiped the tears from off his cheeks with my fingers and said, "I miss you already my love, and I will call you as soon as I'm able."

He kissed me one more time and said, "Be safe Christina, Please!" I returned his kiss then quickly walked away. As I boarded the jet, I blew him a kiss. I stepped back as Julie closed the door, and like the blink of an eye he was out of sight, and I was off to Ghana.

# CHAPTER 10

I wobbled as if I had rubber legs when I exited the Jet in Accra, the Capital City of Ghana, at 1:00pm on October 7$^{th}$. I was surprised to be welcomed by a large group of cheering fans, some holding large signs reading, **"We love you, Christina!"** As my feet touched the ground, I was greeted by a group of armed soldiers, who proceeded to escort my staff and me through the crowd and into the airport terminal. When I finished going through the security gates, I headed down the hall and my heart was filled with excitement the moment my eyes caught Jimmy's. We rushed to one another with open arms and with the exuberance of little children leapt into a whole hearted embrace. In the midst of our loving greeting I whispered into his ear, "I'll get you later you, shithead!"

He started to laugh and whispered back, "I figured, you would." I hugged Richard as Jimmy continued, "Christina, let me introduce you to the American Ambassador to Ghana, Diana Frangella."

I greeted her then off we went to the Princess Hotel. Our entourage had a military escort which led us through the incredibly, beautiful, tropical like paradise, of the Capital City of, Accra.

I was amazed by the obvious wealth of this city, so I turned to Jimmy and said, "I'm surprised Jimmy, I half expected to see a war ravaged city here. This place is far from it."

Jimmy shook his head and said, "I know and so are its sister cities, Secunda and Takoradi. But you go only five-hundred-miles inland and the government is forcing hundreds of thousands into starvation camps. The most barbaric thing about it is all the refugees are the true black native Ghanaians, while the ruling party is completely white. The only blacks you will see in the cities are laborers, who are bussed in from the surrounding slums."

I looked at the Ambassador and said, "Diana, how in the world has this type of racial bondage been allowed to go on?"

She looked at me sadly as she answered, "This civil war between Prime Minister Kwame Nkmah's troops and the rural population in the northeastern hill country has been going on since the ruling party took power in 1957."

I was angered by my own ignorance to this suffering and asked, "What about the U.N. Security Council's Resolution on human rights? Doesn't that apply to Ghana?"

With a sense of frustration she answered, "Ghana has been a political time bomb for America for years now, and no one was willing to talk about it. It appears the American policies of the fifties haven't changed toward Ghana, since the then, Leader of the House, said to Congress, 'after all, they're only ignorant savages, aren't they.'"

I was shocked by her bluntness and it showed as I said, "What you're telling me is if I hadn't brought this to the world's attention, Ghana would still be considered a valued member of the United Nations. That blows me away! If our government knew this was going on, then you can't tell me the U.N. had no idea these atrocities were taking place."

She looked at me dead serious, "That's exactly what I'm saying, Christina."

I shook my head in disbelief and said, "If I've done my homework correctly, the current Prime Minister, Kwame Nkmah, is the son of the former Prime Minister."

She smiled as though she was impressed and replied, "You're right and the war has increased since he was elected to succeed his father in '79, and he has won every election since."

As I listened to her words, I thought, 'My God! Somehow I've got to put a stop to this madness.'

Shortly after the noon hour, I checked my staff and myself into the entire 20th floor of the Princess Hotel, which was located directly across the Boulevard from the Prime Minister's Palace. When we entered the suite, Diana informed me I had a 3:00pm meeting with the International Human Rights Committee, in the conference room of the hotel. She said, "They are anxiously waiting for you to inform them on how you intend to lead this investigation."

I looked at her with a surprised expression, "Are you telling me no one from the U.N. Security Council has a game plan for an investigation?"

She turned my surprised expression into her own and with concern in her voice said, "Yes! We were informed you would be advising the committee on how to proceed with the investigation. As for the advisors from the Security Council, they're all with the British and French, Peace Keeping Forces, in Togoland, which is four-hundred-miles north of here in the interior of the country"

I shook my head in dismay, smiled and said, "Don't worry about it Diana, I'm on top of everything." as I thought, 'Oh well! I'll figure it out later.'

As soon as we settled into the suite, I picked up the phone and dialed the Prime Minister's private number. Diana was asked by the Prime Minister's Personal Secretary to see that I received the number. He also requested she inform me the Prime Minister would like for me to call him personally, as soon as I was settled. So, with the answering of the phone by Prime Minister Kwame himself, I proceeded to dive head first into the entangled web of the Ghana political nightmare, as soon as he said, "Hello, Ms. Powers. Thank you for calling so promptly."

Courteously I replied, "Good afternoon, Prime Minister Nkmah. I would also like to thank you for your private number. It is reassuring to know I will be able to reach you at any time during the investigation, if there should be a need."

With a wonderful use of the English language and a tone which was not very appealing he said, "Ms. Powers, let's understand one another right off. I am not pleased with your presence in my nation. The only reason I am contacting you at all, is because it was requested of me to do so by the U.N. Security Council, and I agreed. Now, I would like to request your presence at a 7:00pm informal dinner this evening at my personal residence here in the Prime Minister's Palace. I would like to know in advance exactly what your plans are for this Human Right's Investigation."

I quickly responded with an authoritative tone of my own, "I'm very pleased you will be cooperating with the investigation, I'm sure you will assist me in any way possible." Just as quickly I changed to a friendly tone as I continued, "I would also be honored to have dinner with you this evening to inform you of my intentions, while I'm here in your beautiful nation." We ended our conversation on a friendly note and it was right to work.

As soon as I hung up the phone I went back into the living room where Jimmy, Diana, Richard, and Pierre, the young man I stole from the Washington Hilton, were relaxing, and called them all into an on-the-spot conference.

When I had everyone's attention, I said, "Pierre, would you please take out the map of Ghana for me?" I opened the map and continued, "Now Diana, please point out and circle all the hot spots for me? I'll need a brief background on them all." She looked at me with a bewildered expression so I added, "You know, the ones where the crimes have been committed." As she circled the hot spots, I began to come up with my game plan for the investigation.

We worked until 2:45pm, at which time we proceeded to the Conference Room for our luncheon with the eighteen international members of the Human Rights Committee. As Diana introduced us all, I was quite pleased with myself because I could actually speak to them in their own individual languages. After our lunch, I walked up to the platform and said in English, "Ladies and gentleman, I would like to say it has been a pleasure meeting every one of you, and as pleasant as this meeting has been, we mustn't forget the gravity of the circumstances which brought us here. Starting tomorrow morning, we will all become very involved in a highly sensitive situation. But I will not be overwhelming any of you this evening. All I will ask for tonight, is that everyone try to enjoy the amenities of the Hotel and get your bearings. I will be having dinner with the Prime Minister this evening, and I will fill you all in on our conversation tomorrow morning at 8:00am, so please enjoy yourselves until then."

It was 6:30pm when a military escort arrived at the door of my suite to accompany me to the Prime Minister's Palace. I was led to the Prime Minister's Office where he was waiting for my arrival. He rose from his seat as I entered the room and impatiently stood there, as I slowly walked the thirty paces toward his large desk. He was a tall, distinguished looking man, in his early fifties, with a stern expression. When I confidently reached him, we graciously exchanged greetings and with sophistication and charm, I quickly put us on a first name basis. I was wearing an off-white Giavani business suit and I made it a point to come across as the beautiful angel who, with a hard hand, would help salvage his crumbling nation. The Prime Minister was dressed in a formal presidential style, black, three-piece suit. He tried to present himself as sophisticated royalty, but he was so taken by my physical appearance that it showed through the eyes of his royal facade, just like any down to earth, red blooded, American male, that I'd ever met. The minute I spotted that look, I knew he was going to end up being putty in my hands!

As Kwame and I chatted, we earned a little respect for one another and what was supposed to be a very formal private dinner, turned into a very informal one. After our cordial dinner, Kwame invited me into his private study, so we might be more comfortable as we discussed our business. I agreed and proceeded to walk with him to his study. As we sat in two side by side, Queen Anne chairs gazing out over the beautiful Gulf of Guinea, Kwame smiled warmly at me and said, "Christina, I must tell you as much as it displeases me to have you in my nation for the reason you're here, it has still been a great pleasure meeting you. May I also thank you for joining me for dinner this evening, because I have discovered for myself you are truly the beautifully, enchanted woman your reputation proclaims you to be."

I smiled with a slightly flattered expression and replied, "I would like to thank you Kwame, for your gracious compliment and I'm pleased to hear it, because my feelings are similar." I then boldly and gently patted his hand, as I gazed into his eyes and with a soft smile added, "Maybe now that we are a little more comfortable with one another, we should consider the reason I'm here."

He nodded his head diplomatically and said, "I agree completely Christina, and my first question is exactly how you intend to proceed with your investigation?"

I turned toward him as I gracefully swept my fingers through my hair, then settled it back in place with a quick shake of the head and said,

"First, I would like to proceed by having the International Human Rights Committee travel into the interior of the country, to eight different regions where Human Rights atrocities have been reported. I would like to get them started on the investigation as soon as possible, and I would also like for you to instruct your military to cooperate with the requests of the committee completely."

As I was speaking, we were interrupted by a house servant who entered, poured us both a glass of white wine, and then slipped away as quickly as she appeared. I took a sip of the wine and continued, "The second thing I would like to do, is come straight to the point with you personally on just where you are leading your nation. You and I both know you're up against a wall now that the world's eyes are upon you. Now as I see it, you have one of two choices to make for your nation's survival. You can either end this civil war and unite your whole nation, or continue with this brutality. Now if you will bear with me just a while longer, I will give you the outcome of the latter, first. If you ignore the U.N.'s warnings to put an end to this civil war, your nation will suffer great sanctions from the International Community. Once this happens, the rebels will become a mighty opponent, backed by the Red Communist Party of China, and I can guarantee the International Community will not come to your aid. You see, the plain truth is Ghana is just not strategic enough for the West to risk a war with China, thus giving China a strong hold in Africa and at the same time enslaving your nation forever."

He was visibly irritated by my bluntness and it showed as he replied, "Well, that sounds like a morbid prediction." Lifting his eyebrows with curiosity he added, "So what is your prediction with my first choice?"

My smile was brilliantly seductive as I answered, "Now on the other hand, if you are willing to rightfully embrace more than three quarters of your population into the mainstream of your Nations' society, then your Nation's future will be quite bright and I will help assure that."

He stood up, reached his hand out to me and said, "Please come with me for a moment, I would like to show you something." He proceeded to lead me through the palace to an open balcony which gazed out upon the Capital City. He waved his hand out toward this splendid city and said, "Do you see all this wealth? If I were to do what you propose, it would be turned into a slum in two years anyway, because that's when the next election rolls around. So, as I and all the residents see it, we have no choice but to continue fighting this civil war."

I embraced his shoulders and with honest sincerity in my voice said, "Kwame, it doesn't have to be like that. You can begin to turn this Nation around just by industrializing the interior of the nation. What you need to do is show the rural population you are truly going to help supply them with the opportunity to make a better life for themselves and their families. Once you treat them with common human dignity they will become an asset to your nation, not a threat."

He looked at me in dismay and said, "Christina, that's impossible. First, most of them are savages, who can't even live among themselves. Just look at their own tribal wars and then you tell me they can live in peace with us."

I shook my head and said, "Kwame, you're still living in the past and you don't even realize things are changing in the interior of your nation. Can't you see how over the last three years the tribes have begun to band together with the Chinese to wage an all-out attack on the Capital? If they can band together against you, then they are a little more intelligent then you give them credit, and one should never underestimate one's opponent." I looked at him with deep sincerity and continued, "If there is one thing I've learned in our meeting this evening, it is that deep inside, you are not an evil man. I also realize for myself you truly believe you have been doing the right thing for your nation."

He smiled and said, "I'm happy to hear that Christina, because I'm truly not the ruthless dictator you've led the world to believe me to be." His expression became helpless and my heart went out to him as a fellow human being, as he humbly said, "My dilemma is I cannot see how to overcome all the obstacles my nation faces."

I gazed at him with compassion as I replied, "If you will allow me to Kwame, I will stand by you and help you guide your nation with dignity, into the twenty-first-century."

I could see his overwhelming feelings of frustration rising from within him as he shook his head, "Christina, I wouldn't have a clue as to where to start."

I smiled and said, "That's because you're too close to the situation to see the big picture. All you have to do is what I've said, and that is to bring life to the interior of this nation. Start by industrializing the war ravaged areas. Bring business there, bring roads, electricity, hospitals, running water, and build health safe communities for the people. Show them your government truly wants to change. Treat them like you really care. Apologize to them and help them understand why you thought you were doing the right thing."

He looked at me with a slight sense of relief and asked, "If I do that do you really believe they will listen to me?"

I answered him with the utmost sincerity, "Yes I do! And I will tour your nation with you, and together we will convince your people this is the right path to follow." I took his hand as I continued, "I promise you right now Kwame, I will personally bring manufacturing plants into the needed areas, and I will also help bring other American Corporate sponsors to your nation." He still had an unbelieving look so I added, "Kwame, all we have to do is create a business like plan, which you can implement over a four-year span."

His eyes widened as he said, "Four years! The people would never give us four years to turn this nation around, and I will be voted out of office in two years. Then it will all end up in the hands of the Communists anyway."

I released his hand with frustration and thought, 'how can I convince this man this is his only answer?' Then it came to me and with excitement I said, "All we have to do is stipulate in a peace agreement that your government must have four years to implement your plans before the next election." I smiled with even more excitement as I continued, "The best part of that is it will put international pressure on the rebels to agree with this peace accord; thus, taking the pressure off your government."

He looked at me with total amazement and said, "If you can prove to me we can convince the rebels to go along with your plan, and you give me six years to complete the task, then I will accept your offer."

I hugged him with excitement and said, "God bless you Kwame, because with courage and dignity you have chosen to do the right thing for your people."

The next morning, I put the International Human Rights Committee to work throughout the countryside in pairs, accompanied by the U.N. Peace-Keeping Force. Kwame and I, along with my staff, began a thirty-six-hour marathon to compose a peace treaty that would be favorable for all concerned. Let me tell you that was not an easy task, but we did it! At the same time I requested the U.N. arrange for immediate peace talks to be held among all the chiefs of the interior tribes with Kwame Nkmah's Government. Kwame had finally agreed to all the changes I proposed for his government and a wonderful peace treaty was ready to be presented at the peace talks. After our marathon, Kwame made a personal request to the U.N., asking the Security Council to allow me to mediate the peace talks, as the official representative for the United Nations. Their reply was they could only do that if I were an 'Official Ambassador to the U.N. The moment President Rush heard this news, he immediately appointed me an 'Official Representative for the United States of America, to the United Nations'.

The next thing I knew, I was overseeing the peace talks in two different African dialects, to the eyes and amazement of the entire world.

At 10:00pm on October 16th, a national peace treaty, which declared each of the twelve tribe leaders, governors of their respective regions, which were to be renamed states was signed. At noon that day, all the governors who signed the treaty, along with the Prime Minister and myself began a nation-wide tour to explain to the citizens exactly what the treaty meant for them. And as all this was transpiring in Ghana, back home the headlines read, **"Christina Powers has proven to be America's 'Angel of Peace!' as she helps bring harmony to a war torn nation!"** Or **"America stands proud as one of her own, Christina Powers helps bring peace to a racially divided nation!"** The peace treaty was ratified on November 5th, and two hours later I put into motion, my prearranged plans to begin to turn this nation into a profit making, free society for all its citizens.

Despite the pace of those few weeks, I tried to stay in touch with Michael as much as possible. With each conversation I could tell Michael was becoming more and more concerned over Joanne's health. It seemed she had experienced the spotting of blood on three occasions and she was still on strict bed rest. Even though I heard Michael's concern, I couldn't allow myself to become caught up in his fear of losing our child, so I chose to bury myself even further into the task at hand. Then, two days before I was ready to return home, while I was touring the nation with the

Prime Minister, I received a message to call home immediately.

So, at 9:06pm on November 16th, when Michael informed me in a devastated tone that Joanne had miscarried our child, I was so far away from the immediate impact of the reality of our child's death, that I could not even feel the emotion of pain my Michael was experiencing. When he finished crying all I could find myself able to say was, "I will be home as soon as possible."

Then I said my goodbyes to the Nation of Ghana, without attending the Prime Minister's planned ticker tape parade for me, took the only ten minutes Jimmy and I had alone together the whole time I was there, to say a sad goodbye, and at 11:57pm I was on my way **home to Michael**.

# CHAPTER 11

Due to the early blustery, winds and snows, of an icy Nor'easter, I was not able to enter the front door of our home until 2:00am, November 17th, 1989. The house would have been quiet, except for the howling of the winds as they roared through the river valley. The bursts of air which crept through the walls with each gust, gave me a cold chill as I made my way to the master bedroom. I was careful not to disturb Michael's sleep, as I quietly opened the bedroom door. The room was dimly lit by the glow of the alarm clock and a small plug-in night light, which enabled me to tiptoe through the room, past the bed and into the bathroom. Once in, I turned up the heat and quietly showered. Afterward, I slipped into my robe and returned to the bedroom without turning on a light. When I reached the bed I slipped off my robe and laid it on the chair bedside the bed. I slowly pulled down the covers and softly slipped into the bed with Michael. My body became cold as soon as I disrobed, so I slowly began to snuggle to Michael's warm bare back. The second my body touched his, the fires of my passion began to heat from within. My desire for Michael rose until I found myself slowly beginning to stroke his body, in an attempt to wake him already aroused. He slowly began to come out of his deep sleep. When he realized I was lying behind him, he turned to me and instantly took on a broken-hearted expression, as he desperately clung to my breasts and began to weep like a little boy.

As he softly wept in my arms, I slowly stroked his head and tenderly whispered, "I'm here my love, I'm here. Everything will work out now that we're back together again; I promise you it will, Michael." As I lovingly spoke these words, he slowly gazed up at me and with tear filled eyes cried,

"I've failed us, Punkie! I've lost our baby. I can't understand how you could go off and help save a nation and I couldn't even help keep our baby alive."

My heart broke as I held him tight and at that moment I felt the pain of his devastation and the shame of his perceived failure. My tears began to flow with his. I wanted so much to comfort him, so in a gentle and assuring voice I said, "Michael, honey, don't do this to yourself. You did everything humanly possible to prevent this from happening, I know you did! But you know as well as I do, sometimes no matter what we do we can't prevent or change anything from happening."

He slowly shook his head as he stopped crying and with disgust in his voice said, "I know you're right Punkie, but it's still killing me that we lost another baby."

I tenderly kissed his forehead as I lovingly replied, "I know it hurts Michael, I feel the pain too, but I promise you we will try again and we will have our baby."

At that, his eyes filled with tears again as he cried in anguish, "No we won't Christina because Joanne has decided she can't go through this again and she's leaving in the morning." Then his voice became weak with a tone of defeat as he continued, "And Punkie, if Joanne won't carry our child, then I don't want to go through the whole ordeal again. I just don't think I can handle it."

I held him close to my heart and with all the love I felt for him said, "Just lay still in my arms and try to get some rest my love. I love you honey, and I promise you things will be clearer in the morning." With that, my heart ached for my love, as I gently rocked him in my arms.

When he finally drifted off to sleep I thought, as I listened to the cold wind outside our window, 'Dear, God, why do you keep taking my babies from me? Are you still punishing me for the abortion I had? I was young when I did those things God! I didn't realize how precious a baby's life was. Nor did I realize how much I would end up wanting to have a baby of my own. God I'm sorry, I know what I did was wrong. My soul is scarred for life because of what I've done, haven't I suffered enough? Lord, help me! I can't and I won't deny Michael a child of his own, and even if it kills me, I will bear him his child.' I lovingly gazed at my sleeping beauty and thought, 'Michael, I want your child my love, more than anything I have ever wanted in my life, and I will give birth to your seed, I vow I will.' After I thought these things, a sense of peace came over me, and I was finally able to join Michael in his restless sleep.

The next morning after a warm welcome home by James and Carman, Carman, served us a delicious French toast breakfast. But, as Joanne, Michael, and I, sat there hardly saying a word, it was apparent I was the only one who appreciated our meal. I quietly ate my feast while waiting for one of them to say something. Finally, I could take the silence no longer so I said, "I know this has turned out to be a very sad situation for all of us, but that doesn't mean we shouldn't talk about it. I think if we talk about how we're feeling then maybe we can walk away from this not feeling so devastated."

Joanne turned to me and in a very harsh tone said, "How do you know how Michael and I are feeling? You weren't here all those hours I layed in that bed, trying to prevent my body from rejecting the implant. Michael and I went through it alone and we cried alone when I had the miscarriage. So please don't sit there with your all-knowing and uncaring attitude, and tell me I'll feel better if I talk, because I'm talking and I still feel like shit."

I quickly tried to understand where this was coming from before getting angry. So, with a calm steady voice I replied, "You're absolutely correct Joanne, I wasn't there. But, that doesn't mean I'm not feeling the same loss you are. It doesn't mean I don't understand what the two of you have lived through in the past three months either. What I'm trying to say is, I do know what you went through and I love you for what you did. I also want you to know, even though you weren't able to give birth to our child, I will still see you receive the rest of your compensation. I also understand why you feel like you can't do this again and whether you can believe it or not, I can accept and agree with your reasons. I just don't want you to leave here hurting, because I do care about you."

The moment I finished speaking, Joanne stood up and walked out of the room without saying another word. As she did, I could feel a sense of desperation come over Michael as he quickly rose from his seat and went after her. I immediately followed and when I reached them, my heart pained as I watched Michael grab Joanne by the arm and pleaded, "Please Joanne, I'm begging you to reconsider! We will give you two-million-dollars if you will please bear our child for us." Tears welled up in his eyes as he continued, "Joanne, why can't you see you're the only hope we have of having a child. If you don't carry our child then we won't have one, because I will not do this again. I could never have another woman carry our child for us, not after knowing you."

As I helplessly watched Michael pleading with Joanne, for the first time in my life I felt inadequate as a woman, and that thought, at that moment, almost stole the pride I had in being a woman away from me. As I stood there feeling like this, I knew Michael had no idea what he was saying was killing me. Watching him plead with another woman for a child, made me want to scream out, "Michael, I will bear our baby!" But I couldn't, because I felt something was not right with this picture. As I watched them standing there together, I struggled to understand the obsession they seemed to have toward one another and I began to feel very uncomfortable with the whole situation.

As soon as Michael finished pleading, Joanne began to cry as she said, "Michael, I love you and Christina very much, and I would love to give you both the baby you desire so badly. But look at it from my perspective, because there is no way I can handle another week of bed rest, and you're asking me to stay in bed for nine months. I just can't do it, not even for ten-million-dollars."

That's when I jumped in with a sharp tone, "Michael, she's right! Now stop making this so hard for all of us and let her leave in peace."

Joanne looked at me with angry eyes as if to say, 'Who are you to speak to him like that.' Then she gazed warmly into Michael's eyes and said, "Michael, because I think you are truly a caring man and would make a wonderful father, I will bear your child for you, but only if you use my egg." With that statement, she smiled, turned to face us both, and continued as if she was also speaking to me, "This way you will both have your child, because I will surrender my parental rights to you Christina, as soon as the baby is born." Once again looking directly into Michael's eyes she added, "Michael, I'm sorry, but this is the only way I can be sure my body will not reject the fetus again."

Michael looked at me with a glow of pure excitement, joy, and relief then said, "Maybe this is the answer to our prayers, Punkie. I know the baby will only be mine biologically, but it will still be ours."

He could see the stunned look on my face, so he hugged me and with the most sincere voice I've ever heard said, "Christina, I love you with all my heart baby, and I would never consent to anything without your approval. But honey, before you answer please know what I've just realized, this may be the only chance I'll ever have of carrying on my father's bloodline."

I stepped back from him, looked into his loving eyes and I wanted to scream, "No, Michael!" But instead I said, "I think it is a wonderful idea too, Michael." We joyfully embraced as I said these words and all the while I was wanting to say, 'Even though I don't want a child like this, I won't keep you from having your own child. I can't bring myself to cause you anymore pain and disappointment than you already have suffered. I love you Michael more than anyone I ever loved before.' Only I kept these words to myself.

After our warm embrace, Michael dragged us to the bar, popped open a chilled bottle of champagne and began to pour three glasses. I smiled as we began to celebrate our decision that morning, but as I smiled, I wondered to myself, 'Will I be able to love this child even though it will not be mine?' As we talked, I really began to look deep within myself for the answer to my question. I looked at how happy Michael had become and how pleased Joanne seemed to be over the fact she could help after all, and at that moment, I truly realized just how much this child meant to Michael and I thought, 'Yes! I know I will love Michael's child, no matter who the biological mother is.' When I came to the awareness of just how much I would do for Michael's love, I was able to come to terms with the idea of having a child in this manner, and as soon as I did, a sense of peace came over me.

Two days later, we were back at Dr. Hart's office to request his assistance in our new adventure. After Joanne's physical, Dr. Hart advised us we needed to allow Joanne's body time to heal properly before proceeding. He felt she might be ready to conceive without a high risk, by her February cycle. So we set our sights on February 1$^{st}$, 1990.

When we returned from our doctor's visit, I whole heartedly invited Joanne to become a permanent guest in our home, until after the birth of our child. I also felt it only fair, to give Joanne her million-dollars and Michael promised another million after the birth of his child. We had also arranged for a new contract to be signed among the three of us, which stated Joanne could never admit to being the birth mother. I wanted this stipulation because I was still terribly ashamed of my infertility. So much so I actually dreaded the thought of my fans ever finding out that the *'Christina Powers'* couldn't bear her own husband's child. Once we signed our contract, Michael and I were once again filled with joy and anticipation for our future family.

# CHAPTER 12

When November 25$^{th}$, 1989 arrived, the news cameras were flashing at the worldwide, headline stealing, wedding of the two happiest people on the planet.

After we said our wedding vows that Thanksgiving morning, I closed my eyes to kiss Michael and as we kissed I became the proud wife of this beautiful man. As soon as we ended our wedding kiss, we gazed into each other's loving eyes and at that moment, for the first time in my life, I knew I was a failure, because I could never bear Michael's child. At that realization my eyes began to tear and my feelings began to spin so fast, I couldn't tell if I was crying because I was happy or because I felt like an empty shell of a woman. In that moment, I went on autopilot as all my thoughts began to ricochet through my mind until they stopped on 'Frank'. Once again, I became able to concentrate on one thought, 'How in the world did I allow my hatred for Frank, to grow so evil that I will be paying for it for the rest of my life?' My mind and heart went deeper into my higher consciousness as my thoughts continued, 'As God is my witness I will never allow hatred to consume my life again!'

Instantly I felt myself being lifted from years of hard heartedness and a glorious strange feeling of harmony and oneness came over me toward every living creature. Finally I understood what Michael once told me about how he knew he was one with God. I came to this realization as I talked with my new mother in-law, Tess Gillespie. As we spoke, a cool gentle breeze brushed my shoulder and I heard a soft voice whispering behind me, "Christina, strength comes forth from those who truly tap into the power of their own divinity. Remember this." I turned so quickly I startled Tess and to my surprise, no one was there.

When we left St. Patrick's church, in that quaint little town of Ravena, New York, there were thousands of people lining both sides of the main street. As we drove past them, they threw Red Roses at the fleet of horn blowing limos, which not only held the wedding party, but the guests as well. As Michael and I waved to my fans, the press caught it all with their cameras, for the whole world to see!

After the reception Michael and I flew to Key West, Florida for a one week honeymoon. We spent the whole week in Barbara's secluded, oceanfront, beach house, which she so graciously offered to us as a wedding gift. That week we spent alone together was a beautiful dream come true for the both of us. Finally, after all we lived through since the night Michael proposed to me, we were legally husband and wife. Throughout that week we spent our days walking the beach for hours planning our future family dreams, and every night was spent in the loving intimacies of our oneness. Our honeymoon was the most incredibly romantic experience I had ever known. When it was time to leave our heavenly bliss, we took with us dreams enough to last a lifetime. So, on the flight to New York when I picked up a pen and paper to turn my thoughts into lyrics, I had a lot to write.

We returned home on December 4th, and on the next day it was right back to the office. While I was in Ghana, Michael managed to stay on top of the business, while taking care of Joanne, but he still had to cancel six pre-arranged business trips, which were the first things I began to reschedule when I sat at my desk.

As I was going through my appointment book that day, Pierre {who had now become a full-fledged staff member of my personal team} buzzed me on the intercom and said, "Good morning Christina, and welcome home. I have dozens of messages for you, when would you like to go through them?"

I answered with a humorous tone, "Why don't we do it now Pierre, because I'll have managed to give us plenty to do by this afternoon."

I began to prioritize my return calls in my normal manner, as Pierre read through the messages in the order they arrived. As Pierre spoke, I was balancing at least twenty thoughts through my mind at the same time and I came to an abrupt stop when Pierre said, "Then you received a call on your personal business line, from a woman who said she was an old friend. She said her name was Mary Everett and she asked that you return her call as soon as possible."

When I heard her name, I instantly thought, 'Johnny! Something terrible has happened to Johnny.' I took the number from Pierre and said, "Would you please excuse me for a moment and I'll buzz you when I'm ready to continue." He nodded his head and left the office. As soon as the door closed behind him I picked up the phone and dialed the number.

When Mary answered the phone and realized who was calling, her voice took on a tone of urgency as she said, "Christina! Thank you for returning my call. I've been waiting on pins and needles to be able to talk with you."

With concern I answered, "What's wrong, Mary?"

In reply she said, "Christina, I know we truly don't know one another. And I'm sorry to contact you like this from out of the blue, but you once told me if I ever needed anything and you could help, that I should feel free to call you. So that is what I am humbly doing, because I am in great need of your help."

As she talked, I found myself wanting to scream at her, 'Well, what is it? Is it, Johnny? Is he, dying? Has he, died? Just stop beating around the bush and tell me!' Instead I answered with a comforting tone, "And I meant it, Mary, so please feel free to do just that and ask me whatever you need."

She sighed with a sense of great relief and said, "Thank you Christina, but I was hoping we could speak in private. If you could only find ten minutes to meet with me, I will drive to New York tonight."

As she continued, I could not hold back my curiosity any longer, "Please just tell me is anyone ill?"

She answered calmly, "No, everyone is well. This is more of a private matter."

I relaxed my tone and said, "Mary, I have a business trip I am scheduling right now, which will take me right to Richmond, Virginia. What if I plan it for December 7th, which is only two days from now? I can stop by your home and save you the trip up here."

With a secretive tone she replied, "Wednesday will be fine Christina, but would you mind if I meet you for lunch somewhere. I feel funny saying this, but I really don't want John knowing I've called you."

I was taken aback by her mysteriousness and I let it be known by saying, "I find it slightly disconcerting that you feel you need to be secretive about our meeting."

She quickly answered, "Please don't feel that way. My reason for the secrecy is to save the man I love from some personal embarrassment. That's all."

By the time we finished talking, we had made plans to meet for a 1:00pm luncheon at The Old Country Inn, which was located in the heart of the historic district of 'Old Richmond Town.'

After setting up the scheduling for a three-week business trip throughout the country, Michael and I decided since we were now three months behind in our plans to revamp our entire holdings, that it would behoove us to have Michael take care of things at our corporate headquarters, while I handled the business trips. We had plenty of reliable people to leave in charge, but I still felt better knowing Michael was at the helm. So when I left at 4:00am on the morning of December 7th, to continue whipping my new corporations into shape, I was not planning to see Michael until he met me in Richmond for my thirty-sixth-birthday on Saturday, December 10th; then it's off to Mississippi and I did not plan to see him again until I returned home on Christmas Eve.

When I arrived in Richmond it was straight to a board meeting, where I immediately began to work my magic on its members. But the whole time I was captivating my audience, I was watching the clock. In the back of my mind, all I could think about was my rendezvous with Johnny's wife. When we finally broke for lunch, I swiftly made my way to the limo and it was off to the Old Country Inn. When I entered the restaurant, I recognized her immediately, even though I had only seen her once in my life, for only two minutes.

She rose from her seat when she noticed me approaching and as I reached her, she warmly embraced me and said, "Christina, it's so good of you to meet me like this, I know you're a very busy woman."

I thanked her as we took our seats then said, "It's nice to see you Mary, you're looking well."

She smiled with apprehension as she replied, "Thank you, you're too kind; but I know what time and working on the farm for the past fifteen years have done to my youthful looks. As for you, you still look like you're twenty-years old. When I look at you, I have to ask myself, how do you do it? I have watched your career and I know you have not had an easy life either, but it doesn't show on you at all."

I finally broke into the middle of her rambling, {as a waitress stood at our table impatiently waiting to take our order} by saying, "I think we should order now, so we won't be disturbed while we talk."

She giggled with surprise, then like a light switch turning on, she saw the waitress standing there and exclaimed with a southern twang, "Oh my, I didn't even notice you there."

Over lunch she went on about her family, the farm, her parents, John's parents and she continued with this litany of her life history, until I finally said, "Mary as much as I'm enjoying our conversation I do have to leave at 2:00pm. So if you need to speak with me about something in particular, then I think we should do that."

She smiled with embarrassment as she replied, "I'm sorry I'm rattling on, I do that when I'm nervous."

As she continued babbling on and on without saying anything, I thought, 'Holy Shit! This is who Johnny married! You poor thing.' Then I thought, 'On the other hand, this is what you deserve for not coming after me.'

Finally she caught my attention when she said, "Christina, I don't know how to say this without just coming out with it."

At that point I had heard enough nonsense, so I abruptly said, "Mary, I'm a very busy woman so would you please get to the point."

Once again, I embarrassed her and when she gained her composure she said, "Okay! It's like this Christina; the last five years have been pure hell for us financially. It has become so bad we are at the point with the bank, if we don't pay them in full by the first of the year, then they will foreclose on our farmhouse. And I know if that happens, it will kill whatever life is left in John." She looked deep into my eyes and spoke from her heart as she continued, "I would never have come to you for help if I had anywhere else to go. The only reason I'm here is to try to save my husband, and if he knew I came to you for help his pride would never let him accept it."

She spoke her words of love with such passion that as a devoted wife myself, I felt her concern for Johnny in my heart. So I took her hand and said, "Of course I'll help, Mary. How much do you need?"

She squinted her face as she timidly squeaked out, "Three-hundred-thousand-dollars. We have two-hundred-thousand-dollars, but the bank won't accept it. They say we must have the whole amount, which is five-hundred-thousand-dollars."

I smiled at her gently and said, "I know how banks can be, I was in your position myself once." Then I opened my purse, took out my checkbook and wrote out a check for five-hundred-thousand-dollars then said, "Please except this gift Mary, and see that the bank gets paid. I want you to keep your money and take the family on a vacation."

She became so excited she nearly knocked my water glass into my lap, as she reached across the table to hug me. With tears in her eyes, she smiled enthusiastically and replied, "Thank you Christina, I will never forget this!"

I kissed her cheek and replied, "I'm glad I was able to help, and don't worry I will never tell a soul of our meeting." Then I deliberately looked at my watch as I continued, "Oh my! Look at the time. I'm sorry to cut this short Mary, but I really must be leaving now." We embraced once more and I walked away thinking, "I would have never lasted all those years on that farm."

After our lunch, I went straight to work for the next two days on corporate negotiations. I didn't have final approval for all my proposals, until 9:00 pm that Friday night. As I walked out of my last board meeting in Virginia, I was totally surprised when I saw Michael standing beside my limo in a black tux, holding a bouquet of Red Roses.

When I reached him, he lovingly hugged me and boisterously said, "Happy Birthday, Punkie!"

My body immediately became rejuvenated and alive with feelings of joy, as Michael kissed me. With a gleaming smile I replied, "It's not my birthday yet silly, but I'm surely glad you're here."

He kissed me romantically and said, "Well, I thought we might usher your birthday in together."

I returned his kiss, "That sounds wonderful, but why the tux handsome?"

He opened the car door and beckoned me to climb in. As we

climbed in, he instructed the driver to take us to the hotel. He turned to me and said, "I placed a new gown in the suite for you, so all you need to do is get ready and leave the rest of the evening to me."

I smiled with sheer delight, then with a slightly seductive tone replied, "OOO! Michael! This sounds like it's going to be a fun and romantic evening. And I love you for thinking of it."

When we arrived at the suite, I disappeared into the bedroom for one half hour. When I reappeared, I was dressed to kill. Michael gazed at me with pure manly pride as I approached him. Then he kissed me gently, took my hand and off we went.

Michael proceeded to take me on the most romantic evening I had in a long time. We started with a candlelight dinner at a quaint little Italian restaurant, in the heart of the 'Old City.' From there, it was ballroom dancing in a 1930's style dance hall. After what seemed like hours of lovingly holding one another, as we rhythmically floated on the dance floor, Michael treated me to a romantic, 2:00am horse driven, Hansom Cab ride. As our buggy took us around the beautiful buildings of the wonderfully historic city of Richmond, Virginia, we were beginning to anticipate the end of our evening. Then right in the midst of this exquisite moment in time, Michael sweetly asked me to close my eyes and hold out my hand. When I opened my eyes, I was holding a small, velvet covered, heart shaped pillow, and in the center of it was a beautiful twenty-four-karat diamond angel pendant! When I saw it, I immediately hugged him as I said, "Oh Michael, it's beautiful and I'm going to put it on right now! Thank you, my love."

I slipped it on my neck chain and as Michael snapped it back on me he said, "I love you more than life itself, Christina." With that, he held me tenderly until we arrived back at our hotel.

When we returned to our suite at 4:00am the morning of the 10th, we wasted no time in fulfilling our passions. We continued in our love making until we welcomed the rays of the morning sun through our bedroom window. That night was incredible and from the time we woke up twelve hours later, straight through to the end of the weekend, Michael treated me to more of the same. Our loving weekend ended Sunday the 11th, at which time Michael returned home and I returned to the hectic pace of my business travel.

# CHAPTER 13

After thirteen days of triumphant corporate maneuvering, I returned home on Christmas Eve to spend a wonderful Christmas at home with Michael and Joanne. The three of us continued to spend almost every minute of the rest of that week together. During that week Joanne became so persistent in her efforts to make herself and the upcoming procedure the center of attention that by the time New Year's Eve rolled around, I was ready to throw her ass out the door.

By the end of that week, I wanted to say to Michael, 'Forget it! I'll adopt before I put up with ten more months of this crap.' However, for the love of my husband I chose to remain silent.

But, when Jimmy called on January 1st, 1990, to wish us a Happy New Year, let me tell you, he got an ear full the minute he shouted, "Happy New Year, Girlfriend! It's your long lost lover boy! How the hell are you?"

I snapped back my response, "Lousy, that's how I am! And how many times do I have to tell you to call me? You didn't even call me for my birthday."

He lovingly snapped back, "Bullshit! I called, but you weren't home. Now stop your nonsense and tell me why you're so miserable?"

At that, I proceeded to take the next hour, to tell him exactly how I felt about this baby plan after spending only one week watching Joanne doting over my husband. I also expressed my new concern over taking business trips and leaving her alone with him.

Jimmy tried to reassure me I could trust Michael and that it would all work out for the best. But for some reason, I was not comforted by his words, so I said, "Well, at least you will be home to help me in July. Hopefully things will calm down some by then."

It was with that statement; he cleared his voice in a disturbing manner and said, "Oh Shit, Christina! I forgot to tell you. Richard and I won't be leaving for home until August 3$^{rd}$. Richard's parents are having their thirty-fifth wedding anniversary on August 1$^{st}$, and they've invited us to come. So we are now going to be leaving Ghana on July 4$^{th}$, for Kuwait instead of America. Richard wants us to spend one month with his family in Kuwait before we come home."

With a surprised tone I replied, "Kuwait! What are his parents doing in Kuwait? I thought he was from New Jersey."

Jimmy laughed as he said, "I know what you mean. We've been together for six months, and I didn't find out myself until two weeks ago. It appears his father works as an adviser to the Kuwait Government, and they have been living there for the last six years."

I replied with a sigh of relief, "Well, at least it's only one month. I think I can hold on that long."

Jimmy laughed at my words at first, then all at once he took on a sad tone, as he said, "Well, I better get off the phone before he comes looking for me. I swear, sometimes he drives me crazy. Christina, the man is always up my ass."

I asked with concern, "Don't tell me you guys are having problems?"

He lowered his voice disconcertingly as he said, "I won't tell you we are having problems because I hear him coming. We'll talk about my troubles next time, okay?" On that note, we lovingly said our goodbyes and I returned to Michael, who I found in the living room watching TV with you know who.

The next morning, it was back to work, only this time it was Michael who went on the road, while I stayed home with Joanne and the home office. During that time I decided to take advantage of my free evenings, which gave me the opportunity to finally get back to the recording studio. Just the thought of singing again was enough to take my mind off the Joanne situation, and I definitely needed to be distracted. Besides, since the day Michael and I returned from our honeymoon, I had written the lyrics to twelve incredible songs. Nine of them were love songs straight from my heart to Michael's, and three spoke of my dreams of one day knowing total peace on earth. Six I planned for ballads, the other six to burn up the dance floor, and I knew they were going to please my begging fan clubs. This soundtrack was going to be hot and I couldn't wait to get it ready for release. So from the moment Michael left on January 3$^{rd}$, 1990, I buried myself into my work, which didn't bother me at all, because as I said, it kept me away from Joanne and at the same time, it kept my mind off missing Michael, who I did not plan to be seeing again until January 31$^{st}$.

The whole month Michael was away, we talked on the phone every night at 11:00pm, and every night I wanted to tell him how I truly felt about our plans to have Joanne carry his child. But every time we spoke, the baby was all he could talk about, so once again I bit my tongue.

On January 30$^{th}$, one day before Michael was to return home, I received a certified letter from the Nobel Institute in Sweden. I quickly opened the envelope to discover that the Nobel Awards Committee had unanimously voted to award me, the 1989 Nobel Peace Prize, for my gallant efforts in helping bring an end to a thirty-two-year, civil war in Ghana. The notification also informed me that because I was a last minute entry for 1989's annual award ceremonies, which I had already missed because it was held on December 10$^{th}$, the committee had decided to hold a special ceremony in my honor on February 10$^{th}$, in Oslo, Sweden. It also graciously stated the Committee was hoping I could be present to accept the Nobel Peace Medallion in person. At the end of the note was a contact number and I was asked to confirm whether I would be available to accept in person or not, by February 1$^{st}$. With excitement and pride, I immediately called to accept their gracious invitation to appear in person.

I was so excited the rest of that day and I could not wait to share my incredible news with Michael. Finally around 7:00pm, I decided to call it an early night. I wanted to get home, get comfortable and call Michael early that evening. When I arrived home, I was still quite excited about calling Michael, so I headed straight through the house on my way to a quick shower. As I approached the doorway which led into the family room, on my way to the master bedroom, I could hear Joanne talking on the phone. Something told me to just eavesdrop on her conversation for a moment.  So I did, and to my surprise, within one minute of listening to one side of this conversation, I knew she was talking to Michael.  As I listened, she was saying, "Oh Michael, I am so excited to be able to carry your child, and the closer it gets to the procedure the more excited I'm becoming."

She was silent for a moment, then in response to something Michael said, she said, "Thank you Michael, very much, and I love you for saying it.  You are the most thoughtful and romantic man I have ever known and if you weren't married I'd sweep you off your feet."

With that, I wanted to burst in and start screaming obscenities, but something held me back.  Instead, I walked in as if I had just arrived and said, "Hi, Joanne.  How was your day?"

She instantly took on a surprised, yet cool look, as she calmly said, "I'm sorry but I have to go now, thanks for calling," Then she swiftly hung up the phone, turned to look me dead in the eyes and said, "Christina, you're home early.  What happened, the place burn down?"

I smiled and in a joking tone said, "No smart-ass, I just wanted to make it an early night tonight" I added with sincerity, "I'm sorry if I interrupted your conversation; was, it anyone I know?"

She smiled innocently as she answered, "That's all right, it was only my mother and I'll call her back later."

I showed no reaction to her **bold faced lie**, as I said, "Well I'm tired Joanne, so I'm going to bed.  I'll see you tomorrow." I walked out of the room and headed for the shower.

My mind was a complete blank when I hopped in the shower, but as soon as the water hit my body, my mind went wild and I thought, 'What's going on here?  Why is he calling her?  Why did she lie to me?  Are they falling in love?  Oh my God!  Have they been having an affair!?'

When I regained my composure, I was once again able to concentrate on details and facts, instead of jumping to conclusions due to jealousy and rage.  I calmly finished showering and headed straight for the phone.  As I dialed the number, my first question was going to be, "Why are you calling, Joanne?"  Then I thought, 'No!  Let me give him a few minutes to see if he starts playing her game.'  So as soon as he said, "Hello."  I said, "Hi honey, it's me."

With a concerned tone he answered, "Punkie!  Where have you

been? I was starting to get worried."

"What do you mean?" I asked innocently.

"I've been trying to find you for an hour now. I called the office and Pierre said you left early. Then I called home and Joanne said you weren't home yet."

I felt an inner sense of great relief as I nonchalantly replied, "You must have just missed me, but I'm surprised Joanne didn't tell me you called."

His voice became calmer as he said, "It probably slipped her mind."

With an emphasis on my words I said, "Slipped her mind! I saw her hanging up the phone when I walked in."

He chuckled and said, "Don't be so hard on her she's just a kid."

I began to choke, as I said, "Just a kid! Michael, she's only a year younger than you. If she's just a kid, what does that make you?"

He laughed again, so I changed the subject by saying with pure excitement, "Oh by the way, I have some great news, Michael! I found out this morning I have been chosen to receive the Nobel Peace Prize."

I proceeded to fill him in on all the details and when I finished speaking he calmly said, "That's wonderful news Punkie, and you deserve it." His tone became excited as he continued, "Oh God Punkie, I can't wait to get home tomorrow! I feel like I did when I was a little boy and I knew Christmas was coming the next morning. I would get so excited I couldn't sleep, and I would be on the edge of the bed all night long waiting for the morning. Punkie, I can't believe just the thought of having our own child is driving me nuts with anticipation."

I answered with a disappointed tone, "Oh boy! I thought all this excitement was over me."

Once again he laughed like a little boy who could only think of one thing as he said, "Christina, that's a given and you should know that, but we don't have a baby every day you know."

"I know," I answered lovingly. Then I added, "By the way, how did today's vote go?"

I heard him take a deep breath as he replied, "I hate to tell you this, but it didn't go in our favor."

With a shocked tone I said, "What! How could they defeat our proposal, Michael? You've been working with them for three weeks now. Can't they see our plans are the only way they're going to survive the competition of the changing markets?"

With a sigh of disappointment he answered, "I'm sorry honey, I guess I'm just not as good as you are at winning people over."

I felt bad I snapped at him so I said, "Don't worry about it Michael, it's not the end of the world, and I think I can fix it."

I guess I didn't comfort him enough because with a very defensive tone he sharply replied, "Please don't patronize me, Christina! I know you're wonderful at everything. And let's face it; I just can't deal with people like you do."

Feeling frustrated, I sighed and said, "I'm sorry, but I wasn't trying to be patronizing. I just didn't want you to be upset over it, because we can decide what to do about it when you come home."

He quickly changed the subject and talked about the baby, until I could take it no more and finally I said, "Honey, I love you, but I need to get some sleep. We can talk more about the baby tomorrow." Then we said our goodbyes and I hung up the phone feeling slightly slighted, to say the least.

When I laid my head on my pillow that night I thought, 'I don't believe him! I just told him his wife has received the phenomenal honor of being awarded the prestigious Nobel Peace Prize, and in two hours of conversation all he could say about it was, 'That's wonderful!' He is so obsessed with having this child, he's becoming totally thoughtless.' That's when I started to really lose my temper and I thought, 'No matter how much I love you Michael, I'm not going to stand for this shit! We are going to be doing some heavy duty talking when you get home later today! If you think you're going to act like this the whole time she's pregnant, you got another think coming.' As much as I hate to admit it, I allowed myself to fall asleep with these angry thoughts.

The next morning when I awoke, I made a conscious decision not to become irrational. I decided I would try harder to understand Michael's position, so that when we talked, I hoped to have had a good idea of how to approach the subject without hurting his feelings. I realized I had to handle the situation in this manner, because I certainly didn't want to be misunderstood. This was too touchy a subject for that, and I knew it.

When Michael entered my office at 4:00pm the next afternoon, he was gleaming from ear to ear. The moment he reached me, he began kissing me with a childlike enthusiasm, as he exclaimed, "I love you Punkie, and just think, before we know it, we'll be having a baby! And as he rambled on I thought, 'This is going to be a bigger challenge than I **ANTICIPATED**'

After our loving embrace, he kissed me passionately then said, "Hi, sexy! How would you like me to rescue you from this mad house for the rest of the afternoon? Maybe we could take a ride up to the Catskills, and I'll treat you to a romantic dinner."

I kissed him back and sincerely said, "Now that sounds like a proposition I can't refuse." I grabbed my coat and off we went.

It was 4:10pm when we left for what I hoped would be a wonderfully intimate afternoon. I figured this would be the perfect time to talk with Michael about my concerns, but he talked so much about having the baby, that I still could not find the appropriate time to bring the subject up. We didn't return home until 11:00pm that night and believe it or not, the whole time, Michael never said another word about the news I received from the Nobel Institute.

When we did enter our home that night, I watched in total amazement, as Michael and Joanne instantly climbed up each other's butts like two love birds, the minute they laid eyes on one another. And at that moment, I knew we were heading for trouble.

The three of us talked about the baby until midnight, at which time I said, "Well it's been a long day and I think I'm ready for a quick shower and a warm bed." I turned to Michael as I continued, "Are you ready, Michael?"

He gave me an incredibly sexy wink and said, "Why don't you take your shower and I'll be up in a minute."

I smiled, kissed his cheek and replied, "Okay sexy, I'll meet you in bed." I said goodnight to Joanne and left them alone.

After my shower, I climbed in bed feeling quite amorous and waited for Michael. As I lied in bed, I found myself waiting and waiting for Michael. As I waited, I once again started to lose my temper. Michael finally entered the room at 1:30am and he went straight into the shower. At 1:45am he climbed into bed, snuggled up to my back and began kissing my neck. The moment I felt his lips touch the back of my neck, I sat up in the bed and all my self-control and how I would handle this situation, went right out the window when I sharply said, "You've got a lot of nerve! I'm sorry, but I can't keep quiet any longer! Do you actually think I'm going to make love to you after the way you've been treating me?"

A shocked look, come over his face as he said, "What do you mean, the way I've been treating you? I don't know what you're talking about? Didn't we just spend a wonderful afternoon together?"

With that, my voice rose an octave as I said, "I can't believe, you! How can you not know what I'm talking about, Michael?"

He shook his head in frustration, "Well, if taking you out for a romantic dinner is treating you bad, then I'll never know how to please you!"

At that point I climbed out of the bed, turned the light on, headed for my dressing room and began to get dressed.

When Michael realized I was dressing, he came flying into the room and demanded, "And where do you think you're going at two o'clock in the morning!?"

I looked at him as I brushed my hair with dramatics and replied, "I have got to get out of here before I say something we may both regret."
He grabbed my arm forcefully, "You're not going anywhere unless you tell me what this is all about!"

I ripped my arm out of his grasp, grabbed my purse, looked him dead in the eyes, and with real anger in my voice, said, "You've just pushed me over the edge Michael, because no one talks to me like that, not even you!"

This time his voice became panicky as he said, "Please, Punkie! Don't walk out like this without telling me how I've made you so angry. That's not fair to me at all."

His words struck my heart, so I took a deep breath to calm myself, "Michael, it blows me away to think you could hurt my feelings like you have, and not even be aware of it." Then like a child, my eyes began to tear as I continued, "Do you even realize I told you, I was going to be honored with a Nobel Peace Prize and all you said was, 'That's wonderful'! And you haven't said another word about it since. All you talk about anymore is the baby. All I hear is the baby this or the baby that.

I'm to the point of being sick of hearing about the baby and she hasn't even conceived it yet."

His face showed his sincerity as he said, "Oh God, Punkie! I'm sorry! I had no idea I was acting that stupid."

I gazed into his eyes and with tears in mine, I replied, "That's just my point Michael, and I don't like it. Can't you see you're so obsessed with having your own baby, you've become totally consumed with it?" I took a deep breath and thought, 'If I'm going to let him know how I truly feel about Joanne, then this is the time to do it.' So I dove right in as I continued, "Another thing I don't like is the coziness you and Joanne seem to have together. I have got to be truthful, Michael. This whole baby thing with Joanne is starting to worry me. I don't trust her anymore. I know she's falling in love with you, and if she thinks she can find a way to have you, she'll try."

He gazed at me with an unbelieving expression and said, "Christina! You're my Punkie, and I love you. I would never knowingly give you any reason to worry about my faithfulness to you. And as far as my friendship with Joanne, that's all it is." He took me in his arms and kissed me and as I reluctantly surrendered to his charms, he continued, "Punkie, Joanne is a good person and she's not falling in love with me. The only reason it might appear as if we're, 'so cozy', as you so eloquently put it is because this is just as exciting for her, as it is for us. Don't you see she is doing such a wonderful thing for us, that I don't know how to adequately thank her."

I looked into his eyes and proceeded to tell him how Joanne had lied to me. Afterward, he looked at me sadly and said, "I don't know why she would lie to you and that concerns me. But as for trusting her to fulfill her contract with us for our baby, I'm more than certain she will."

I gently hugged him comfortingly, as I said, "I hope you're right, Michael." We made our way back to the bed where we tenderly made love before drifting off to sleep in each other's loving embrace.

# CHAPTER 14

Two days later on February 2$^{nd}$, the three of us were back in Doctor Hart's, office, where Joanne was artificially inseminated with my husband's seed. Doctor Hart told us we should wait two weeks to see if she has conceived, so he gave us an appointment for February 16$^{th}$. The day after the insemination, I was back in the recording studio finishing up what would be my first new album in more than two years, which I entitled, 'One Voice, One World and Love Enough for All.'

I stayed in the recording studio sixteen hours a day, because I wanted it ready for release the day I would receive my Nobel Peace Prize. While I was burning the midnight oils in the recording studio, Michael was back to handling our corporate headquarters, and Joanne. After much deliberation, we decided it would behoove us financially, to have Michael continue to man the main office, while I would resume our now, four months behind business schedule, on February 17$^{th}$. I didn't care for this plan too much, but we really had no choice. Michael just could not handle that side of the business. He was a behind the scenes man and we both knew it. Finally, on February 7$^{th}$, we completed the entire soundtrack, plus six videos to accompany my first six planned releases. On February 8$^{th}$, Michael and I were off to Oslo, Sweden for my Nobel Peace Prize acceptance.

At 10:00am, on February 10$^{th}$, 1990, in front of the eyes of the world I received the prestigious Nobel Peace Prize.

As the chairman of the Nobel Institute presented me with the

Medallion of Peace he said, "My dear Ms. Powers, it brings great pleasure to the Nobel Institute, to bestow the honor of the Prestigious Nobel Peace Prize to such a deserving candidate. Your work in Ghana has proven to the world that all races can learn to live together in peace and harmony. The Nobel Peace Prize is the way the world is saying thank you, Christina Powers, for the tremendous strides you've made in helping to bring the light of peace to a war ravaged nation." He placed the peace medallion around my neck, as tears of pride welled up in my eyes.

Afterward, I kissed his cheek and said to him, "Mr. Chairman, I would like to thank you, and all the notable members of the Nobel Institute Committee, for this distinguished honor. And may I say that I have never felt prouder of my accomplishments than I do at this very moment." At that point I gave a speech of why I believed, there was no reason why the whole world shouldn't be able to live in peace. I added, "Now I would like to thank everyone in my own very special way. I have written the lyrics to a new song which was inspired by my experiences in Ghana. Now if I may, I would like to sing that song for the first time, right here, as my gift to everyone listening?"

Just then the curtains behind me opened to reveal my entire orchestra and to the applause of everyone in the auditorium, I began to sing the first release off my new soundtrack to the entire world through the cameras of the media. I entitled this single which I wrote as a ballad, 'Love Grows in the Arms of Peace.' My performance was captivating and the song was so filled with emotion, the entire audience cheered for five minutes.

When I walked off that stage, Michael embraced me, passionately gazed into my eyes, and with pure love said, "You are the most remarkable person on the face of this planet, and I am proud to tell the world you are my wife." He kissed me with enthusiasm and added, "I love you, Punkie!"

The next day, I was praised by world leaders in the headlines all over the globe, for my wonderful contribution to peace in the world. And to top it off, the Pope himself said in a public statement, ***"Christina Powers* has proven herself to be a beacon of light in the midst of man's darkness."**

Even President Rush, at a news conference that same day, praised the Nobel Institute for their choice by saying, **"*Christina Powers* has earned the right to be called America's 'Angel of Peace.'"** He also informed me, as well as the entire country, he was going to honor me with the Achievement of the Year Award for 1989, at the White House on March 1st." He ended his news conference that day with, **"I hope and pray that the work *Christina Powers* has done in Ghana, will be a call to all nations to stand against human rights violations, whenever and wherever they may occur in the world."**

When we arrived back home at Stewart International Airport, on February 12th, we were totally exhausted and just wanted to get home. But, to our surprise we were welcomed by thousands of cheering African Americans, and the cameras of every news station across the country. We walked through the crowds shaking hands and receiving grateful hugs all the way. Then finally, after a short news conference we headed for home. Joanne greeted us both warmly with open arms when we entered the front door, and for the next four days the three of us got along wonderfully whenever we were together, although most of that time Michael and I spent working on my up and coming business trips.

On February 16th, with great anticipation, the three of us went to Doctor Hart's office to see if Joanne had conceived. Not five minutes after her blood test, the three of us were crushed when the test result came back negative. Doctor Hart set up another appointment for March 3rd, to try again. Only this time, I would not be accompanying them. I would be in Dallas, Texas securing another one of our new companies. After that, I was beginning a six-month business tour, which included periodic charity benefits, and addressing student bodies in as many universities as I could. I was now considered a scholar on human rights and peace, and I wanted to take my message of peace for all mankind to the youth of America while the current mood of the country prevailed. So when February 18th, rolled around, once again I was sadly kissing Michael goodbye, because we would only be seeing one another periodically. To our dismay our visitations would remain this way, until all our planned business trips would hopefully be completed by August 1st.

While I was away, Michael and Joanne's second attempt on March 3rd was also a failure, and they had to reschedule the procedure for April 4th. They would not know the results of the third insemination until April

18<sup>th</sup>, which happened to be one of the weeks I planned to be home with Michael, and do my work from the main office.  In the midst of my business trips and personal appearances, my popularity soared and so did the sales of the soundtrack 'One Voice, One World and Love Enough for All.'  And the single, 'Love Grows in the Arms of Peace,' stayed at number one for fifteen weeks after its worldwide debut in Sweden.

I arrived back home on April 18<sup>th</sup>, in just enough time to accompany Michael and Joanne back to Doctor Hart's office.  This time we left cheering because Joanne had finally conceived.  As soon as Michael heard the words that he was going to be a father, his eyes lit up like a plane's headlights.  He took Joanne in his arms, swung her around in the air and shouted, "We finally did it, Joanne, and I love you for it!"  He then grabbed me and shouted, "We're going to have a baby, Punkie!  Isn't that the best news in the world?"

I kissed him and with joy in my voice said, "It sure is the best news Michael, and I love you."

Doctor Hart gave Joanne an appointment schedule for her to keep, which included an appointment for a sonogram to be taken on July 5<sup>th</sup>.  As soon as I could, I changed my business plans so I could be home for the sonogram, and the rest of that week the three of us spent walking on cloud nine together.  Joanne treated me with such respect and love that week that without realizing it herself, she put all my fears to rest.  Then on April 23<sup>rd</sup>, I was back on my business trip schedule.

When I arrived back home on July 3<sup>rd</sup>, I was only planning on staying five days before resuming my business trips.  The three of us spent the Fourth of July at my mother in-law's annual barbecue.  We were having a wonderful day right up till 7:00pm, that's when without asking me first, Michael proceeded to inform his entire family of my infertility and how Joanne was carrying our child for us.  After the initial shock wore off, his family congratulated us on the baby.  Then, with open arms, my in-laws welcomed Joanne into the Gillespie family, almost as if she were Michael's second wife.  As Michael's family lovingly welcomed Joanne with hugs and kisses, her face lit up like a bride on her wedding day.

When my mother in-law turned to congratulate me, she looked at me sadly and whispered in my ear, "I know it must be a disappointment for you not to be able to bear children any longer, but no matter how much you wanted a child, you should have never talked Michael into having a child in this manner. It's wrong."

I whispered back, "Tess, I respect your opinion, but as far as I'm concerned, you're mistaken. As for your son, he's a big boy with his own mind, and no one can talk him into anything he does not want to do."

Ten minutes later I came down with a headache and I asked Michael to take me home. That's when he and Joanne complained we would miss the fireworks if we left now. So, first I apologized for causing them to miss the fireworks; then, I insisted we leave.

As soon as we climbed into the car, I lost all my self-control and proceeded to blast Michael for telling his family. He was speechless as I said, "How could you tell them without consulting me first, especially since you knew I didn't want anyone knowing!?"

When I finished my tantrum, all Michael could say was, "I'm sorry Punkie, but you said you wanted to keep it from your fans, I didn't think that meant keeping it from my family too."

I shook my head in frustration and replied, "Well, if you knew me as well as I thought you did, you would understand why I didn't want anyone knowing, not even your family."

Just then Joanne snapped at me from the back seat, "Christina, I don't know why you're acting like such a child. You didn't really think you could hide your infertility from Michael's family, did you? Besides, no one said anything derogatory, everyone was happy for us."

I didn't even turn to face her when I said, "Joanne, this has nothing to do with you, so please keep your opinions to yourself."

Michael turned to me and said, "Christina, there's no reason for you to take your frustrations out on Joanne. And if you plan to continue this tirade, then please save it until we're in private."

This time I didn't even look at Michael when I said, "That's the most intelligent thing you've said in months Michael, and you won't hear another word from me." After that no one said a word the rest of the way home.

Later that night in the privacy of our bedroom, the first thing Michael asked me was, "Why in the world did you snap at Joanne like that?" I guess I didn't answer him as quickly as he would have liked, because he sarcastically added, "You don't even know why, do you? Do you realize you talk about me being obsessed, but you're the one who's obsessed? You're so jealous Joanne can give me what you can't; you're distorting everything I do and say. Now I'm going to ask you to stop acting like the child this time, because if you don't get a hold of your own insecurities, you could mess this up for both of us with Joanne. I'm surprised she's not packing to leave right now."

I looked at him with an expression of total disbelief, "Why you stupid ass! All this time and you still don't know what I'm all about." I shook my head in disgust as I continued, "Now let's go to sleep Michael, because I'm just too tired for any more of this tonight." Then I rolled over and ignored every word he said from that point on.

He became so frustrated that I would not answer him that he climbed out of the bed and began to get dressed. As he walked out of the room he said, "I'm going for a ride, and maybe I'll be back by morning."

As the door closed behind him, I decided I was not going to allow myself to feel anything at that moment. I didn't want to give him the satisfaction of seeing me upset. But needless to say, I didn't get a moment's sleep that night, and as for Michael, he didn't come in until 5:00am that morning. I was so angry with him that when he climbed in the bed; I climbed out.

Michael and I were still not on speaking terms when we entered Doctor Hart's office later that morning, at 11:00am with Joanne. Remarkably, that whole morning we were both able to keep Joanne from sensing our hostilities' toward each other. Doctor Hart personally escorted the three of us to the sonogram room and proceeded to perform the procedure. First, he moved the screen so we could all watch as he videotaped the fetus. Then he proceeded to explain to us exactly what we were looking at. When we could actually see the baby moving in the uterus, my heart melted as my eyes teared, and I instantly fell in love with that little fetus.

With these feelings flowing through me, I drifted close to Michael, took his arm in both my hands, squeezed it tightly, and with tears of joy in my eyes, said, "That's our baby. Michael, I'm sorry I've upset you honey, because I love you more than life itself."

At that he lovingly took me in his arms and with a gleam of joy in his eyes said, "I love you too, Punkie!" Then we turned our attention back to the fetus on the screen.

The procedure only took ten minutes and when it was finished, Dr. Hart handed me the video tape with some snapshots he took of the fetus. I passed the snapshots to Michael to see, who passed them to Joanne. After Joanne looked at them, I watched as she opened her purse and casually slipped them in. At the moment she snapped her purse shut, I knew all my fears would soon be my reality. So in a calm voice I asked, "Joanne, why did you put those snapshots in your purse?"

She snapped at me like a rattlesnake as she shouted, "For God's sake Christina, I'm giving you my baby and I can't keep the fucking negatives? What the hell is wrong with you?"

As she hatefully spit these words at me, Michael's eyes almost popped out of his face with anger toward me as if to say, 'How could you dare!' So I quickly apologized for being so insensitive to her feelings and when I finally stopped her from crying, I said, "You're absolutely right Joanne, and I want you to keep these photos."

She wiped her alligator tears with a tissue as she replied, "I'm sorry if I was overly emotional, it must be the baby." She turned toward me as she continued, "Thank you for the snapshots, Christina. I'm glad you can see that because this is not your biological child, the snapshots should come to me. I also feel I deserve to have the tape as well. After all, I am allowing you to raise my child, aren't I?"

In reply to her cruel statement, I handed her the tape with a reassuring smile and said, "Joanne, you're welcome to the tape as well. I want you to know I do realize what you're doing for us and once again I thank you for it."

She hugged me gratefully as she replied, "Thank you Christina, now would someone please feed me? This fasting when you're eating for two doesn't make any sense at all."

I turned to Michael and nonchalantly said, "Honey, why don't you take Joanne for a bite to eat and just drop me off at the office? I have too much to do before leaving tomorrow to go with you guys." And that was what he did.

# CHAPTER 15

When they dropped me off, I went straight for a company car and took off. As I drove around that day, I was feeling so hurt by what had transpired that I had no idea how I was going to handle it. I wished I could just run away and never come back, but I loved Michael too much for my own good, to be able to just walk away from him and the baby. At the same time, I wanted to be as far away from Joanne as I possibly could. I knew one more outburst from her could push me over the edge, and I feared for her life if that should happen.

It wasn't until 6:00pm, when I finally calmed down enough to pull into the driveway of our home. As I reached the house, I could see Joanne frantically throwing her suitcases into the trunk of her car, with Michael trying to take them out. I quickly stopped the car right next to the action and when I jumped out, to my shock, I found Joanne crying hysterically, and Michael pleading with her not to leave.

I immediately stopped their struggle over a suitcase, by shouting, "What the hell is going on here?"

Joanne threw her suitcases into the trunk, slammed the lid and started to walk toward the driver's door. This time, I grabbed her arm and demanded, "I asked you a question, and I expect an answer before you go anywhere."

She pulled her arm out of my hand and with hatred in her voice shouted, "You really want to know what's going on? Well your husband and I have been having an affair for months now. We've spent every night together when you were out of town, and now that you're home, I'm not good enough anymore."

Michael instantly grabbed my arm, looked dead into my eyes, and with panic in his voice said, "She's lying, Christina! I swear I've never slept with her. She just tried to seduce me and when I refused, she went nuts. She started screaming at me yelling, 'You told me, you loved me!'"

I trustingly gazed back into his eyes and soothingly replied, "I believe you, Michael."

That's when Joanne tried to slap my face. I blocked the slap, swung her arm behind her back, pushed her up against the car and shouted, "Don't you ever try to do that again or you will find yourself at the bottom of the river. Now you have a contract with me and you're going to keep it! So please calm down and start talking!"

I let her go and she screamed at me, "I'm leaving and you can't keep me here. I don't care how many threats you issue."

I shook my head in dismay as I said, "You're right again Joanne, I can't keep you here. But if you leave, you will be breaking a contract with me and no one does that and gets away with it."

She opened the door of her car, climbed in and shouted, "Fuck you, *Christina Powers,* and you can shove your contract up your ass because neither one of you will ever get this child now." Then she started the car and sped away.

As she drove away, Michael took me in his arms and pleaded, "I swear to you again Punkie, I never slept with her."

I squeezed his hand reassuringly and said, "Michael, honey, you don't have to do this, I know you're telling the truth." What Michael didn't know was that after 'the phone call incident' back in December, I had the house wired. I wasn't going to leave them alone again without being sure there was nothing going on between them. But I didn't need to tell him that, I preferred for him to believe I just took his word for it.

As soon as we went into the house, I immediately had a tail put on Joanne. Then, I called my attorney Tom Davies, and informed him of our dilemma. During our conversation, I discovered the only way we could get the baby from Joanne now was through the legal system. Afterwards he added, "But if you're going to fight her for the baby, you'd better do it now before she takes off."

There was no way I wanted to go public with this headline, but I had no choice. So, with a completely disgusted voice I said, "Go ahead and do whatever it takes. I'll just have to learn to live with this one too, I guess."

Two days later, the whole country knew I was infertile, and in the middle of a custody battle with the surrogate mother of my husband's child. To top that off, Joanne took her distorted version of the facts to the tabloids, and they had a field day at my expense.

Michael became so distraught over the situation, he was put on antidepressants, which left him almost unable to function, no less take care of business. So once again, I put my business trips on hold and on July 15th, 1990, I dove head first into the hottest custody battle in American history. And let me tell you, everybody had something to say about it. Even the Pope himself, who only a few months earlier had praised me publicly for my peace efforts, released a new statement saying, **"Christina Powers is suffering at her own hand for trying to have a child in an immoral and sinful manner."**

To that I was compelled to issue a public statement of my own, saying, **"I believe the Pope and the Christian community should read their Bible a little closer before passing judgement based on it. Because if I recall correctly Abram's wife Sara, had the Egyptian slave girl named Hagar, bear Abram's child for her, because she was unable to conceive herself. After that God blessed the child and Sara, He didn't condemn them."** But all they heard were their own little naive words of condemnation.

As the court battle heated up, so did the battle between Michael and me. Little by little, it became quite evident Michael was blaming me for what transpired among the three of us. But it all came to a head on July 27th, after one particularly bad day in court, where Joanne superbly portrayed me as the 'wicked witch' who caused it all. When we arrived home that evening, I was feeling totally defeated. But I guess that didn't matter to Michael, because as soon as we entered our house he finally blew-up at me and said, "If you hadn't opened your month like you did the night we left my Mother's house, none of this shit would have ever happened."

I burst out in sarcastic laughter as I said, "I think you'd better take the blinders off Michael, and see things for what they really are. I'm not what caused this at all! I told you before we went through with the procedure I feared something like this might happen; but no, you wouldn't listen! You had to have your own child whether I was part of it or not. And because I listened to you, our private lives are once again an open book and I've been humiliated in front of the entire world. Thank you very much! So don't you dare stand there and tell me it's my fault. Now wise-up and stop trying to blame me because we're both at fault here and the sooner you realize that, the sooner our relationship will improve." I tried to hug him and his body became rigid; which made me even angrier, so I pulled away and said, "Michael, I will do everything in my power to bring your child back to you, but I will tell you right now, as long as she is the birth mother, that child will never be part of me."

With that harsh statement he looked at me and started to cry like a baby, "I'm so sorry, Christina! I'm feeling so confused, I don't know what I'm really feeling anymore."

I held him with compassion and softly said, "I'm sorry Michael, I didn't really mean that. I love you and it will work out for the best, I promise you it will."

The next morning on Friday, July 27th, it was my turn to take the stand. Upon the first question, I proceeded to strategically, yet gracefully tear her story to shreds **so badly** that by the end of the day, we were sure we were going to win the case. At 2:00pm the Judge called for an adjournment until Monday, August 1, at 10:00am. Michael and I both had a feeling of confidence that whole night and right up till 2:00pm the next day; when, I received a call from the tail I had on Joanne, informing me that she gave them the slip.

With that news, I hung up the phone and within ten minutes I had every police officer in the state, unofficially looking for her. We frantically searched for her that whole weekend! But to our dismay, no one saw her again until she entered the courtroom with her attorney, on the morning of Monday, August 1st. As soon as Joanne's attorney approached the bench, he informed the court that his client aborted the fetus in question, at 7:00pm on July 30th, and after viewing the official medical records, our courtroom custody battle came to a devastatingly abrupt end. Especially for Michael, who went into a deep depression the moment he heard the news. As we walked out of that courtroom, the press charged us.

Michael turned to me with tears in his eyes and said, "I have to get out of here, Christina."

I took his hand and replied, "We don't have to make any comments at all. We can just get in the limo and take off." And that was exactly what we did.

When James pulled into the driveway, Michael looked at me and sadly said, "I can't go in yet. I think I'll just take the car and ride around for a while."

I grabbed his hand as we climbed out of the limo and with concern asked, "Why don't you let me come with you, Michael?"

He looked at me as if he were going to cry again as he answered, "I need to be alone right now, Christina." He pulled his hand from mine, walked to his car, and drove away without saying another word.

At that, I went in the house and straight to our room, where I laid on the bed and cried my eyes out for several hours. I was not only living through the death of this child, but I was reliving the deaths of all my babies. I decided not to go anywhere for the rest of that day because I wanted to wait for Michael at home. I waited from 11:00am that morning, {on pins and needles} until he finally called me from his Mother's home in Ravena, at 11:40pm that night. He told me not to wait up, because he was not sure when he would be coming home. So with a sad voice I said, "Michael, please come home honey, I really need you here."

His voice cracked as he replied, "I can't yet, Christina. I have to figure out how to deal with this cruel blow."

I nearly pleaded, "Michael, listen to me, honey. I'm your wife and I love you so much I would die for you if it would take the pain away, but it won't. The only way we are going to come through this is if we do it together, honey. So please come home to me?"

With a bit stronger voice he replied, "I'll be home Punkie, I promise. I just need a little more time by myself."

I sighed and with a small sense of relief replied, "All right, my love. Just please be careful and come home to me safe." We finished our conversation by saying, "I love you."

Not five minutes later, I received a call from Jimmy, and as soon as I heard his voice I exclaimed, "Oh thank God, it's you, Jimmy! You won't believe what happened today."

His first words back to me were, "With you girlfriend, nothing would surprise me." I filled him in on all the details and he reassured me, "Just hang in there two more days girlfriend, and I promise I'll be home for good. Then as you would say, 'we will figure it out together'."

With that news, I took a deep breath and said, "I hope so, because if Michael doesn't come through that door soon, I'll be weaving baskets, so you'd better come home in two days."

As Jimmy started to laugh, a sharp squeal came over the line and we lost our connection. I tried to redial the number he gave me for Richard's parents, but I couldn't get through. Then I laid my head on the pillow and as I waited for Jimmy to call me back, I fell asleep.

# CHAPTER 16

It was shortly after 2:00am when I was startled awake for I heard Carman's panicked cries as she banged on my bedroom door yelling, "Christina! You have to get up! It's urgent!" I flew out of the bed fearing the worse had happened to Michael.

I opened the door in a flurry, grabbed Carman's shoulders, and with fear in my voice shouted, "Where's Michael, Carman?"

With the panic of your typical older Italian woman, she shouted back at me with her hands shaking, "It's not Michael, Christina!" At that, she put her hands to her face and cried, "Dear God, Christina! It's our boy Jimmy! Something terribly dreadful has happened!"

I looked at her strangely and asked, "What are you talking about, Carman? I was just talking to Jimmy two hours ago and he was fine."

She grabbed my hand with the force of a halfback as she said, "You have to come see for yourself." With that she dragged me into her attached servant's quarters, where James was riveted to a news broadcast on CNN.

Immediately I took a seat beside James and asked with a concerned tone, "What's going on, James?"

He turned to me with an expression of horror and replied, "At 1:00am, five-hundred-thousand Iraqi forces, with hundreds of tanks and heavy artillery, swept across the Kuwait border. They say the fighting is fierce and the Iraqi Air Force has destroyed the Kuwait International Airport." Then, he shook his head with shear concern as he continued, "That means Jimmy is probably a fugitive in hiding already, and if they find him they may kill him."

I became glued to the TV, as well. A deep sense of great fear came over me for Jimmy as I watched and listened to the blow-by-blow details of the invasion, live on CNN.

The three of us watched TV like until 3:42am that's when the announcer said, "Our unofficial sources state that the Sultan and his family escaped into Saudi Arabia minutes before the Capital fell into Iraqi control."

I was so horrified by what I was seeing and hearing that I knew I had to do something. So I got up and dialed President Rush's private number. I paced for the next twenty minutes praying the whole time for Jimmy's safety as I waited for a return call.

I grabbed the phone on the first ring to hear George say, "Christina, as much as I enjoy them, I don't have time for one of our quaint chats right now. So please make it quick."

I answered him just as swiftly, "I can't make this one quick George; not when my dearest friend's life is at stake. George, do you remember my business partner Jimmy Severino? Well he is somewhere in Kuwait at this very moment, and I'm sure you're aware of what's taking place there! What I want to know is what are we going to do about it?"

He cleared his voice and said, "I'm sorry Jimmy got caught up in this Christina, and I promise you I'm going to do everything possible to get him out of there safely. My staff and I were working on how to respond to the crisis when you called."

Once again I was swift to respond, "Have you talked to Lussein to see why he is doing this?"

His voice was not optimistic as he answered, "Lussein is desperately trying to save his own political ass, that's why he's doing this. I have been trying to prevent him diplomatically from invading Kuwait for months now, and he has ignored my every attempt to meet with him personally. I'm already at the point of deciding where and how many American troops to send over there."

With that statement my heart shot up to my throat because I realized he was about to throw our nation into another 'Vietnamese-style' conflict. So with a sense of desperation in my voice I said, "Please forgive me George, but if you send American troops in now, you'll be making a big mistake. Please listen to me. This is not America's war. This is a transgression against the statutes of the U.N. That means this problem belongs to every free nation on earth, not just us. This must be handled through the U.N. Security Council, or it will end up looking as though America is trying to rule the world. If we go through the U.N., then we'll have the backing of the entire international community. Once we do that, Lussein won't have a prayer of staying in Kuwait."

I could tell by his voice, I had caught his interest when he said, "That sounds great, but if I do that; then, we will have to turn large numbers of American troops over to the control of the U.N. and our Joint Chiefs of Staff would have a real problem with that scenario."

I answered with complete optimism in my voice, "This is true George, but you're the President of the United States, and you can sure as hell tell the U.N. that you want American generals in control of all American troops."

His voice was very clear when he said, "Do you really think we can rally the whole world into storming the deserts of Kuwait?"

"Yes I do, George," I answered assuredly.

With a respectful laugh he said, "I thought you would say that and I'm sure if anyone could, it would be you. So I'll make a deal with you Christina; if you will be my mouth piece to the world, then I will hold back our military response and do it your way."

Without a second thought of anything I replied, "When and where do you need me, Mr. President."

Quite relieved he answered, "The sooner you get to Stewart Airport, the sooner I can have a military escort bring you here."

I hung up the phone, told Carman to pack my suitcases, and I headed for a shower. As I dressed, I thought, 'Oh my God! I'm forgetting about Michael.' I sat down and wrote him a note explaining what happened and where I was going. I also told him I loved him with all my heart, and that I would be home as soon as I could. I placed it on Michael's pillow and headed out of the room.

As I was coming down the stairs, James entered the foyer and said, "The car is packed and ready to go whenever you are, Christina."

I grabbed my briefcase from the hall closet, "Pull the car around front would you please James, and I'll be right out." I grabbed a mug of coffee to go from Carman's shaking hand, kissed her cheek and said, "Keep us in your prayers, Carman."

I headed for the front door and as I opened it, Michael was standing there getting ready to open it himself. Instantly his expression turned to one of surprise when he saw me dressed, and he asked, "What's going on? Better yet, where are you taking off to at 4:30 in the morning? I thought you were going to be waiting for me?"

I drew him tightly and passionately to my body, kissed him gently and lovingly said, "Michael, honey, I don't know if you've heard, but there's a war going on in Kuwait. I have already talked with the President and I have to leave for Washington, D.C. right now. I left a note on the bed for you explaining everything."

He pushed himself out of my arms and in a loud, angry, voice he screamed, "You're what? You can't just kiss me then tell me there's a note on the bed and walk out the fucking door! You told me to come home! You told me we would get through this together! How could you be leaving me now!?"

I felt his pain so deep within my soul that it threw my emotions into a state of confusion, and I started to cry as I pleaded, "Michael, please don't do this to me now. I love you honey, with all my soul and I know how much you're hurting, but I still have to go, can't you understand that?"

With a plea of his own he shouted, "I'm hurting, Christina! Really hurting! And now you're tearing my heart apart even more. You told me you needed me! I finally got my head together enough to come home to you, because I need you as much as I thought you needed me, and now you're telling me you have to leave?"

I grabbed his arm and cried, "Please Michael, you have got to listen to me and understand!"

He only shook his head in disgust as he exclaimed, "Understand what, Christina? That you don't give a fuck about me!" Then, he turned his face away from me.

I grabbed his jaw and turned his head to force him to look at me, "Listen to me! I love you, but I have got to go, Michael! Jimmy's life is on the line here, that's what I want you to understand. Don't you realize that hundreds of people are really dying and I have to do something to help stop it?  Now, please, just kiss me goodbye Michael, so I may leave knowing I have your blessing."

He turned his head out of my hand and angrily said, "No, Christina!  Because if you can walk out that door on me now, knowing how much I need you; then, I won't be here when you get back.  I just can't take this shit anymore, no matter how much I love you!"

He began to walk away from me and as he walked away I shouted, "Fine then, Michael!  Once again we'll have it your way!"

I was so angry at him for not being reasonable that when I slammed the door the glass panels shattered.  I looked back to see Michael angrily staring at me through the broken glass and I thought, 'Thank God they're not mirrors!  I sure as hell don't need any more bad luck.'

As James pulled out of the driveway that morning, I put my feelings on hold and dove head first into what would soon be known to the world as, **"Desert Storm!"**

# CHAPTER 17

When I arrived at the White House, I was escorted by security guards straight to the Oval Office. I was greeted by the President, who with his all male staff, stood up as I entered the room. I held myself tall and confident as President Rush proceeded to introduce me to the Vice President, the Joint Chiefs of Staff, and the Secretary of Defense. Our introductions were formal to say the least and the aura in the room was thick, so thick it was quite apparent at least to me, my presence was not appreciated by everyone in the room. So, I immediately attempted to cut through the bad vibes by saying, "May I say it is an honor to be in the same room with so many distinguished gentlemen, and I humbly thank you all for allowing me this opportunity to express my feelings concerning this crisis."

At that we took our seats. Then George turned toward me as he said, "Christina, I have shared our conversation with everyone in this room and we've been brain-storming since. Most of us have come to the conclusion that your suggestion to go totally through the U.N. with this crisis is the best way for America to proceed. That's if it can be done."

Vice President Pigeon interrupted with an attitude which was strongly adamant and slightly hostile as he said, "Pardon me Mr. President, but before we go any further with this, I must strongly protest. Lussein is a mad man, sir! If we delay our military response, he'll take it as an open invitation to send his troops right into Saudi Arabia. Then you won't have to worry about getting the U.N. involved, because that will do it nicely."

I was taken aback by his willingness to jump into a military conflict, so I looked directly at him and said, "How can you be so anxious to throw American troops into a war alone, when this is not just our responsibility? Yes we are a super power, but we're not God of this earth. We are one nation, and there are other counties who must accept their responsibility for protecting the welfare and freedom of all nations. That's the reason why the U.N. was established."

Directing my words toward George and the others, I continued, "Gentleman, we must go through the U.N. Security Council and do this with the cooperation of its members, or this will explode," then turning to George, "in 'your face' Mr. President."

With a little more irritation to his voice, the Vice President, in an attempt to intimidate and humiliate me said, "Please listen to me Ms. Powers, because I know what I'm talking about, and obviously you don't have a clue. This is not Ghana and you will never convince the U.N. members to commit troops against such an awesome opponent. Do you realize Lussein has the second strongest military power in the Middle East? And the time we waste with diplomatic bullshit, will only give Iraq more time to dig into Kuwait."

His condescending remarks angered me, so I tried a little intimidation of my own when I said, "I think 'you're' the one who's not seeing the entire picture here Mr. Pigeon. Can't you see those are the exact reasons the U.N. is the answer? Don't you realize if we take on Iraq without the U.N.'s full support, then you will be inviting the Russians, as well as the Chinese, to confront us over the Middle East? Now, if you would just stop being so bullheaded and listen for a change, you might understand what I'm saying."

Frustrated, he slammed his fist on the table and nearly shouted, "I understand exactly what you're saying, Ms. Powers! I also understand you have a personal friend in Kuwait, and I'm telling you he may not survive if we wait. Do you realize how long it will take to get the world's military support on this?" Then he shouted, "Iraq has already over thrown Kuwait! If we lose any more time, it will not only be too late for Mr. Severno, it will be too late for Saudi Arabia as well."

With that slap in the face I stood up and forcefully said, "Mr. Pigeon! That was totally uncalled for, unprofessional, and I expect an apology. And please don't you ever speak to me with such disrespect again."

That's when George cleared his voice deeply and the moment he did, Mr. Pigeon began to apologize. I accepted his attempt to be civil by once again taking my seat. Then, with a much calmer tone of my own I replied, "Before I answer your question Mr. Vice President, I have one of my own. How can you be so sure Iraq is going to invade Saudi Arabia?"

He looked at me as if I were an idiot and with a tone of contempt replied, "Ms. Powers, if he gains control of Kuwait and Saudi Arabia, then he can hold the industrial countries of the world hostage, because the world relies on these two nations as its primary source of petroleum."

As soon as he finished speaking, I stood up, turned to look at everyone in the room, and very calmly said, "If you were all listening to the Vice President's words, you should now realize under the circumstances he just described, going through the U.N. is the only legal way for the United States to handle this situation. Under International Law, Iraq is threatening the security of many nations, not just ours. These are the reasons why I believe it will only take a few hours to rally the world's support against Iraq." Glancing at my watch I continued, "And I could be in New York to address the U.N. Security Council by 11:30am to do just that, if I left now."

Just then the Secretary of Defense, Mr. Breaner joined the conversation by saying, "Mr. President, I agree with Ms. Powers completely. We have to go to the Security Council to ask the U.N. to condemn the Iraqi invasion anyway, so why not try to get our allied nations involved on the military end of this as well. Besides, I think a military action of this size would sure as hell pass congress a lot faster if they knew we weren't footing the entire bill alone."

Mr. Mickie, the Chief of Naval Operations, spoke up, "My only problem is if we do a joint military response through the U.N., then we will be putting substantial numbers of American forces under the guidance of the U.N. Security Council."

I confidently spoke up, "Sir, there is no nation on the face of the earth more capable of handling a military action such as this, than ours, and I'm sure the U.N. Security Council will look to America for strategic guidance on how to proceed with an invasion, if it comes to that. But, it is still our responsibility as a member of the U.N., to do everything possible diplomatically, to prevent this from escalating to that point."

George stood up and said, "All right, let's not waste any more time. We're going through the U.N. all the way with this one and that's my final decision." Then he looked at me as he continued, "Christina, I'll call for an emergency meeting of the Security Council right now, if you're ready to go?"

I looked at him proudly, smiled confidently, and answered, "I'm past ready, Sir."

He smiled at my enthusiastic answer and replied, "I thought you'd say something like that. Now if you will head to New York for me, I'll have a fax waiting for you on what issues I want you to discuss, and the ones I want you to stay away from. I also want you to keep in close contact with me. I need to know every response you get from individual countries. Clear?"

I stood up, shook his hand firmly and answered, "I'm on my way, Mr. President." Then I said my goodbyes to everyone, and out the door I went.

I arrived by Presidential chopper on the roof of the U.N. building at 11:04am, and as soon as I got off the chopper, I dialed the number to Michael's hand held cellular. When there was no answer I called the office for him. Lucille Karatzas, his secretary answered and told me, Michael said, 'he had to leave town and he was leaving Ann Markel in charge.'

I immediately had her connect me to Ann's office, and when she answered I said, "Ann, tell me what's going on and how come Michael isn't there?"

With a confused tone she answered, "I'm not sure Christina, I thought you knew. Michael called me this morning, told me you had to go to Washington and that he had to leave town. He left me in charge and told me if anything comes up I can't handle that I should call you, because he would not be available to be reached."

Sadly I asked, "Ann, did Michael leave you anyway for me to get a hold of him?"

With a hint of concern in her voice she answered, "No I'm sorry Christina, he didn't. But I could tell he was hurting really badly over the abortion of his child. Christina, is there anything I can do on a personal level to help you guys through this?"

I answered quickly, "Yes Ann, there is. If Michael calls please tell him I love him, and I need to speak with him."

We finished our conversation, just as I reached Jean Fitzpeters office, the American ambassador to the U.N. As soon as I opened the door, she handed me an envelope and said, "Hi Christina, this just came in on the line from the President for you. You better read it fast we only have a few minutes before the Assembly gathers."

We talked for another ten minutes as I scanned through the fax. Afterward, I was once again off to address the U.N. Security Council, on a matter which I saw strictly as another violation of human rights, thus falling under the jurisdiction of the U.N.'s Statutes.

As I waited to be called to address the U.N. Assembly, I found it difficult to place my thoughts of concern for Michael on the back burner of my mind. Which, for a moment caused me to completely forget even where I was, when I heard my name called as the speaker introduced me to the Assembly. I quickly regained my composure as I confidently approached the podium. I greeted the Assembly casually, and then proceeded to call for the world to condemn Iraq's aggression and demand Iraqis' immediate withdrawal from Kuwait. I was so dramatically convincing that by 1:00 that afternoon, that's just what the U.N. did.

The next day the headlines read, "***Christina Powers* once again leads the band wagon for the Rush Administration, only this time it's against Saddam Lussein's invasion of Kuwait!**"

The only problem was, Iraq ignored the U.N.'s demands and proceeded to do exactly what the Vice President predicted, and began to move thousands of troops to Kuwait's border with Saudi Arabia. So, on August 3$^{rd}$, 1990, I was on a two-day trip to six European nations, to try to convince them to stop all international trade with Iraq.

Then it was back to New York, to address the U.N. on the 6$^{th}$, at which time I helped convince the U.N. Security Council to declare an economic embargo against Iraq. Right after I finished addressing the Security Council, I received a message from the President asking me to come directly to the White House. I said I would and by 1:00pm, I was on a military flight back to Washington, D.C.

The entire time we were in the air all I could think about was

Michael. It had been four days now and I had not heard a word from him, even though I had left numerous messages on his pager for him to call me. I wondered how he was and if he had listened to the world news. I hoped he had the opportunity to see for himself what I was doing. Maybe then, he would realize I had no choice, but to leave him like I did.

As I sat there thinking over the loud roar of the chopper's blades, my eyes began to tear and I thought, 'Oh God, I miss him so much! Won't you please bring him back to me Lord, I promise I will never leave him alone and hurting again. I need his love and strength so badly right now and I know he needs mine, so please send him home to me.'

All at once, I was abruptly snapped out of my thoughts as the chopper bounced at least twenty feet on landing, leaving the remains of my stomach in my throat. My nervous system was so upset after that shock it took me several minutes just to unbuckle my seat belt. When I finally stopped my shaking, I looked up to see the crew nonchalantly laughing as if it were a common occurrence. So I shook my head at them as I said, "Next time I want Air Force One." With that, I exited that noisy monstrosity laughing along with the guys.

The next thing I knew, I was once again being escorted by White House Security to the Oval Office. When I entered President Rush immediately rose from his seat to greet me with a warm embrace as he said, "Christina, thank you for coming so quickly." He gestured for me to take a seat as he continued, "Please make yourself comfortable. I've asked you here because we are approaching a very delicate stage with our U.N./Iraq operation. You see, I will be announcing to the U.N. tomorrow, the United States will be sending troops to the Persian Gulf to defend Saudi Arabia from a possible attack by Iraq. I will also be asking for the members of the U.N. to form a military coalition under the guidance of the U.N., and then authorize that coalition to use force to carry out the embargo against Iraq. Now, I've spoken to the leaders of all the member nations with veto power, and the only problems we have are the Chinese and the Soviets. Neither country is willing to allow the U.N. to use force against Iraq. I have already been warned by both nations' leaders if we use force, then it could escalate the situation rather quickly. Now as I see it, the only way we can pull this off is if we keep the human rights issues at the core of this crisis. This is where you come in, because I'm hoping with your help, we will be able to convince both nations not to use their veto power against the formation of a coalition."

I lifted my eyebrows with concern as I said, "It sounds like it's already a crises." I shook my head in dismay and added, "I'll do whatever I can to help George, just name it."

He grinned from ear to ear and said, "I'm glad you're on my side, because you're a little dynamo lady."

I smiled graciously and replied, "Why thank you Mr. President, I'm pleased you noticed. Now how may I serve my country?"

We both smiled at that one, then he said, "I have a great come back for that, but since I'm a gentleman I'll get right down to business. I would like you to leave this afternoon for Moscow. I have arranged for you to meet with President Gorbasoff tomorrow morning. I would like you to convince him, and the Soviet People, in only three days that this invasion is a violation of human rights, and as a member of the U.N. they must support the Security Council to stop this atrocity. After that, I'll need you to take three more days and do the same in China. I've heard you speak both languages fluently, I hope that's true?"

I was overwhelmed by his request, but I chose not to show it when I said, "I really need to stop by my home first, do I have time to do that?"

He put his hand to his chin as he replied, "Not really, Christina. If you're going to make the meeting with Gorbasoff, you will need to leave now."

He handed me a large envelope from off his desk and continued, "Here is an outline of our strategies and goals for the embargo. I would like you to give a copy of each to both leaders, as a show of good faith."

With that, I took a deep breath and said, "Oh Well, I guess National Security must take precedence over the heart every time." I smiled, took the envelope and added, "So how do I get there?"

Within ten minutes of our conversation, I was on a military jet to the Soviet Union. Eight days later I returned to Washington a victorious woman. I had gracefully charmed the citizens of both nations, and I received a verbal promise from their leaders, that they would not veto the formation of a U.N. coalition. After that, I had two days to go home before heading off to the Arab countries of Jordan, Libya, and Yemen, who opposed the involvement of non-Arab nations on Arab soil. George

123

hoped I could use my powers of persuasion on them as well as I had on my last mission.

While I was home I tried to get in touch with Michael over the phone, but I decided not to look for him. I figured if he truly loved me he'd come home on his own. I only went into the office twice and for one hour each time. Thank God for Ann Markel, because I couldn't concentrate on work if my life depended on it. All I did in those two days was mope around the house hoping Michael would return my calls, but he never did.

On the 20th, I was off to my mission in the Middle East, where I was able to at least convince Jordan, Libya, and Yemen, not to join Iraq in fighting against the coalition, if it should come to that.

I returned home just in time to accompany the President, as he addressed the U.N., and on August 25th, at 11:00am the U.N. Security Council passed a resolution to allow enforcement of the embargo by military means.

Before retiring to our suites that night, President Rush and I celebrated our U.N. victory over a private drink in the lounge, of the Plaza Hotel in Manhattan. As we toasted one another he said, "Christina, words cannot adequately express my gratitude for your help with this crisis, and your efforts have proven the U.N. truly has the ability to play a leading role in world affairs. I know that's the purpose the U.N. was created, but because the world is so diverse, it's still something I never thought would become a reality." He took my hand in his as he continued, "You truly are a remarkable woman *Christina Powers,* and I'm impressed by how much you really care about people. If you should ever desire to get into politics with the Republican Party, I'll support you all the way."

Starting to laugh I said, "Thank you kindly George, but you can keep the politics. My life is crazy enough as it is, so I certainly don't need to add the responsibility of a public office to it. Oh by the way, since we are speaking of hectic lives, I must tell you I have to do something to slow this pace of mine. George, now that things seem to be on the right track, I need to ask you to send me back to my civilian life. I have a husband I have not seen since the day this started, and I need to find him."

He graciously brought my hand to his lips, gently kissed the back of it and said, "I will definitely miss your presence on this Christina, but I understand your circumstances completely. I have a wife at home I hardly see also."

Shortly after that, I kissed his cheek as we said our goodbyes and off I went. I decided not to stay in the city that night. Instead I drove the four-hour trip to Michael's family home in the Catskills, in the hope he would be there. I was missing him just too much and I could no longer wait for him to come to me.

I arrived at the mountain house at 1:00am, and my heart began to pound with excitement, when I saw Michael's car in the driveway. I quickly parked and as I opened the door to climb out, my body began to shake, and I thought, 'What if he doesn't want to see me?' Then I remembered the night I went after Johnny and I thought, 'What if he's not alone? Oh my God, what if Joanne is with him? What do I do? What do I say?' I immediately, yet gently slapped myself across the face and chuckled as I thought, 'Just stop this you asshole, before you talk yourself right out of going in.' Shrugging my shoulders, my thoughts continued, 'Oh well! If she's with him I'll react tonight and figure it out tomorrow.'

With that thought, I pulled out my key to the front door and headed for the house. When I opened the door, I could hear the sounds of a CNN news broadcast on the TV, so I slowly walked toward the living room. When I entered it, the light from the TV helped me see Michael sleeping on the sofa, completely dressed with shoes and all. I walked over to the sofa, and kneeled down beside him. I noticed he hadn't shaved since I left, and the growth of his beard looked mighty good on him. I just watched him sleeping for a few minutes; then, I began to slowly kiss his forehead. He was startled by my first kiss which made him jerk up quickly. He looked at me, and with a surprised tone said, "Punkie! What the hell took you so long?" At that, he pulled me into his arms and began to kiss me passionately.

As we melted into one another's embrace, I slid my hand behind his head, pulled him close enough to whisper in his ear and said, "Michael, my love, I've lived and learned a lot throughout my years on this planet, and I've always known I could face anything life threw at me. But over this last month, I've discovered you are so much a part of me, that I am an empty shell of a woman without you. So I am asking you now Michael, please come back to me. I love you with all my heart, and I need you desperately."

Gazing lovingly into my eyes as he replied, "Christina, honey, I love you and I'm sorry we both had to go through this. But after you walked out on me like you did, I couldn't just return your calls like nothing had happened. I hate to admit this, but more than anything I had to be convinced you really love me, Punkie. So I gave you the time you needed to decide for yourself how much I really meant to you. As for me, I needed you to show how much you loved me, by coming after me." Then he held me tightly and added, "Punkie, I love you and I thank God you came back, because my soul has been slowly dying every second I've been without you."

My heart melted, as I lovingly said, "Let's not ever do this to one another again."

We kissed with the passion of angels in love and proceeded to gently disrobe each other. As we made love that night, I kept from Michael the fact I had gone off my birth control the day I left for Washington, D.C. We shared in the passions of our flesh until dawn that morning, and at the height of our love making Michael screamed out in ecstasy as he forcefully bore himself within me. As I felt his explosion, I prayed in my thoughts, 'Please God, let me conceive his child this night.'

Later that morning, I fixed us a lovely little breakfast and as we sat down to eat I took Michael's hand and said, "I love you baby, and thank you for last night, you were incredible."

He kissed my hand, smiled devilishly and replied, "I didn't get there alone."

I smiled back and it hit me like a flash, so with excitement I said, "Michael! Ann is doing a fine job handling things, and while the rest of our business trips are still on hold, why don't we spend all of September up here together? We have some lost time to make up and in more ways than one."

His face lit up with love as he replied, "There is nothing I would love more, than to spend an entire month alone with you."

He led me back to the bedroom, slipped off my robe, laid me on the bed, spread my wings with his thumbs, and began to devour my essence with his warm moist lips. He drove me to the point of actually pleading with him to plunge deep within me. The moment he did, my emergency code rang on my pager and we chose to ignore it. He went wild as he loved me with every ounce of his strength, and my body screamed with ecstasy as I took every explosive inch of him.

When I did finally answer the fourth emergency ring, to my surprise I discovered it was President Rush, and the first thing he said was, "Christina, I have some bad news for you. It seems Jimmy has been taken hostage with a number of foreign diplomats in Kuwait. Lussein has ordered these hostages moved to military and industrial sites throughout Iraq. He is using them as human shields to discourage attacks by coalition members."

I gasped loud enough to alarm Michael who was sitting beside me and said, "Oh my, God! No, George! Not Jimmy! What are you going to do about it?"

With a hint of urgency he replied, "I'm going to try and force Lussein to release them through international pressure. That's why I am calling you. I don't know how you did it, but you seemed to have created a good personal rapport with the Arab nations of Jordan, Libya, and Yemen. This fact could prove to be quite useful, because the only way we're going to have even a slim chance of obtaining the release of the hostages, is if these nations put pressure on Lussein. Now I'm going to ask you to visit them again and convince them to pressure Lussein for the release of all the hostages. I thought you would want to be the one to try to convince them, especially since Jimmy is one of the hostages."

I looked at Michael with tears in my eyes as I said, "Mr. President, I will call you with my answer in ten minutes."

I hung up the phone and proceeded to tell Michael everything. Afterward I said, "Michael, all I will say is I feel I must go, but if you'd rather I let the President send someone else, knowing Jimmy's life is on the line; then, I will call the President and tell him to find someone else."

He looked at me sadly, "Well I guess you better not unpack." And not two hours later I was on my way back to the Middle East.

# CHAPTER 18

The next month, I spent hopping across the Arab Nations of the Middle East like a jack rabbit, and on September 29th, I was the first Westerner since the invasion, to have a personal conference with Saddam Lussein in Baghdad, the Capital of Iraq. When I arrived at Lussein's palace, I was escorted to his office by several high ranking Iraqi military officials. As I was led in, I could see Lussein standing by some large windows on the opposite end of the room, and from the moment our eyes met I began to study him. I had heard so many conflicting stories about the man that I had no idea how to handle him. So once again, I was playing it by ear, and you know how I hate doing that.

As we greeted each other with a bow, I thought, 'Shit! What am I worried about? He's just another man.' At that I smiled at him softly and laughed to myself as my thoughts continued, 'I'll probably end this war in ten minutes,' and the first words out of his mouth were, "You are an imperialist pig, *Christina Powers,* and if I hadn't vowed to my fellow Arab brothers I would negotiate the release of the hostages with you, I'd have you assassinated right on the spot! If you hadn't gotten involved, I would be ruling OPEC already. Now please keep these things in mind, before you attempt to use your trickery on me."

I was so completely taken aback by the ruthlessness of his tone that for one moment, I, *'Christina Powers'* was speechless. I quickly changed gears, realizing I needed a new approach, so I removed the smile from my face, and in his native tongue firmly said, "Somebody had to stop you, because what you're doing is wrong."

His response to my answer was even more hateful as he growled, "You have not stopped me **WOMAN**! You've only succeeded in slowing me down."

I took a deep breath and tried another angle by saying, "King Lussein, if we continue to hurl insults at each other, we'll never accomplish anything.  So may we at least try to be civil as we discuss the reason why I'm here?"

He put his hand to his chin as he silently studied me.  Then all at once, he slapped his hands together loudly, and shouted, "Everyone leave us!"  And the room cleared in seconds.

When the room quieted, I turned to Lussein and said, "King Lussein, you mentioned negotiating the release of the hostages with me.  But I have come to ask you in good faith, to show the world you are not the barbarian everyone believes you to be, by letting me take these individuals with me when I leave.  I believe if you do this, you will gain some support from the International Community.  Then if you will air your grievances with Kuwait to the U.N., maybe together in the harmony of worldwide brotherhood, we can come to an acceptable settlement between your two nations."

He looked at me sternly and said, "How would you like me to address you?"

I proceed to stare him down, because I refused to allow him to intimidate me with his evil eyes, and the second he looked away, I answered his question with a firm voice, "You may call me, Christina."

In response he lifted his eyebrows with amazement; then, turned and walked over to his desk.  When he reached it, he invited me to take a seat, at which point he outright refused to release the hostages, and he promised Iraq would never submit to American pressure.  After three grueling hours of trying to reason with a nearly unreasonable man; I finally convinced him to at least allow me to see the hostages. By 9:00pm that evening, he was personally escorting me to where the hostages were being held.

The moment Jimmy saw me he leaped from out of the group of hostages and landed right in my arms.  He clung to my breast like a baby nursing and began to cry.  I tried to nonchalantly hold him like a stranger as I whispered in his ear, "Jimmy, try to be cool, I don't want them to realize we know each other." I began to pat his head as I very loudly said, "I understand how you feel sir, and I promise the international community is doing everything possible to obtain everyone's release."

Jimmy jerked his head from my shoulder and with a petrified look said, "Doesn't the fact you're standing here, mean we're going home?"

I was fighting back my tears and Jimmy knew it when I said, "I'm very sorry sir, but King Lussein is refusing to release anyone at this time." I looked at them all and added, "Folks, I know this is a horrendous ordeal you're living through, but I give you my word we will not stop trying to obtain your release. So, I must ask everyone to please be patient with us and remain strong."

The second I stopped talking Lussien slapped his hands together and immediately his guards came between Jimmy and me, and abruptly ended our visit. I was quickly ushered out of the room, without even being given the opportunity to say goodbye. It happened so fast I was stunned.

The next thing I knew, I was on my way to the airport, and all the way I tried my best to convince Lussein to release the hostages. As I spoke with this man, I felt like I was talking to a wall. Just before I was helped out of Lussein's limo I turned to him and said, "King Lussein! Please listen to me. I don't want to play games with you, so I'm going to be blunt. The world realizes what you stand to gain from annexing Kuwait. First, you will have acquired Kuwait's oil wealth, plus Iraq eliminates a two-hundred-billion-dollar debt to Kuwait. Second, you become a major power in OPEC." As I spoke, I put my hand to my chin, and with a slight touch of sarcastic humor added, "And would you just take a look at the increased access your Naval Forces will have to the Persian Gulf."

I slowly changed my approach and as my words intensified, so did the expression on my face. I gently shook my head and with conviction said, "The people of the world will not stand for this. I'm telling you the international community will truly do battle against you and for one reason only, what you're doing is morally and ethically wrong. Won't you please reconsider and release some of the 'steam in this pressure pot', by releasing those innocent people?"

I could tell I was getting through when he slowly lifted his eyebrows, shook his head and in a calm voice said, "You have proven to be everything I was told you would be, and you have given me much to think about." He slapped his hands again, and I was immediately escorted to my waiting jet.

October 2$^{nd}$, I was back in Washington, D.C. for a six-hour debriefing with the President and his advisers. From there, it was onto a one hour international news conference, and finally by 6:00pm that evening, I was in the air and on my way home to Michael. As I tried to make myself comfortable on the jet, I grabbed the phone to call Michael.

He answered the phone with a hopeful, "Christina, is it you?"
The moment I heard his precious voice, and knowing I would soon be with him, brought tears of joy to my eyes, which flooded forth from a fountain of pure love for my man. With a tone of absolute sensuality I said, "Hi, baby. It's your Punkie, and I'm longing for your touch."

I received quite the erotic response, "Well I just happen to have something throbbing, and it's longing to touch you too!"

I sighed, "Aaa," and with my famous May West interpretation replied, "I can't wait big boy. I should be landing at Stewart by 7:00pm, meet me with that gun in your pocket fully loaded and I'll help you fire it."

With a tone of pure excitement he answered, "I'll be there baby."

As we talked, I began to feel slightly dizzy, then nauseous. Ten minutes after we ended our conversation my nausea turned into lower abdominal cramps. By the time we landed the cramps became so intense, I could hardly walk off the jet. I managed to make it through the airport, and when I reached Michael I nearly collapsed in his arms. He grabbed me to hold me up and with a concerned tone said, "Christina! Baby, what's wrong?"

I grabbed at my abdomen and cried, "I don't know Michael, I started feeling sick to my stomach on the flight, and it's been continually getting worse."

He proceeded to help me to the car and when we reached it, I doubled over in pain and I cried out, **"OH GOD, MICHAEL!** Something's wrong!"

Swiftly he lifted me up, placed me in the car seat, and as he climbed in he said, "We're going to the hospital right now."

He hit the gas pedal and the moment he did, my lap filled with blood as I began to hemorrhage. I grabbed Michael's arm and cried, "Honey, help me!"

I heard him say, "Oh my God! Baby, hold on!" And that was the last thing I heard before losing consciousness.

# CHAPTER 19

I woke up two days later at Vassar Brother's Hospital in Poughkeepsie, with Michael once again sitting beside my hospital bed. I glanced over at him, managed half a smile and said, "Well how was that for an exciting reunion?"

His blue eyes and glorious smile brightened up the dimly lit room, as he gracefully came to my side. Taking my hand gently in his, and looking deeply into my eyes, he lovingly said, "You're going to be the death of me yet, Punkie."

We both managed a smile, then he gently kissed my painfully dried out lips, and in a soft voice said, "I love you Punkie, and I know why you did what you did. I only wish you would have talked to me first Christina, before risking your life for me."

I looked at him with a completely bewildered expression, as I mustered up the strength to say, "What are you talking about, Michael?"

He gave me a surprised look, and proceeded to inform me that I had just had a miscarriage and nearly bled to death. As he spoke, a horrifyingly sick feeling came over me. I put my hands to my face and cried, "Oh God! **Michael no**! I can't believe I let myself become so caught up with trying to obtain Jimmy's freedom, I completely forgot I deliberately tried to conceive our child."

All at once a fear hit me from deep within my soul, so I squeezed Michael's hand with all my strength, and with intensity in my words I asked, "Did Dr. Hart perform a hysterectomy on me?"

He shook his head as if he were disappointed by my deep concern over the welfare of my uterus, and it showed in his voice as he answered, "Dr. Hart told me after the surgery he wanted to perform one on you, but since he didn't deem it a necessity to save your life, he elected not to risk your wrath. He asked me to help convince you to have a hysterectomy done as soon as you recover. So Punkie, I'm asking you to agree to the surgery right now, for your own safety." Then he slowly dropped to his knees and with a look that told me he was truly troubled said, "Punkie, how could you endanger your life like this without talking to me first?"

I explained I had forgotten to take my pills when I left for the Middle East, then I added, "I remembered as we were in the heat of our passion and I didn't know how to stop things to bring it up. I also wanted to have your child."

He kissed my hand and with half a smile replied, "I can understand everything you just said, but I'm still having a problem accepting it. I thought neither one of us would ever do anything involving our personal lives together, without discussing it first. Don't you see that keeping something like this from me is just the same as if you were purposely deceiving me?"

I looked at him sadly, realizing what he was actually saying and said, "Michael, honey, I wasn't keeping this pregnancy from you, I didn't know myself. So that's why I never thought of it as lying to you, and I promise you I will never keep anything from."

His smile was loving and sincere as he said, "Please, Christina! Never deliberately put your life in harm's way again. I love you so much Punkie, it would kill me to be without you."

I took his hand in mine, brought it to my dried lips, kissed it once and said, "I love you too, Michael."

Michael looked open heartedly into my eyes and with complete integrity said, "Punkie, I need to know something. I have not kept one thing from you since the day we meet, can you say the same?"

I gazed back at him confidently and answered, "Yes Michael, I can say the same." After that I continued to reassure him I have always told him everything, all the while knowing I had just lied to him. As I spoke, I thought, 'Michael, I wish I could tell you everything, including all my fears. But I have been betrayed and hurt so badly in the past, I don't know if I can ever completely trust anyone again, even you my love.' These words I kept to myself as Michael kissed my cheek, and laid his head down on the pillow beside mine.

The first thing I did the next morning was spend twenty minutes listening to Dr. Hart and Michael, trying to convince me to have a hysterectomy. After their plea, that it was for my own safety, I politely said, "No!"

With frustration in his tone Dr. Hart responded, "Why are you being so obstinate, Christina?"

"Obstinate," I snapped back. "That's spitting in the wind, isn't it Dr. Hart? I will say this but only once more, this is my body and I will decide what is best for it."

He looked at me as if I had slapped his face and said, "You're absolutely correct Christina. Please forgive me, it's only because I'm your physician and I care."

I could see in his eyes I had hurt his feelings, so I took his hand in mine and said, "I understand that, Dr. Hart." And in that moment, I could feel through his hand the anger of his soul begin to fade, and I realized this incredibly handsome young man, was desperately in love with me. So I released his hand to keep his knees from forcing him to the floor. I could sense he knew I had discovered his secret, so I continued as if I hadn't, by saying, "I also want you to know I respect your opinion Robert, not just because you're my physician, but Michael and I, consider you a close family friend as well."

He smiled with a sigh and said, "Well then maybe you will at least listen to this. I don't want you going back to work or traveling anywhere for the next month. That's when I want to see you back in my office." With that, he gave us both a warm friendly hand shake, and gracefully left the room.

The next morning as we left the hospital, we were surprised to say the least, when a mob of reporters charged us. Especially since Michael assured me, he kept a lid on this one. But to my dismay, it appeared someone from the hospital staff had informed the press twenty minutes before my discharge, that I was a patient in the hospital and that I had a miscarriage. I was horrified and humiliated as I openly dodged questions like, "Christina! With all the children who need to be adopted in this world, why would you risk your own life to have a child?"

Thank God for Michael, because I froze up so badly from that question, I could hardly move. Michael rescued me by swiftly ushering me into the limo. The second we climbed in he shouted, "James, take off!"

James sped away and he didn't stop speeding until he finally lost the paparazzi. After our escape, James drove Michael and me to the Catskill Mountain family home, with enough supplies to last a month.

Michael gave Ann Markel full power over our entire empire for that month and told her not to call us unless the world was about to end. He was so determined to keep me from running myself into an early grave, that for the entire month he was my 'knight in shining armor', as well as my servant boy. And let me tell you, I loved every minute of it!

On November 5th, Dr. Hart gave me a clean bill of health put me back on the pill, and the next day it was back to work. When I saw how well Ann had handled the helm of Powers Incorporated, I called her into my office to meet with Michael and me. When she entered the office, I invited her to be seated and said, "Ann, I can remember when you, Jimmy, Bobby, Joe Aiello and me, all worked together on my first U.S. tour back in the seventies, and you have been a loyal employee ever since. That's why I want you to know I think very highly of you as a friend, as well as an employee, and as an employee you have proven yourself to be more than capable. Because of this, Michael and I would like to offer you the position of fourth executive vice president and increase your salary to five-million annually." With a joyful smile, I reached for her hand as I continued, "Congratulations Ann, you deserve it."

She hugged me and with tears of pride said, "Christina, I don't know how to thank you." She hugged Michael with sincerity and added, "Thank you for giving me the opportunity to prove myself, Michael."

He happily returned the hug as he said, "You don't have to thank me. I thank you for doing such a great job." When Ann went back to her office that day, her feet were not touching the floor.

Although we were back at the office, it was not work as usual. Michael insisted we begin delegating much more of the top brass responsibility to others, which gave us more time to be together as a couple.

Michael delegated so well that by November 13th, we had

everything running fairly smoothly, including our marriage. Yet at the same time, I always had a sick feeling inside, because I would never allow myself to forget Jimmy's plight for one moment.

On the evening of the 17th, as Michael and I watched the evening news together, Tom Brokoff said, "The President announced today he would be visiting Saudi Arabia, November twenty-first, through the twenty-second, to celebrate the Thanksgiving holiday with American troops deployed in the Kingdom of Saudi Arabia as part of Operation Desert Shield."

The second he finished speaking Michael watched with amazement, as I grabbed the phone like a possessed woman and began to punch the numbers. As soon as I heard the beep of the answering machine, I excitedly said, "Hi George, its Christina. Please call me on my private line as soon as possible."

At that, I put down the phone, turned to Michael almost breathless and exclaimed, "I can't believe this, honey!"

He looked at me strangely and with bewilderment in his voice said, "What are you talking about?"

Just then the phone rang, so I quickly grabbed it and said, "I hope it's you, George?"

He chuckled as he answered, "You'd better make this one quick too Christina, because you caught me in the middle of preparing for my trip."

With excitement I said, "Take me with you, George!"

Sounding slightly confused he asked, "What?"

I answered quickly, "You heard me right. Take me with you. I want to perform for our troops. I think it would aid in your task of building moral, by showing them every American is behind them on this, not just the government."

With a disappointed tone he said, "I can't take you with me. Saudi Arabia law forbids live performances of any kind on their soil."

I slightly wined my response, "Come on, George! You're the President of the United States, and they're American troops. I find it hard to believe you can't convince King Fehd to allow it. After all, their law also forbids foreign troops on their soil, doesn't it?"

I was calling his bluff on that one, because I had no idea what

Saudi Arabia law stated. But by his momentary silence, I knew it was a good guess; then, he said, "I'll tell you what Christina, I'll do it if you do one for me?"

I thought to myself, 'Here we go!' As I said, "Name it, George."

He cleared his voice and said, "I want you to be standing beside me with your full support when I announce my bid for re-election in January."

I started to laugh then I controlled myself and said, "That's a good one, George."

With that he said, "You're laughing at me! I can't believe you!"

I quickly replied, "You know I love you George, it's your party I'm not too fond of. But my answer is still yes."

He laughed, "Great! I'll see you here on the 19th."

After we said our goodbyes, I placed the phone down on the coffee table, turned to Michael with a smile of pure excitement, and before I could utter a single syllable he shouted, "What the fuck do you think you're doing? Call him right back and tell him you're not going!"

I was taken aback by his outburst, but I still answered calmly, "Honey, I have to go."

He snapped back, "I don't care what you think you have to do. You're not going!"

I tried to make him understand by saying, "Michael, there is something telling me I have to go."

He shook his head with utter frustration, and in an extremely angry voice said, "You've got to stop this, Christina. I know you're upset over Jimmy, and so am I, but you're driving yourself mad with this. Can't you see you're killing yourself?" His voice began to calm as he took me in his arms and continued, "Punkie, I'm just worried about you. You almost bled to death on me only a month ago, remember? I can't let you go charging off to Saudi Arabia to perform, when you're not even totally recuperated yet."

I looked at him sincerely and said, "Michael, my health is fine, so please listen to me and try to understand. I know that for some reason, I'm being guided there and I must go."

With that statement, he pushed me out of his arms and shouted, "Guided! Are you a nut!? You're being guided all right, by your own obsessions, and if you don't pick up that phone and make that call, then I'm washing my hands of you. If you don't give a damn about yourself, how can you expect me to give a damn about you?"

This time I lost it, so I shouted back, "Nuts huh! I must be nuts, to live and breathe for someone like you."

He began to laugh sarcastically as he shouted, "That's why you're always so willing to drop me on a dime and take off. Shit Christina, this is a marriage and it's meant to be a mutual partnership, that means we're supposed to discuss this stuff, remember?"

I flung my hands in the air and shouted, "I can't take this anymore, Michael. I'm tired of you trying to run my life. You're my husband, not my master. So if you want to walk out the door go ahead and walk."

I could see the fire in his eyes as he yelled, "You know what? That's just what I'm going to do!"

My own anger flared with his as I answered, "If you do Michael, don't expect me to come after you!"

He shouted back, "Do us both a favor this time and don't bother!"

He stormed out of the room and as I watched him go I thought, 'What the hell are we doing?' So I quickly went after him, grabbed his hand as he reached the front door and said, "Michael, wait a second please."

He pulled his hand from mine and angrily replied, "Christina, I don't give a damn anymore!" Then he slammed the door in my face and he walked out.

I stood there speechless, not totally believing what had just occurred, and feeling completely bewildered I thought, '**Oh Well! I'll figure it out tomorrow!**'

# CHAPTER 20

I gave Michael two days to cool off, and on November 16th, I thought, 'All right Michael, that's long enough!' I figured he should be a little less obstinate and a little more reasonable by now, so at 9:00am that morning my search began with a phone call. As I guessed, Michael did not return my call and since I didn't have time to play games, because I was leaving on the 19th, I called my security firm and asked them to locate his whereabouts for me. I told Frank Rossi, the Director for Powers Security, all Michael's normal hideouts, and I expected he would be found in a matter of hours. But to my dismay, Frank never called me back until 9:00pm that evening. When he did, he informed me Michael was nowhere to be found, and the search would take a little longer than anticipated.

The longer it took to find him the more concerned I became. So, at 8:00am the following morning I decided to call my mother-in-law, who unbeknownst to me, absolutely could not manage to rise and function before 10:00am She wasted no time informing me of that fact when she answered the phone with a groggy, "Hello, who is this?"

"Good morning Tess it's Christina," I said with a slight hint of urgency.

Sharply she asked, "What time is it, Christina?"
"8:00am I apologize for waking you, but I really need to speak with you." I answered.

With the sincerity of an angel in her tone she replied, "Christina, it takes me ten minutes just to get moving in the morning, so please don't ask me to solve your family problems before 10:00am, okay?" And all I heard was {click!} as she hung up the phone.

As I stood there holding the phone with my lower jaw touching the floor, I thought, 'What the hell was that?' I proceeded to work my thoughts into a fury as I paced through the house for the next two hours wondering, 'Where the hell are you, Michael? I know you love me asshole, so why are you being so damn stubborn. Oh my God! This man has a power over me that's frightening.' My mind went wild like this until finally the 10:00 a clock hour came and I hit redial. The phone was answered on the third ring and I heard,

"Good morning Christina, and don't ask me where he is."

"That's not fair Tess," I protested vigorously, "Michael's my husband, how can I not want to find him?"

Just as forceful she replied, "Well, from what I have seen and heard, you've nearly destroyed my son. Now from a mother's point of view, if your son had been swept up by a worldly woman as yourself, and you watched as she broke his heart time after time; then, he finally comes to his senses and tells you that he never wants to see this woman again; then, this woman calls you and wants to know where your son is, I wonder if you would wonder, is she coming to finish the job? What would you do?"

I answered her with an air of integrity, "After having met the woman in question I would hopefully be capable of looking past the hype which precedes her, and still be able to make a clear decision on the woman's true intent toward my son."

With integrity of her own she simply replied, "Then you will understand when I refuse to answer your question. Now, I am a seventy-six-year-old woman Christina, but I will still fight to protect one of my children. I'm going to do just that by saying goodbye, I have much too much to do for an old lady as it is, and I certainly don't need this worry."

"Please! Tess! I'm begging you don't hang up!" and I heard (Click!) With that I slammed the phone down feeling totally frustrated and I began to cry.

The next morning over my first cup of coffee, James brought in the local newspaper the Poughkeepsie Journal. I took two sips from my cup, as I unrolled the paper. I took two more sips as my eyes caught the headlines and the moment they did, I choked so hard, I showered the article with coffee.  Once I caught my breath, I quickly wiped off the paper and in big bold print it read, **"Michael Gillespie, the husband of our local celebrity *Christina Powers* Gillespie, has hired the law firm of Laforge and Han of Middletown, New York to file divorce papers against his famous wife."**

My first response was shock, than anger, and after finishing the article I thought, 'Christina, what are you worrying about?  This can't be a true story.  You know Michael loves you.  He's a reasonable man when he's calm.'

Just then the doorbell rang and not two minutes later, Carman entered the room with a certified letter from the law firm of Laforge and Han.  I ripped it open and sure enough, there were divorce papers inside.  I stuffed them back in the envelope and ran for the shower.  I was dressed and on my way to Tess' house with letter in hand, in only twenty-two-minutes, and I was looking hot to boot.

As I drove through the sleepy village of Ravena, I remembered how the main street was lined with people the day of our wedding and I thought, 'Michael, there is no way you're getting away from me, I love you too much you pain-in-my-ass.'  At that I pulled into Magnolia Circle and proceeded with determination to my mother in law's home, only this time I wasn't laughing when she opened the door.  I was dead serious, and it was my turn to show it when I said, "Tess, please listen to me because I don't have much time.  I have got to find Michael!  I love him Tess, and I don't want a divorce.  I know if I can only see him I could convince him of that."

She looked at me with disbelieving eyes and said, "To do what Christina, say hello for ten minutes then leave him again?  Do you realize you will be out of the country on your first anniversary?  How do you think that's making Michael feel, knowing you would rather be in Saudi Arabia on your anniversary then with him?"

I gently touched her hand as I said, "Tess, what Michael is refusing to see is that if by my taking this trip I am able to save even one life, then that's worth giving up every anniversary for the rest of our lives.  I know if I could just speak with him, I could make him see that.  Tess, I love your son, my husband, more than life itself, but he's got to understand the lives of thousands of innocent people are at stake. I would be less than human, if I did nothing to help try to bring a peaceful conclusion to this crisis."

She looked at me and as tears welled up in her eyes said, "He's at his sister's camp house in a town called Indian Lake, in the Adirondacks. I misjudged you Christina, and I'm very sorry I did. I know if you talk to Michael he will understand, he loves you just as much Christina, I know he does."

I opened the door all the way so I could hug her, and with tears of relief in my eyes I said, "Thank you, Mom. I know I have never said it before Tess, but I do love you." And for the first time since the day I met her, she returned my hug with an open heart. She gave me directions to the camp and sent me on my way with God speed.

# CHAPTER 21

After spending two hours driving around the back roads of Indian Lake, I finally found the driveway which led up to a quaint little cabin, nestled in the woods, with Michael's car parked at the end of it. I climbed out of my car, walked to the door and knocked. Michael answered the door and the moment our eyes met, I wanted to leap into his arms, but the look of disgust on his face and the tone of his voice, forced me to conceal my true feelings, because the first thing he said was, "What are you doing here? I thought we agreed not to come after one another."

At that I shook the divorce papers in his face and forcefully said, "What is this Michael, a plea to get my attention? Well you have it! And I'm here! Now, would you please stop this nonsense and listen to me, I know you don't really want a divorce and neither do I."

"I'm not pleading for anything, Christina." He answered sarcastically.

"Then what is this all about, Michael? Is it just to keep me from going because you think I'm rejecting you? You know I love you with all my heart, how can you truthfully stand there and honestly think to yourself that I am putting you second, especially since you know world peace is at stake."

With a look of deep sincerity in his eyes and a voice to match he said, "Christina, I told you! If you go to Saudi Arabia again we're finished, you told me you were going, so there's your divorce papers. Since you're here, please just sign them and be on your way."

I looked at him, started to laugh at his performance and said, "Don't expect an academy award Michael, and please don't expect me to sign these papers. I'm telling you again Michael, I love you and I know how difficult being married to me has been. I also understand why you're so upset, and that's why I'm not going to give you a divorce."

He nearly became irate as he shouted, "Would you fucking listen to me for once! All I want from you is a divorce! Damn it, Christina! I don't want you or all the bullshit that comes along with you. Don't you get it? I don't want anything that will make me think of you even once, including your precious empire. Just let me leave with my self-respect and dignity." Tears came to his eyes as he continued, "My heart can't handle this life with you any longer Punkie; you're destroying me."

I felt the pain of his heart, so I reached out to comfort him with all my love, and as my voice cracked I said, "Michael, please honey, listen to me, I'm not trying to hurt you, I love you. Don't you remember, Michael? You're the one who told me you knew God had a higher calling for me in this life. After knowing that, how can you now ask me to turn from that calling, when I finally realize I'm truly hearing it?" Passionately I grabbed his hand and with fear in my voice, "Michael! I don't know why I must go, I only know I must!"

With his strong firm hands trembling, he grabbed my shoulders and with a voice as hurting as a little boy lost, said, "I know that, Christina. I also know you're my soul mate, and even though my love for you springs forth from the depths of my being, if you go for whatever reasons, we will not be together in this lifetime. Christina, I'm constantly filled with fear for your life when I'm not with you, and I can't deal with it anymore. So as much as it's breaking my heart to say this I must, if you're still planning to be on that jet in the morning, then sign these papers before you leave and I will know we're just not meant to be. But if you choose to stay here with me, I will rip up those dammed divorce papers and love you with all my heart every day of my life."

My tears began to flow like a fountain as I looked at him and pleaded, "Michael, Honey! I love you, but I can't stay. Please, just let me do this one more thing, and I promise you, I will never leave you again."

He dropped his hands from my shoulders, and with a tone of utter frustration said, "One more thing! Never again! How many times have I heard those words before!? Don't you mean until the next time and the time after that!? Well I can't, and I won't, be the man behind the woman, Christina. I just can't, so at least you can let me keep whatever self-respect I have left, and grant me this divorce."

This time 'I' was the one to become irate, and it was apparent the moment I opened my mouth, "You, bastard! You totally refuse to give an inch, don't you?" I stomped my foot with pure anger as I continued, "Well, I'll tell you what you stubborn male, you're my husband, and if you think I'm going to let you walk away from me that easily, you have another think coming!" I ripped the divorce papers into pieces, threw them in his face and shouted, "If you want your freedom from me that damn bad, then you better find a reason that's going to hold up in court because you're going to have to fight me for it. Now dammit Michael, listen to me! I have something I must do and I'm going to do it! I want you to take some time to get your head together, and I'll expect to see you at home when I get back." I grabbed the door handle and shouted, "This time, I think I'll slam the door in your face!" (Crack!)

At that I turned away, stormed to the car, threw it into drive and flung gravel thirty feet in the air all the way to the main road.

At 6:00am the next morning, I forced thoughts of Michael to the back of my mind as I boarded Air Force One with the President and the First Lady. To my surprise it was off to Paris, before Saudi Arabia. The President invited me on behalf of himself, and President Gorbasoff of the Soviet Union, to attend as their personal guest, the history making summit being held to mark the end of the cold war. Our twenty hours in Paris were the most exciting hours for true global peace, the world had ever seen, and I was elated to be part of it.

We left Paris at 10:00pm on the 20th, and headed for Jidda, a city on Saudi Arabia's Western Red Sea Coast. This time on Air Force One, we were joined by National Security Adviser Brent Scowcroft, Gen. Norman Schwartoff, and four senior bi-partisan leaders of Congress: Senate Majority Leader George J. Nikcall (D, Maine), Senate Minority Leader Robert J. Zole (R, Kan.), House Speaker Thomas S. Boley (D, Wash.) and my ex-husband, House Minority Leader Lee Bradford (R, N.Y.). Needless to say neither one of us was pleased to see the other, but we did manage a civil greeting.

As this cheery group talked in the main cabin I thought, 'God, I pray Michael and I don't end up like Lee and me.' I thought some more, 'Oh Shit! This is the way all my relationships end up.' At that, a chill of fear shot through me as my mind began to race with thoughts of losing Michael forever. Just before the verge of insanity, I hit the brakes of my mind and thought, 'Stop it! Our souls have soared through the heavens together our love could never end like the others.'

Sometime around 2:00am on the flight to Jidda, as all the guests dozed in the dimly lit main cabin, George came to me and touched my shoulder as he whispered in my ear, "Christina, Sorry to wake you, but I'd like to speak with you alone in the conference cabin now, if I may?"

I woke quickly as he spoke, nodded my head 'yes' in response to his request, and quietly followed him into the conference cabin. As we made ourselves comfortable, he softly smiled as he said, "Finally, we have the opportunity to talk. I need to fill you in on the rest of our agenda and what we can expect to pop up next."

I chuckled with total sensuality as I said, "Oh yeah!"

He turned as red as a beet and started to laugh as he struggled to say, "You know what I mean."

I stopped laughing and with a girlish smile said, "Yes, I know what you mean George, I just couldn't pass that one up." I continued with eagerness, "Now please tell me, what's next? You know how I hate being kept in the dark; I have this phobia over leaping into bed before I know what's in it."

He smiled that famous ear-to-ear smile and replied, "You're a bad girl, *Christina Powers!*"

I gave him one of my own famous smiles and with an emphasis on my Texan accent said, "Oh stop George, you know you love it. Now stop fooling around and start explaining!"

From that point on our conversation became serious as he said, "The first thing on the agenda when we arrive in Jidda, is a 9:00am meeting with King Fehd and Sheik Jabir Al-Ahmad Al Sebah, the exiled Emir of Kuwait. From there we have a 1:00pm luncheon with Saudi Arabian and Kuwait dignitaries, until 4:00pm. Then we will begin a two day, whirlwind tour of four different U.S. Military sites in the region. Our schedule is set up so we first meet the troops with handshakes and autographs; then, we'll have a quick Thanksgiving meal with them. Afterward, I'll give a short tough anti-Iraq speech, turn it over to you, and you can wind up our visits with a half-hour performance at each site. The preparations for our visits are already complete, so all you and your crew will have to do is jump up on the platform when I introduce you."

Impressed, I smiled and said, "Great! It sounds like you've covered all angles."

He lifted his eyebrows as if he thought he was overwhelming me and continued, "Do you think you can handle this schedule?"

With an air of confidence and a slight chuckle I replied, "Without a doubt, George."

He slightly blushed as he said, "Please forgive me. For a moment I forgot with whom I was speaking. Now maybe we should try to get some sleep before this day starts, I think we've covered everything."

He gazed around the room aimlessly, as if he were forgetting something, then finally said, "Oh yes! There is one thing I neglected to tell you. In order for me to get the approval for your mini concerts, I had to agree ahead of time that you would grant King Fehd's son, Prince Mohammed Fehd a private meeting with you. King Fehd told me personally his son Mohammed has been obsessed with following your career. He claims to be your biggest fan."

I found myself intrigued by the news of this request, so I said, "A Prince, huh! That's interesting, what do you know about him?"

"Just that he's heir to the Saudi throne, and the most vast fortune on the face of the earth."

"You're kidding! What else do you know?"

He smiled mischievously, "Christina, I heard about the divorce; don't tell me you're looking already?"

"No, George, I'm not, I'm thinking of the bigger picture," I answered devilishly, "what if you thought a prince was after your wife?"

He started to laugh then said, "You're too much, Christina! I guess that's why I enjoy your company as much as I do."

I winked with a seductive smile, "I enjoy your friendship too, George. Now will this Mohammed suit my needs or not?"

He shook his head and with a big smile answered, "Well if your goal is to make Michael stand up and take notice, then you picked the right guy. He's a thirty-six-year-old genius, who graduated top of his class at Harvard Law. From what I hear, he's the most sought-after bachelor in the world."

With wide eyes I said, "Whoa! It sounds like I'll be meeting my male counterpart instead of a fanatical fan."

"All you have to do is meet with him sometime during our luncheon; then, you can sing your heart out on Saudi soil."

With that I yawned then said, "I think I can handle the prince, George, as long as I can have a little sleep first." He chuckled then we said good night and I passed out the minute I hit my seat.

The next morning, we received the most incredibly intense military escort to the King's palace that I had ever witnessed. Everywhere the eye could see, there were armed soldiers guarding the entire route of our motorcade, through this incredibly beautiful and wealthy city of oil sheiks. When we reached the palace, everyone in the President's entourage were swiftly ushered from their autos straight into the main greeting room of the palace. From there, those of us who were attending the meeting with King Fehd and Sheik Jabir Al-Ahmad Al Sebah, were led from the group and into the King's private chambers.

The four-hour meeting which followed proved to be deplorable as Sheik Jabir showed us graphic photographs of Iraqi atrocities in Kuwait. Immediately after the meeting, George held a news conference where he strongly condemned Iraq and called for the United Nations Security Council to pass a new, anti-Iraq resolution by the end of the month. He also assured the world that any differences between the U.S. and the U.S.S.R. on Persian Gulf policy were extraordinarily small compared to our mutual commitment to see an emboldened withdrawal of all Iraqi troops from Kuwait. After the news conference, we joined some of the most powerful men in the Middle East for lunch in the formal dining.

Shortly after lunch, George stood on the platform at the head of the room and began to address those present. As he did, six heavily armed soldiers came to me and asked me to accompany them to the prince's private chambers. I looked at their weapons; then, I looked at George feeling a sense of apprehension. I guess he sensed it too, because he winked at me in an attempt to ease my concerns. At that I smiled, and proceeded confidently and fearlessly, following my escorts to a prearranged rendezvous with the prince.  As I walked in the center of my six towering guards, through a large hundred foot long, thirty foot tall and wide, oval shaped corridor, I looked with astonishment at how this entire palace was lined with detailed solid gold trimmings, and I thought, 'Oh my God!  The wealth in just this one corridor could probably put an end to world hunger.' I got a quick cold chill as my thoughts continued, 'What an incredibly vulgar waste of wealth and at the same time it's mighty enticing.'

At the end of this massive corridor hung two large, fifteen foot oval shaped African redwood doors, with the family crest molded on each door, and you guessed it, they were in solid gold.  The doors opened into the large, pearl white, and purple, hexagonal shaped chambers of the prince.  The ceiling was a solid gold dome, with six golden hexagon chandeliers, dropping twenty feet from the ceiling, to illuminate the center of the room, where stood a large throne.  Seated upon the throne some one hundred feet ahead of me, was the most beautiful man I had ever seen.

As I glanced at him in his golden attire I thought, 'This man's physical beauty rivals my own, while his strength and wealth towers that of mine.  Whoa!  This is exciting!'

He looked to be a six-footer, with deep Mediterranean blue eyes. I could just see the edges of his jet black hair, peeking through his hand woven golden turban.  He was gorgeous!

The moment I stepped into the room a feeling of apprehension came over me, and my heart rate increased with every step I took closer. As these unexplained feelings swept my emotions, I felt myself wanting to run out of the room.  So, I mentally slapped myself across the face and thought, 'Pull it together girl before you pass out on the spot.  He's just another man.' As I reached the foot of his throne, I swallowed hard, took a deep breath and thought, 'I don't know what's going on here, but whatever it is you can handle it Christina.'

As I curtsied, I kept my smile cool and calm, just like the perfect performer I was born to be, in an attempt to conceal my true inner anxieties.  Our eyes met with intensity as I completed my curtsy.  He rose from his seat and gracefully approached me with his hand stretched out. Taking my hand in his, he brought it to his lips and never letting his eyes leave mine once, he kissed the back of my hand with such passion, that I felt it in the core of my being. When he opened his mouth, the words flowed forth like a chorus of angels as he said, "How honored I am to have the incomparable *Christina Powers,* curtsy before me. And I must say your beauty is more radiating in person, than any likeness of you could ever hope to capture."

I thought, 'Whoa! You called that right,' as I replied, "Your words are too kind Prince Fehd, but I thank you just the same."

He smiled gracefully, "Modesty in a woman with your physical attributes is a precious rarity, which is refreshing."

He was attempting to immediately sweep me off my feet, and I knew it the moment he said, "I have adored you from my first glimpse of you, and now that I've kissed your hand, I will not rest until I make you mine, body and soul."

I stepped back, put my hand to my chest, caught my breath and said, "You certainly don't waste time beating around the bush, do you?"

He gently took my hand and with excitement said, "Come with me my love, I must show you something." He continued to speak words of his undying love for me, like lyrics of my own songs as he led me on a tour through the palace.

I was nearly enchanted by this man's charms by the time we reached the roof of the main towers of the palace, which overlooked the entire city. He gently held my hand as we stood there gazing out over the sun glistened rooftops, which like a mirage, gave the city the sparkle and appearance of pure gold. I looked at this powerfully bewitching man, in the middle of this awesome setting, and I found myself spellbound by his beauty and charisma. At one point as we spoke, his eyes looked right through me with such clarity, I felt myself drifting into every word he said. He took me in his arms and kissed me so passionately, I thought I'd melt.

I felt myself almost helplessly being utterly devoured by this man's ferocious appetite, right up until he said, "Your destiny *Christina Powers,* is to be my bride and bear my son; the son which will one day rule the world from the throne of Persia."

With that statement, I put up the stop sign by gracefully slipping out of his grasp and saying, "Slow down, Prince Fehd! I'm flattered, but I'm a married woman and I cannot accommodate your needs."

I could see sadness come over his face as he replied, "Christina, if you were mine, I would be so empowered by our union, I could catch the light from a star to adorn your bridal gown."

It finally dawned on me he was serious, so I said, "Forgive me Prince Fehd, but I must ask you to please take me to the President's luncheon now. It's getting late."

Then all at once, with force he grabbed my hand, pulled me back into his arms, and with passion to his words said, "If you marry me, I will stop Lussien tomorrow."

I knew I had to try to handle this situation on the humorous side, so with a chuckle I said, "Oh yeah!  What makes you think you can do what no one in the world has been able to accomplish?"

He started laughing only his laugh was frightening, and when he stopped laughing his face took on an evil expression and with viciousness said, "You really don't know who I am yet, do you?"  He squeezed my shoulders to the point of pain and laughed as he shouted, "You don't even realize who you are yourself yet!"

I became more then concerned when I looked into his eyes and realized there was nothing but black space behind those Mediterranean blue eyes, so I quickly said, "You're absolutely right, Prince Fehd!  I don't know what you're talking about, and at this point I don't really care to know.  All I want you to do is let go of my arms, and stop hurting me before I start to become upset."

In response to my demand he applied more pressure to my arms, and with anger in his voice said, "You don't have a choice Christina, because you were born to be mine.  Your destiny lies with me, and together we shall conquer and rule the world."

All at once he began to bodily drag me to the edge of the tower as I shouted, "What are you doing?  Please let go of me, Mohammed, you're scaring me!"

When we reached the edge, he forced me to look over the side as he said, "Do you see all this?  If you marry me and bear the child we have been pre-destined to bring into this world together, I will give it all to you."

Realizing I was in the hands of another Arabian madman I said, "It's beautiful Mohammed!"  Then I turned my head to gaze romantically into his eyes and continued, "You would really give all this to me?"

He slowly released his tight grip as I gently kissed his lips, and the moment I could slip out of his hands I did. And as I backed away from him I said, "You don't want to give it all to me Mohammed, I'll only give it to the less fortunate souls on this planet anyway."

From out of the blue he lunged for me, grabbed my neck and I could see the hatred flare in his nostrils as he shouted, "Jesus Christ, Christina! You're just like him, and if you refuse to unite your gifts with mine, then you will die the martyr like him as well."

I pushed him off me with all my strength and shouted, "What the hell is this, the twilight zone? Well if it is all I can say is I don't know who you're comparing me to, but I can tell you I'm not like anybody you've ever met. So you better keep your hands off me."

As fast as lighting, he grabbed my hand and this time he flung me up against the chains, which held one back from falling to their death and shouted, "If you don't agree to marry me right now, I vow one day you will be on your knees pleading for your life at my feet!" Then his eyes radiated unquenchable evil as his voice thundered, "Remember this, *Christina Powers*! I will be standing as the divine ruler in the temple of David, when I have you beheaded!"

My anger gave me the strength of ten men, as I once again pushed him off me and screamed, "You're a **sick fuck,** Mohammed!" Then, I took off running toward the elevator we came up on, and when I reached for the down button my hands were shaking so badly I could hardly push it.

I had myself somewhat composed as I swiftly exited the elevator on the main floor of the palace. I immediately began to search for the dining room where the President was and as I walked down a large corridor, I could see two armed guards approaching me from up ahead. From behind me I heard the prince yell, "Guards, retain her at once!"

My heart almost stopped when I realized I was trapped in this corridor and all I could do was pray in my thoughts, 'Dear Lord Jesus! Please get me out of this country alive and in one piece!'

I struggled to keep my composure as Prince Fehd reached me. To my great relief he gently took my slightly trembling hand and said, "Christina, my sweet, you're heading in the wrong direction." With a smile that could tame a lion he added, "Please allow me to escort you?"

At that, he led me back to the dining room where the President was, and proceeded to carry on amongst his father's guests, as if nothing had happened.

I watched his graceful transformation back to the charming man I first met and I thought, 'My God! This man is scary! He's a better performer than I am.' From that point on I stuck to George like glue. I actually feared for my safety with this madman still in the room. Finally, that long bizarre afternoon ended around 4:00pm when the President took his entourage, via a convoy of helicopters, to our first military site about two hundred miles inland.

On the flight, George turned to me and said, "Why don't you tell me what it is? I know something's wrong! You haven't left my side since you came back from your meeting with the prince."

I gazed at him and with an obvious look of concern on my face said, "George, we think what Lussein is doing is mad, but mark my words, the world hasn't seen anything like it's going to see when that fruitcake takes over his father's throne!"

His expression was one of complete surprise, "You can't be talking about the same Prince Mohammed Fehd I know."

I shook my head as I replied, "The one and only! Let me tell you, he's U.S.D.A. certifiably insane."

His face reflected my concern as he said, "Man! The implications of that are frightening."

I lifted my eyebrows, "Tell me about it! I just experienced it first-hand."

"What happened?" He asked with curiosity.

"Nothing worth repeating; all I ask is that you keep a close eye on my back while we're here."

He laughed and said, "Well I guess he's not going to be replacing Michael too soon."

Feeling much more relaxed I allowed myself to laugh at George's attempt to be humorous and said, "Not if my life depended on it!"

I finally felt completely relaxed the moment I was back in my element, surrounded by cheering fans. I'm sure the fact they were all armed American soldiers, had a lot to do with my confidence level. When

154

I took the stage to perform, the first live performance on Saudi soil in its history, I was deliberately so seductively hot I could almost hear Prince Fehd's ancestors turning in their entombed temples. The desert had been brought to life by the cheers of the young Americans for whom I performed that night, and when I took my last bow, I blew the crowd kisses as they chanted, "We love you, Christina! We love you, Christina!"

When I finally quieted them down, I said, "I love you too! And from the depths of my soul, my thoughts and prayers shall be on each and every one of you, until the moment you all return home safely. I also vow to continue to work hand-and-hand with the President, to bring a peaceful end to this crisis. But I know in my heart if Lussein forces a confrontation with you guys; he'll regret it for the rest of his life." At that the cheers rang out and I shouted, "*I love you, and may God bless you all!*" I waved goodbye as I walked off the makeshift stage, in the seemingly barren and tranquil Saudi Arabian desert.

With all the encores, I ended up performing that night my show went 'twenty minutes past my half hour allotment. When I did finally leave the stage, I discovered the President and his immediate entourage were forced by time restraints to depart ten minutes prior. He had left three choppers for my staff and me, along with those who stayed behind, with instructions for their pilots to take us to the next military site when the show was over.

As we were being escorted to the choppers, I asked the sergeant if I might be allowed a few minutes to freshen up before taking off, and of course she said yes. As the others went to the choppers the sergeant led me to a makeshift latrine, which was about three hundred yards from the parked choppers. I had been washing the sweat off for about five minutes, when I heard the sergeant yell, "Ms. Powers, I'm going to have to ask you to please pick up the pace a little; we need to be on our way."

The sergeant was a tall muscular black woman and I was not about to challenge her; so, I yelled back, "I'll be right there, Sergeant Dexter!"

Not two minutes later I emerged feeling much cleaner and I said, "Thank you sergeant, I needed that and I'm ready to go!"

She smiled, "You're welcome Ms. Powers, but we'd better hurry."

We proceeded with a gentle but steady side-by-side trot through the open spaces of the desert toward the choppers. Our path was well lit by a bright full moon and we could clearly see the others standing by the chopper, as we approached. When we reached the halfway mark between the latrine and the choppers my heart almost stopped, as a pack of ferocious sounding desert wolves appeared from out of nowhere, cutting off our path to the choppers. We both simultaneously stopped dead in our tracks, the moment we spotted them.

I looked at the growling pack of wolves, then at the horrified face of Sergeant Dexter and said, "I hope they're part of security?"

"No, they're not!" And the moment she spoke, a big black one who seemed to be the leader stood out with a ferocious howl. Sergeant Dexter pulled out her gun to shoot and it jammed. She turned to me with a look of horror and shouted, "How's your running legs!?" And at that point, they began to charge us.

I let out a blood curdling scream when I realized the black one with the sharp fangs had his eye on me. Everyone around the choppers came running toward us and from out of the corner of my eye; I saw the black one lunge for me as I started to run back to the latrine. I screamed in terror as I ran, knowing at any moment I would soon be feeling the sharp fangs of this beast on the back of my neck. From behind me there was a horrendous explosion {**BOOM**} and the force of it threw me flying at least twenty feet forward, and I landed head first into the sand. I quickly turned and I could see flames bellowing hundreds of feet into the air, directly over the spot where the choppers were parked. In the midst of the sound, flames, and heat, I looked frantically for the black wolf and his pack, and to my astonishment, with the entire sky lit up there were none to be found.

My body became filled with fear as I looked back at the burning chopper and realized, one minute sooner and I would have been in those flames. I gazed up into the heavens, feeling completely humbled before the throne and power of God, and I thought, 'Thank you, Lord Jesus!' It was at that moment, I felt my mortality and realized "God must truly have a higher calling for my life, this time around!"

Remarkably, not one person was killed in that explosion, which was eventually declared a mechanical defect. But that's not how the reporters, whose lives were saved because they ran to my aid, put it. The headlines read, **"Dramatic Wild Wolf Attack on *Christina Powers'* Life**

**remarkably saves the lives of passengers and crew alike, from the ill-fated military helicopter, which exploded in the Saudi Arabian desert!"**

Of course I shook the experience off like it was nothing, and twenty minutes later I was in the air and on my way to completing the tour with the President. But underneath my cool exterior the rest of that trip, I was a frightened little girl just longing to be safely home and in Michael's arms.

Finally at midnight on November 23$^{rd}$, 1990, we were landing back home in America on the Presidents' private runway, in the great city of Washington, D.C. When I exited that jet, I was so glad to be back on American soil, that I knelt down and patted the pavement. After that I shook my head, looked up at the President and the First Lady, who were watching, and with a relieved smile I said, "There's no place like home!" I stood up, still looking at the two of them and continued with a chuckle, "I must thank you both for the most incredibly exciting trip I have ever taken in my life. But thank God, even the most sensational adventures must end and now I shall say adieu. I'm sure I have a husband at home desperately awaiting my arrival." I winked at the First Lady and added, "After all, he did almost lose me you know!"

She smiled at me and with utter charm said, "I'm sure you do, Christina! He'd be a fool not to be." We said our goodbyes with genuine sincere hugs and kisses, and as they headed toward the terminals, I headed for my private jet which was waiting to take me home.

# CHAPTER 22

I pulled into the driveway of our home at 3:00am on the morning of the 24th, which also just happened to be our first wedding anniversary. When, I entered the house, it was quiet and dimly lit, so I swiftly made my way to the master bedroom without making a sound. I opened the bedroom door with my heart in my throat, totally expecting beyond a shadow of a doubt, to find Michael lying in the bed. When I discovered he was not, I was completely crushed. I couldn't believe he wasn't there and I thought, 'He had to know I was almost killed! How could he not be here, waiting for me? Dammit, it's our anniversary, Michael.' I shook my head as my heart pained and my thoughts continued, 'I even wired you to let you know when I would be home Michael, why aren't you here?'

The awakening effect of that thought caused me to lie across the bed and begin to cry. My mind went on, 'Could it be he truly means what he's been saying?' At that, my personality seemed to split and I don't have a clue as to what happened to the real me from that point on, as my thoughts took over, 'Wait just a minute, Christina! He couldn't have known you were coming home, the Michael you know would be here. Stop kidding yourself, he's a man and all men show their true colors sooner or later! You've always known you could never really trust anyone, so why are you so shocked? Now stop it! He didn't get my wire and I know he didn't! Michael's not like the rest!' I somehow snapped myself out of that moment of madness; then, confidently grabbed a tissue, wiped off my face, blew my nose and proceeded to page Michael.

I woke up six hours later at 8:16am, still waiting for a return call. By 10:00am no call had arrived, and that's when I decided to call my mother-in-law. When Tess answered the phone, her voice perked up the moment she realized I was on the other end, and she said, "Christina! Thank God, you're home safe."

First, I thanked her then I asked if Michael was there.

Her tone seemed to sadden as she answered, "No honey, he's not here. He was here the morning we heard the news bulletin that you had nearly lost your life in a fiery helicopter explosion. The minute the story ended, he grabbed his coat and started to walk out. I tried to stop him, and he told me to let him go because he needed to think. Christina, I haven't heard from him since and he never received the telegram you sent, it's still sitting here on my counter."

I thanked her again; then, told her I would be staying home the rest of the day to wait for Michael and that if he should call her, to please have him call me. We said our goodbyes and I spent the rest of that entire day, just waiting for Michael who never came or called.

After a night of feeling extremely sad, I decided it was time to put Michael out of my mind and go back to work. After some hoopla from my staff when I entered the main building, I went straight to my office. I sat there for the first twenty minutes not doing anything. I slowly began to go through my messages, but I was still not really caring about what I was doing. All I could think about was Michael. I missed and wanted him so badly, and the pain was so intense, I felt as if someone were to look at me in the wrong way, I'd just start crying.

As I felt these things I thought, 'Michael, please come home. I feel so insecure and confused since my trip to Saudi Arabia. Honey, can't you feel in your soul how much I'm hurting?' I softly shook my head as my thoughts continued, 'You've just got to come home, I need you!'

At that point, Pierre, my secretary buzzed me and said, "Christina, there is a courier out here with some legal documents for you to sign."
"Send him in Pierre," I answered disconcertingly.

A tall Hispanic man entered my office and said, "Good morning Ms. Powers, I'm sorry it's under these circumstances, but it's a pleasure meeting you." I thanked him as I took the large yellow envelope he handed me. I opened it and inside were divorce papers from Michael's law firm, with a note clipped to them asking me to sign and return them with the courier.

I picked up my pen and wrote, **"If your client wants these papers signed, then he'd better bring them in person."** As I thought, *'You want to play games Michael? I'll play games with you!'* I slipped the papers back in the envelope and handed it to the courier.

From that point on I became angry, and I allowed that emotion to fuel my energies. And when I was completely juiced and fuming nicely, I decided I'd better dive head first into my work, realizing I needed a diversion from thinking about Michael and I needed it fast. I resumed going through my messages, only this time with real fervor, and I stopped when I came to one which read, "Tom Davies called, says he has some puzzle pieces for you."

I quickly dialed his number and I said with enthusiasm, "Hi Tom, how many pieces did you find?"

He proceeded to rattle off a list of interesting things, but nothing seemed to make any sense. As he talked, a shiver shot up my spine as my eyes spotted the next name and number on my message list. So I thanked Tom for the good job, asked him to keep up the good work, and it was quickly off to the next message.

As I dialed the number, I glanced at the message again which read, **"John Everett called, urgent personal matter. Please call ASAP!"** As the phone rang, I thought, 'You're making this call without thinking about it first!' "CLICK" 'You better think about it first! This is Johnny, you're calling.'

I took a deep breath and thought, 'All right Christina; you can handle this like an adult. Now just pick that phone back up and proceed with this call as if it were to any business associate.' At that, I took one more deep breath and hit redial.

I could feel my heart rate increasing with every ring and on the fifth ring I heard a woman's voice say, "Hello!" For a moment I couldn't speak.

"Hello! Is anyone there?" Came a second reply.

I cleared my voice, "Excuse me, I had something in my throat."

"Who's this?"

"It's *Christina Powers*, is this Mary Everett?"

Her voice instantly became panicked, "Christina! I'm so sorry John called you. He found out I lied to him; so I had to tell him the truth."

With a reassuring tone I replied, "It's nothing to be upset about Mary, take a deep breath and tell me what happened?"

She took that breath and did just as I feared, took off like a jackrabbit with a story that zig-zagged just as fast, "It happened like this! I told John I won the Lottery for five-hundred-thousand-dollars and that I took the money to pay off the bank. He believed my story up until two weeks ago, when he looked at our savings account for the first time since I paid off the loan. When he saw we still had our original two-hundred-thousand-dollar balance, he came to me and said,' Mary you told me you won five-hundred-thousand and paid off the bank with it, is this true?' I told him yes and he said, 'Well, then you should have only received about three-hundred and fifty-thousand-dollars after taxes. The rest of the money I assumed came from our savings, but I see you haven't even touched it. Now start talking and tell me where you got the money!' So I had to tell him the truth. Once I told him the money was a gift from you, he became irate and demanded I tell him how I got in touch with you, so I gave him your number."

When she finally finished talking, I said, "Don't worry about it Mary, I'm not upset and if John wants to talk about it with me, I'm more than willing to listen to what he has to say. Is John there now?"

"No, but he will be coming in from the fields at noon for lunch. Can I have him call you then?"

"That will be fine Mary, tell John I'll hold off going for lunch until I hear from him." I said a quick goodbye and thought, 'No big deal,' as I went right back to work.

At 12:00pm on the nose, I received a call from Johnny whose first words were, "Christy, I mean Christina. It's John Everett. How are you?"

"Hi John, I'm fine, how are you?" I answered nonchalantly.

"I've been better," he answered abruptly. "And that's why I'm calling you. I need to speak with you about this loan you gave Mary."

I quickly interrupted, "John, it was a gift not a loan. We were friends at one time, remember?"

With a tense tone he replied, "I remember. Just the same, I'd still like to speak with you in person if I may. I'll be in Manhattan on December 8th, and 9th, for business, I should be free sometime after 10:00am on the 9th. If I took the ride up to your office in Milton, I could be there around 12:00pm, is there any possibility you could meet with me then?"

Casually I answered, "Hold on John, while I check my schedule." I took a few moments just to keep him waiting then said, "That would be fine John, and since it's the noon hour, why don't we do lunch while we chat."

"Thank you Christina and lunch sounds good," he replied with a more relaxed tone.

I gave him the directions to my office, and told him I looked forward to seeing him after all these years. Our goodbyes were casual to say the least, but I was still intrigued by the thought of seeing him alone for the first time, since the day I threw him out of my bedroom, almost seventeen years ago.

At 3:00pm that same afternoon, I finally received a call from Michael, and as soon as I heard him say, "Christina, why are you playing games? Can't you just sign these damn papers, so we can get on with our lives?"

I thought, 'Up your's, buddy!' but very calmly and business like I said, "I'm not playing games with you, Michael! I want this divorce just as much as you do, especially since I've realized what a jerk you really are. To think, I once thought you loved me, but you don't even have a clue as to the meaning of that word. Michael, you know as well as I do, I don't have time for you anymore, so if you want me to sign your papers, meet me here at my office on December 9th, at 2:00pm!" I said these things, all the while thinking, 'we'll see how much you want me to sign those papers when see me walk in with Johnny on my arm.'

With a high pitch in his voice he responded, "December 9th! I'll be there in ten minutes!"

`"Don't bother!" I quickly replied, "I won't be here, I'm leaving in two minutes and I won't be back until the 9th."

With sarcasm he snapped, "Where are you going now?"

With just as much sarcasm I answered, "I don't think that's any more of your business Mr. Gillespie. I must leave now, so if you want your papers signed, then you better be here for our appointment, or you might have to wait months for that signature!"

He shouted, "Wait one minute, Christina!"

I deliberately cut him off real fast, by saying, "I've got to go, Michael! Till the 9th." (CLICK!) And that was the end of that.

I sat there at my desk with a smirk on my face bright enough to light up Time Square at midnight, and I thought, 'Well, since my loving and reasoning sides haven't reached you, maybe the bitch in me will.' Then, I thought, 'Now to set this trap just right! But first I'd better get out of here.' I got up from my desk, quickly gathered my stuff, and headed out the door before Michael could get to me. I figured it was now his turn to wonder where I was for a change, and I hoped it would help him see he would be throwing away the best thing that had ever happened to either one of us.

As I ran out of the office I turned to Pierre and quickly said, "I have to get out of here before Michael comes. So do me a favor, rent me a villa on the French Riviera for the next week, and only page me if something urgent comes up, otherwise wait to hear from me. Oh yes! Make sure you tell Michael I had to leave town to help an old friend who's going through a divorce." At that I was on my way out the door, and as the door closed behind me I thought, 'That story should do nicely for starters with setting a good trap, and a great suntan couldn't hurt either.'

# CHAPTER 23

When I entered my office on the morning of December 9th, 1990, I was tanned to perfection and dressed to the max, for today would be 'D-day', in my ongoing saga of love with Michael. And just as I anticipated, 12:00pm on the nose, Johnny walked into my office. He was dressed in a distinguished looking three piece black pinstripe suit and besides the signs of a little roughness around the edges from the years; he still had that twenty-four-year-old smile. We gazed at one another with childlike fear in our eyes and smiles on our faces, as we both stood there momentarily speechless.

As he approached me, I could see he was struggling to keep his composure, so to help ease both our discomfort from this stressful meeting, I stood up from the seat at my desk to greet him with a fearful yet relaxed hand-shake. With a warm friendly smile I said, "John! It really is good to see you after all these years." I looked straight into his eyes with complete sincerity, "You look as if the years have been good to you John, I hope that's true?"

Keeping his composure he smiled gently as he answered, "I can't complain Christy, but I can see they haven't been as good to me as they have to you. You're looking just as beautiful today as you did the day we met."

"Thank you John! That's nice to hear, especially coming from you," I answered with a cheery smile. "Now I hope you brought your visa card, because you're taking me to the best seafood joint in the area, and I'm starving."

He chuckled with that same boyish grin I instantly remembered so well, as he said, "Don't tell me you still have that ferocious appetite?"

I smiled graciously, "I guess some things never change, so let's go eat. I have my car, do you mind if I drive?"

He shrugged his shoulders, "Not at all." And off we went to Marine's Harbor in Highland, New York.

When we arrived, we were immediately escorted to my favorite table which, overlooked the beautiful Hudson River, the majestic Mid-Hudson Bridge, the glistening city of Poughkeepsie, and of course, Michael's Townhouse.

As we were seated, I looked at John and said, "You're going to love eating here the food is great; I know, I'm their best customer."

He smiled, "I like the view!"

"I know that's the other reason I like it here so much."

"Do you know what you're having yet?" He asked innocently.

"Nope!" I answered as the waitress handed us our menus.

We both opened up our menus and as we looked through them, he glanced over his at me and said, "Would you care for some champagne with your lunch?"

As I gazed back at him, I struggled unsuccessfully not to burst out laughing. But of course I did, and when I could speak again I said, "No, John! I like vegetable juice with my lunch, remember?"

After he stopped laughing, he said, "Now that you mention it, I do remember something like that."

With childlike curiosity I replied, "After all these years I have got to ask you, what is it with you and champagne with your lunch?"

He gave me that southern boy look that could melt butter and said, "When I was a boy my mom took me to see the movie 'Lunch at Tiffany's', and as I remember all the sophisticated people were having champagne with their lunch. So, I thought it was the proper thing to do when having lunch with a sophisticated woman."

I smiled, then chuckled at his charming answer, "You're too cute, John! But I think it was 'Breakfast at Tiffany's', and they were most likely drinking grape juice, not champagne." With that we laughed some more.

Over our luscious seafood lunch, I discovered what I automatically assumed would be a difficult encounter was actually turning out to be quite an enjoyable one. As we ate, we talked about things which took place in our individual lives over the last seventeen years, as if our bond of friendship had never ended. He told me he and Mary had raised a happy family of five children on their farm together, and that he hasn't missed the ball playing at all since he was forced to retire, due to an arm injury ten years ago. I told him how hectic my life has been of late, but that I also had high hopes things would someday settle down.

At one point in our conversation he looked sincerely into my eyes and said, "I have watched you from afar for years now, and I'm completely amazed and totally impressed at the way you have led your life." He took my hand as he continued with gentle passion, "The memories I have of the two of us, are still some of the most precious memories I hold. I often wonder what our lives would have been like if we did reach our dreams together." Realizing what he had just said, he swiftly let go of my hand and in a soft embarrassed tone added, "Shit, Christy! I'm sorry! I didn't come here for this. I came to give you a check for two-hundred-thousand-dollars." He reached into his pocket, took out a check, and handed it to me as he continued, "I would like you to take this and set up a payment plan with me, so I can pay you back the rest of the money."

I handed it back to him, "I've already told you John, it was a gift, I can't take this and I would consider it a slap in the face if you were to insist I take it. Please don't do that to me John, I gave it from my heart for someone who will always have a special place in it."

He looked at me with his mouth hanging open. Catching himself, he closed his mouth and said, "I guess I can't argue with that." He tore up the check as he continued, "If there is ever anything I can do for you Christy, please don't hesitate to ask."

I smiled and said, "As a matter of a fact John, there is. First, please call me Christina. I haven't been called Christy in years and it sounds strange. Second, when are you heading back home?"

"Tomorrow morning; why?" He asked curiously.

At that, I told him what I wanted him to know about my situation with Michael. Then, I added, "It's just this, John. Tomorrow happens to be my birthday and if Michael doesn't take me out for dinner tomorrow night, I don't want to spend it alone, and there is no one else I'd rather spend it with than you. But only if Mary gives her okay."

He smiled at me, "I'd love to take you for dinner on your birthday and I'm sure Mary won't mind. After all, we never did get the chance to go dancing on your birthday, did we?"

"No, we didn't!" I answered matter-of-factly.

"So when will you know if you will need an escort or not?"

I smiled mischievously, "Shortly after we return to my office. Michael will be meeting me there at 2:00pm and I'm going to ask him to take me out then."

He glanced at his watch then exclaimed, "2:00pm! Christina, its 1:45 now! We'll never get back before 2:00pm!"

"Don't be too upset John. I had no plans on being there when Michael arrived." I smiled again, only this time it was a devilish one as I continued, "I was hoping I could convince you to escort me arm-in-arm back to my office. I think it might give Michael something more to think about, before he asks me to sign those papers again." I squinted as I added, "Do you mind?"

He chuckled, "So you want me to help you make him jealous, do you?" With a playful wink he continued, "I'd be honored to play the other man for you, Christina."

I stood up, kissed his forehead and with excitement said, "Okay my new partner in crime; let's go pull one off." And off we went.

We entered my office arm in arm at 2:15pm and just as I planned, Michael caught the whole sensitive scene. And believe me; I made sure it looked good. I had an adoring look on my face as I clung to Johnny's arm, pretending to be on cloud nine as we strolled in chatting. Michael was sitting in my outer office talking with Pierre as we approached. With an act of genuine surprise, I pretended to just notice Michael, only three feet before reaching him. Putting my hand to the right side of my face I said, "Oh, Michael! I totally forgot about our meeting."

He immediately stood up, taking notice of Johnny's closeness to my person and said, "I'll bet you did! Who's your friend?"

At that I took front stage, "Where are my manners?" Turning to them both I continued, "John Everett, I'd like you to meet my husband,

Michael Gillespie."

I released my hold on Johnny as he reached for Michael's hand and said, "It's nice to meet you Michael, and I've got to tell you, you have one incredible wife. A word for the wise, I wish I'd never let her slip out of my hands when she was mine."

Michael snickered as he smiled and said, "Maybe you were wiser than you think."

Johnny rubbed his hands together and said, "Well I think that's my cue to leave." He kissed my cheek and added, "Thanks for lunch it was great."

I gave him a peck on the lips then said, "Thank you, I love those two hour lunches. Now don't forget. I'll call you tonight to let you know about tomorrow."

With a cute wink he replied, "I'll be waiting." I walked him to the door, gave him one more huge to tighten my snare, and off he went.

When the door closed, I turned and began to walk back toward Michael as I asked, "Do you have your papers?"

He handed me an envelope, "Yes I do, Christina. Now how about signing them?"

I gestured to him to lead the way, "Let's go into my office, so I may read them first."

I took my seat as I opened the envelope, and gazing up at him impatiently standing there I said, "This may take me some time Michael, so why don't you try to make yourself comfortable and sit down. After all, we did share this office not too long ago and in more ways than one as I recall." He just ignored me and continued to stand there.

After deliberately leaving him standing there for several minutes as I slowly read the two page document, he shook his head in frustration, "Can't you just sign it!? You know damn well what it says!"

With anger I sharply focused my eyes on his and snapped back, "We've spent several years together in love and you can't spare me ten minutes now!"

That's when my act fell apart and tears slowly began to escape from my eyes as I added, "Did you ever really love me at all, Michael?"

I could see his huge muscles straining as he fought to hold back his tears while saying, "Don't do this to me, Christina!"

"Don't do this to you!  You're the one who wants this damn divorce, not me!  Do you realize tomorrow is my birthday?  Is this really the birthday gift you want to give me?  I can't believe this from you, Michael!  I thought we were one!"

"Oh please!"  He shouted, "Don't sit there and tell me you don't want this divorce, or you would not have spent the last two weeks helping your divorced friend. And I'll bet money it's that asshole ball player. What did you think, just because you never told me anything about him yourself, I didn't know he existed?  I always knew he was once your lover. The fact you never told me anything about him, told me you still loved him.  Especially since we told each other about all the rest of our past lovers, but I still noticed how you conveniently left him out of the stories you shared."

I quickly reached out and grabbed his hand, as I wiped the tears from my face with my other hand and said, "Michael, honey!  Please, let's not turn this into another fight."

He pulled his hand out of mine, "Then sign the damn papers, let me vanish out of your life, and we will never have to fight again, Christina!"

I could feel my blood beginning to boil as I clenched my fist, "You stubborn Irish are all the same, **Stubborn**!" Once again I ripped his divorce papers up, and as I threw them in his face I yelled; "Now I really mean it!  If you want a divorce then you're going to have to fight for one, because you know me, I like to do things the hard way."

He shouted, "That's the whole problem with us, Christina!  You think you're my husband.  Well if you want to wear the damn pants in the house, then you go right ahead and wear them.  But I give you my word, as long as you insist on wearing the pants, no matter how much I love you or how much it breaks my heart, they will never be my pants again!  So I guess if it's a fight you want, then a fight it will be!"

I took a deep breath and struggled to calmly say, "Michael, why won't you understand I wasn't trying to wear the pants in our relationship when I went to Saudi Arabia.  I had to go and now that I'm back I need to talk with you about what happened to me over there.  Don't you realize I was almost killed when I was there, and when it happened I immediately called you, but you never called me back!  How do you think that made me feel?"

He slammed his fist down on my desk with such force he nearly frightened the life out of me as he shouted, "I can't listen to this! I asked you not to go! I begged you not to go! I tried ordering you not to go! None of that meant enough to you to keep you from going then, so none of this is going to keep me from divorcing you now!"

I felt the pain of his words shoot through my heart and the only thing I could do was scream, "Get out! Get out! The longer I look at you the madder I'm getting, you stubborn asshole!"

For one moment I could see my Michael coming through in his eyes, as he reached out for my arm, with his true feelings showing on his face. Catching himself he stopped just before touching me, and as if in slow motion turned and gently walked away.

As I watched the door close behind him, I slowly sat back in my seat feeling totally dazed by what had just transpired, and once again all I could do was cry.

Later that evening after my third White Russian, I picked up the phone and dialed Johnny's number. He answered the phone with a cheery "Hello!"

My reply was a groggy, "Hi, Johnny. Oops! I mean John. It's Christy. Oops, I mean Christina."

"You sound as if you're two sheets to the wind. Are you all right?" I immediately started to cry, and the moment I did he said, "I guess it didn't work out." And I cried even harder. "Don't cry Christina, he'll come around." He said with a reassuring tone.

I blew my nose and with a drunken whimper cried, "No he won't! You don't know Michael, he's more thick-headed then I am."

"Are you going to be all right?" He asked with concern.

I thought about his question for a moment then replied, "No John, I don't think so. I don't think I'll ever be all right again."

He gently chuckled then said, "That's the alcohol talking, not the Christy I know, oops, I mean Christina."

I gently laughed finding humor in his *oops* and said, "I'll bet you've charmed a number of the ladies on the side, you little devil you."

"Ha! Not me! I learned my lesson a long time ago." He answered assertively.

James Aiello

"I'm glad to hear that, John. So tell me, what did Mary say about our date?"

"She was fine with it."

"Great! I'll pick you up at your hotel around 5:00pm tomorrow evening. Now before I pass out, I'm going to say goodnight. I'll see you tomorrow."

He chuckled again, "Don't tell me I'm getting the bum's rush for turning your tears into laughter."

"Like I said, I'll see you tomorrow! I'll thank you properly then, now go to sleep because you're going to need your rest for this date." On that note, we ended our conversation.

# CHAPTER 24

I wasn't planning on going into the office on my birthday and it's a good thing, because I couldn't have dragged myself out of that bed before noon, unless the house was on fire. When I did get up, I headed straight for the medicine chest and nearly choked on three aspirins as I struggled to get them down. It took me another hour and four cups of coffee before I could even climb into the shower. I felt a little more like a human when I returned to the kitchen for a cup of Carman's chicken and rice soup, which I requested with hopes it would help settle my stomach. I took my last sip of soup around 2:10pm; then, I headed back upstairs to prepare for my trip into Manhattan and my date with Johnny. By 3:40pm I was dressed to impress and on my way out the front door. When I opened it, I was stunned and excited at the same time to see Michael reaching for the door with his key.

His face lit up with amazement when he saw me standing there, and with a tone of delight he exclaimed, "Wow! You look phenomenal." His expression and voice immediately changed to one of suspicion as he continued, "Where are you going dressed like that?"

I finally struck a chord of jealousy, and my face couldn't conceal my pleasure as I smiled and said, "You know it's my birthday Michael, and I told you I was not going to spend it sitting in this house alone." As I continued, my voice took on an air of curiosity, "So what are you doing here?"

Without any detectable reaction at all, he answered, "I've come to pick up a few of my things."

I chuckled and sarcastically said, "Well that's great! After all this time, you pick today to come get your stuff."

With a slight sense of his own sarcasm he replied, "Yes! Do you mind?"

As a feeling of disappointment came over me, I sadly answered, "No I don't mind, come on in."

He entered the house and I followed him as he headed up to the bedroom. I watched as he took out his black tux with all its accessories from the closet, and laid them on the bed. At that, he started to unbutton his shirt, and as my body temperature began to climb I asked, "What are you doing?"

He knelt down, untied his shoes, then gazing up at me with that look that slays me he answered, "I'm going to take a shower, get dressed, and take you out for your birthday."

My heart leaped with joy as I softly said, "Really, Michael?"

He slipped off his pants and in his already bulging, 'Fruit of the Loom,' he beckoned me to him as he said, "Really, Punkie."

I went to him like a quivering love struck damsel in distress, longing for the touch of her gallant knight in shining armor. When I reached him, I stood in front of him gazing longingly into his eyes, and softly said, "I'm here, Michael."

He put his arms around me and as he gently pulled me to him he said, "Happy birthday, Punkie."

My tears began to flow, and with every quiver of my body, I melted deeper into his powerful arms. I could truly feel our souls reuniting as he held me, and I whispered, "I love you, Michael, and if you come home, I'll take off the pants."

He kissed me in the way only he could then said, "I love you too, Punkie."

He swept me off my feet, and carried me into the bathroom. Our lips were one as he placed my feet on the floor, then slipping off the rest of his attire he began to massage his groin against mine as he masculinity said, "Come join me in the shower. You have a lot to catch up on."

I nearly over heated on the spot by his forceful command, and as I covered his face lovingly with baby kisses I said, "Just let me take this outfit off, make a quick phone call, and then I'm all yours."

He pulled his head back from mine and said, "A phone call, now! What's so important about this phone call it comes before making love to your husband?"

I shook my head as I placed my right index finger horizontally across his lips and said, "It's not, Michael, and your right, I don't need to make it now."

I watched helplessly as his excitement dissipated and he said, "Well who is it you have to call, your baseball player?"

I stroked his shoulder as I carefully said, "Yes, Michael. He's waiting for me to pick him up, but he can wait forever for all I care. It was out of courtesy, I automatically thought to call, and that's all."

He backed away from me and said, "I must be nuts to think you could ever put me first in your life." He shook his head as he pushed past me and continued, "Get out of my way! I've gotta get out of here before I throw up!"

As he proceeded to get dressed, I pleaded, "Michael, don't leave me. Please, I'm sorry I upset you honey, but honestly I wasn't putting anything or anyone before you."

He jammed his feet into his shoes and said, "Save it for someone who believes you, like your lover boy."

I became so infuriated by his comment I actually hauled off and slapped him right across his face as I shouted, "Why you creep! If you want me to go to him that bad, then I will!" I headed for the bedroom fireplace, where I grabbed one singed bottle of champagne from off the mantel and dashed out of the room.

As I did that, Michael grabbed his stuff from off the bed, and came charging behind me. When I reached the driver's door of my car, I heard Michael yell, "I hope you have a great birthday, Christina!"

I opened the car door and yelled back, "Don't worry I will!" I slammed the door and proceeded to burn rubber all the way down the driveway.

# CHAPTER 25

When I arrived at Johnny's room in the Newark, Holiday Inn, I was carrying a bag with an eight-piece bucket of Kentucky Fried Chicken extra crispy, with all the trimmings in one hand, and in the other was a seventeen-year-old singed bottle of champagne.

Johnny was wearing a black tux when he opened the door, and he had a bouquet of roses in his hands. And guess what! There were two dozen red ones with one white one in the middle. He gazed at me standing at his door with my chicken in hand, and started to laugh, so I said, "Well are you going to invite me in, or would you rather I'd stand here so you can keep laughing."

He gestured me in as he controlled his laughter enough to say, "I thought I would take you out for a fancy meal, and you come to my door looking like a million, with a bucket of Kentucky Fried Chicken."

I smiled as I unpacked our meal and said, "You got that right! So I hope you're in the mood to lick your fingers." I handed the champagne to him and added, "Would you put this on ice for us please?"

He took it from me and said, "This looks like it's been through a war, are you sure we should drink it?"

I turned to him with a mysterious grin as I fixed our plates and said, "Yes! Now please chill it and I'll explain why after dinner."

At that he headed for the ice machine, and by the time he returned, I had the small table in his room set for a romantic chicken dinner for two, with candlelight to boot.

We chatted as we ate, and after our meal I took the champagne bottle out of the ice, handed it to Johnny and said, "There is only one person in this world who may open this bottle, and that's you, but before you do there is a little story I need to tell you first. The singed champagne bottle you hold in your hands and are about to be asked to open is the same bottle of champagne you gave me the day we met at the Tavern-on-the-Green."

His face took on a look of complete surprise as he gazed into my eyes and said, "You really kept this all these years, and you want me to open it tonight? Wow, Christina! I'm truly moved and honored by this. Now that you've shared that, I need to share something with you." At that, he unbuttoned his shirt to reveal the chain he had around his neck with a ring on it and said, "I know you remember this ring! You're the only other person besides my grandmother who has ever worn it, and it hasn't left my neck since the day I received it back from you in the mail."

I softly smiled as I said, "And I thank you John, for sharing with me, that's sweet of you and it really means a lot to me to hear that. Now would you please do the honor of opening this bottle, so we may both finally find out what it tastes like?"

He stood up holding the bottle, braced it between his arms and as he slowly pushed up on the cork with his two thumbs he said, "May the shadows of our once fantasy life together, live on in our memories forever." "*POP!*" Then, he poured two glasses and as he handed one to me he added, "The toast is on you."

I smiled as I clicked my glass to his, "To memories! Good and bad."

As I slowly took my first sip, feelings buried seventeen years ago came rushing to my consciousness like a flash flood in the deserts of Nevada. And as I watched him sip his, I began to feel myself wanting to be touched by him, and I thought, 'What the hell are you getting yourself into now, Christina? Don't forget you're both married.' At that I said, "Hmmm! Not bad after all this bottle has been through."

Taking a second look at the bottle he said, "I guess this must have survived your tragic fire."

Sadly I replied, "You're right, as a matter of fact it was one of only a few things which did survive that fire." I took another sip from my glass and let my emotions show when I said, "John, since we're being open with our feelings, I wonder if you would tell me something?  Why did you send me the roses with the 'ditto' note, the night I preformed 'The Love I lost', and yet you never called me after Tony's death?  Did the words on that note truly come from your heart?"

I could see in his eyes he knew my question was coming from a place of great pain; then, he gently took my hand in his and said, "Christina, with all my heart I didn't just want to call you, I wanted to come running to you.  But I couldn't!  When you recorded 'The Love I lost' Mary was three months pregnant with our second child.  When she saw you sing that song to me that night at the concert, she became distraught and she cried for days.  The night I heard about Tony's death, I had to make a choice to be there for one of you.  She was my wife and carrying my child, what could I do?"

I gently squeezed his hand as I said, "Thank you for being honest with me, John."

He slowly shook his head as he replied, "You know what I don't understand is after knowing how Mary has feared you for years, how could she come to you for that loan?"

I let go of his hand, smiled, and said, "It's because she's madly in love with you, you big jerk."

As I spoke, he refilled our glasses and when I finished, he handed me mine and with the look that once captured my heart said, "Let's make this one to new memories!"  We drank to his toast and as we put our glasses down he slowly leaned toward me still gazing into my eyes and added, "I love her too, I guess that's why we are still together, but my love for her never compared to what I've felt for you since the first instant our eyes meet."

The moment he stopped speaking, he leaned closer and softly began to kiss my lips.  I felt myself slipping into my passion as I slowly began to surrender to memories of powerfully embedded feelings.

All at once realizing what was happening, I caught myself and went for the quick save by slipping out of his embrace and excitedly saying, "Do you know what I would like right now?"

He gave me his southern country boy smile and very seductively said, "I hope it's the same thing I do."

With playful force I grabbed his arm, pulling him up from his seat I said, "For us to go dancing at the Plaza Ballroom, just like we once did."

Gallantly he replied, "If that's what my lady would like, then that's what my lady shall get."

At that, off we went and as we walked toward my car I thought, 'Man-oh-man! That was a close one.'

We arrived at the Plaza shortly after 10:00pm, and you should have seen the heads turn and the tabloid cameras flash, when the two of us walked in together. Marcel the head Maître' immediately came to us with open arms and a big smile. The moment he reached us he said, "Christina! John! I can't believe this!" He gave us both a warm, hardy, Italian hug as he continued, "My heart is filled with joy, seeing the two of you walk in here together again!"

I smiled graciously, "Thank you, Marcel, it's good to see you as well. Is there any chance we could have our old table?"

He smiled his answered, "Of course you may! Even if I have to throw someone out. Just give me one moment and I'll be right back."

Within two minutes Marcel was happily escorting us to our table, then the second we were settled he took our drink orders, and off he went. I glanced into Johnny's sparkling eyes as from the vantage point of our balconied table we watched the orchestra play and all the enchanted people dance on the open dance floor below us.

Within moments Marcel returned with our drinks and when Johnny picked his up, he gazed romantically into my eyes and said, "May I offer a toast to the most beautiful woman in the world on her birthday. Happy birthday Christina and may-you be blessed with many, many, more!"

"Why thank you John, that's quite the toast." I replied with wide eyes.

He smiled, "Don't be so modest. I know you've been People Magazine's choice for most beautiful woman-of-the-year, thirteen times in the last fifteen years."

With a look of surprise I said, "You're kidding! I didn't know that." As I thought, 'Yeah, I know! I lost in '85 to Princess Diana, and then again in '88 to Kim Bassinger. Can you believe that? Kim Bassinger!'

At one point during our conversation, I smiled softly as I gently touched his hand and said, "You showed me something, now I'd like to show you something." I unfastened my necklace, the same one he gave me in the dugout so many years ago and I continued, "Do you remember this? Well I haven't spent a day without this around my neck since you gave it to me in the Dodger's dugout."

He took it from my hand and said, "I always knew our love would somehow last for all eternity." As he examined my chain he added, "Where are these other pendants from?"

I took it from him and as I showed him each one I said, "This Heart pendant came from my best friend in the entire world, Jimmy Severno, and inside it reads, **"Your A fucking Genius! Love Jimmy**!" I held out the medallion next, "See this! It's of a golden goddess standing on top of a flaming ball of fire. She is breaking the cords of gold which bound her to the inferno. I found this on a white water rafting trip in Lake Tahoe with my late ex-husband Tony. But the strangest thing about this believe it or not, is the fact that I buried it over Tony's grave, and the day I buried my daughter Joy, I found it lying on top of the headstone. I took it home, washed it and I've had it on ever since!" As I touched the last one I added, "And this dainty little guardian angel here was a gift from my Michael."

Smiling he replied, "Christina, you're a sentimental romantic, just like I am." Just as he said that the orchestra began to play 'Johnny's Love,' and when Johnny heard it his eyes lit up as he asked, "Would you please give this dance to me? I requested it because our memories would not be complete without it." I gracefully accepted, and he escorted me to the dance floor.

As we danced the memories of dances past brought tears to my eyes and when Johnny saw I was crying he held me tight and said, "I must call you Christy one more time. I need to tell Christy I love her with all my heart. Christy, I have regretted hurting you like I did, every day of my life since you told me to leave."

He brought his hand to the back of my neck and slowly began to move his head toward mine as we danced. The moment his lips met mine, he was ripped out of my embrace by a crazed Michael, who belted Johnny so hard, he went flying into the wall twelve feet from us. Michael shouted, "You bastard! Until the divorce is final, she's still my wife, and if I catch you touching her again, I'll kill you." Cameras were snaping all around us and as they flashed Michael turned to me and with a tone of hatred shouted, "Thanks for giving me grounds for divorce!" He turned and began to walk away.

I followed him saying, "Michael, it's not what it looked like! Not really!" Right in the middle of all the sophisticated people I grabbed his arm, swung him around to face me, and sharply added, "You're not going to just walk away from me like this! We need to talk!"

He pulled his hand out of mine, "Oh yea! Watch me!" And at that he turned, and continued to walk away leaving me standing there looking like a fool.

I stamped my foot in frustration; then, turned around to see Johnny standing beside me holding an ice pack to his nose. I looked at him and exclaimed, "Oh my God! Are you all right?"

"I'll live" he answered, and hile looking at all the on lookers he added, "The shows over folks, you can mind your own business now."

I took his hand, "Come on, I think we better get out of here."

When we arrived back at Johnny's motel, I parked next to his room, leaned toward him and said, "This was certainly an interesting evening, and I thank you for it very much."

He smiled as he replied, "Well at least you got a reaction from Michael. Maybe not the one you wanted, but it was sure a doosie."

I started to laugh as I stroked his arm once gently then said, "I'm sorry for laughing, but if I don't think about this as something funny, then I'm going to start crying again, and I'm tired of all the crying I've been doing lately."

He took my hand and passionately said, "Christina, please come in with me. I want to make love to you again so badly I can taste you." All at once he began to lean toward me with the look of love in his eyes.

I put my hands up to stop his approach, "John, I'm in love with Michael, and no matter how enticing your offer may be, I can't make love with you. I may do a lot of things behind Michael's back, but I can't and won't cheat on him." I gently kissed his forehead and continued, "I thank you again John, for an incredible evening, but I have to go now. I still have a long ride ahead of me."

"I'm sorry, Christina," he said apologetically. "I was thinking with my heart instead of my head.  I hope I haven't put a damper on our evening?"

I smiled warmly, "No John, you haven't, but it's already 2:00am and I'm really very tired."

"Well if you must go would you please wait until I get in the room?  I didn't know it at the time I rented here, but I heard this is a gay neighborhood.  The last thing I need tonight is to be arrested for punching somebody out."

I assumed he was kidding, so I chuckled and said, "Sure, I'll wait big boy!  Now get going."  Finally, we said our goodbyes and I was on my way home.

# CHAPTER 26

Of course the press had a field day with my latest public escapade, and the headlines on the front page of the next mornings 'New York Post' read, in big bold print, **_It looks like Christina Powers is up to her hips in dueling men once again!_**" When I unfolded the paper I was horrified to see a full-page, color photo of my unflattering, shocked, expression, which the camera caught so well of the three of us, and Michael's now famous punch that I wanted to go into hiding.

And that was just the start of my day. My next humiliating experience took place only twenty minutes later, the moment I sat at my desk and answered my private line. When I picked it up, I was hoping for Michael, but instead I heard Johnny's wife, Mary Everett say, "I should have known better then to trust a woman like you. John is my husband and a Christian family man, why would you seduce him and destroy us in one night."

"Wait just a minute now Mary, and listen to me," I protested. "It was nothing at all like the papers put it."

"No miss big shot, _Christina Powers,_ you wait! I don't care to hear what you have to say, I know you could talk your way out of a crocodile pit. So you just listen to me and stay away from my husband, or you will see just how tough we country girls can be." "_Click!_"

I thought, 'Was that really the same little mousey woman I know? My God! Is it me? Could I really have some kind of strange effect on people, or is everyone going nuts?'

The next incident came around 10:00am, when Michael walked into my office escorting a process server, and without saying a word she placed an envelope in my hand. The two of them turned around and walked right back out. I opened it to find a summons to appear in the Ulster County Court House for divorce proceedings at 9:00am on February 28, 1991. I placed the summons on top of a pile of papers, placed my head on my desk, and as tears slowly fell I thought, 'Okay Michael, I give up, you win. I don't have the heart or energy for this. I'm so tired of the heartache, I can't even think about trying to fight you anymore.'

As I sat there with my head on my desk feeling utterly depressed, Pierre buzzed me with a very nervous voice and said, "Christina! The President is standing out here, and he would like to see you now!"

Quickly I grabbed a tissue, wiped my eyes, and headed for the door thinking, 'What now!?'

When I opened the door, I wore a big smile, and immediately invited him into my office with a warm embrace. As we sat down, I looked at him with a suspicious expression and said, "It's good to see you George, but I know damn well this isn't a social call."

He smiled, "Once again you're absolutely correct, this is not a social call. I'm here in person because I'm hoping my presence will make it impossible for you to turn down my request."

My eyes opened wide as I said, "Don't tell me you want me to go back to Saudi Arabia, because if that's it, you've wasted a trip. There is no way I'm going back there George, and you know why."

"Well that's good, because that's not what I need you to do."

I sighed as I exhaled and said, "I'm glad we got that out of the way, because nothing you might ask could be that bad."

His face took on a strained look as if the pressure of it all was getting to him, and he said, "Actually it's a lot worse than that, Christina. As you know, the U.N. Security Council has given the coalition members permission to use all necessary means to expel Iraq from Kuwait if Iraq doesn't withdraw by January 15, 1991. So, as you can see, it's imperative we free the hostages before that date. I have been frantically trying to reach Lussein personally, since the U.N. made that announcement.

Finally, I had a private phone conversation with Lussein at five o'clock this morning, and in his own very convincing words he said, "I will agree to release the hostages only if *Christina Powers* comes in person, and on her own private jet to take them out of my country."

My initial reactions to his words were split right down the middle to either extreme. I was elated to think of Jimmy and all the hostages coming home, but I was mortified to think I had to go get them. It took a few moments to let it all register; then, I looked at him without hiding any emotion and said, "Why me?"

"He says he trusts you."

"What's to stop him from keeping me with all the others this time?"

He began to shake his head with utter frustration and answered, "Honestly Christina, nothing. If he wanted to have you executed the moment you walked off the plane, he could. That's why it's tearing me apart to ask you to do this, but if I want the hostages out alive; then, I have no choice but to ask you to take this chance with your life."

Realizing he was right, I looked him straight in his eyes, and with my own frustration showing asked, "What is it I'd have to do?"

He gave me his famous Texas smile and said, "That's my girl! I knew you'd go. All you have to do is fly over there in your corporate jet, with our military pilots in civilian clothing at the controls in the cockpit; then, personally take possession of the hostages from Lussein. He will be waiting at the Baghdad Airport for you; then, the air force pilots will bring all of you to a U.S. Military base in Germany."

"When is this trip scheduled?" I asked calmly.

"That's the other reason I'm here. I wanted to escort you to the airport personally right now."

I shook my head as if I were shaking off a punch to the jaw, and with a stunned tone said, "What!? Now!? George, my personal life is turning into a shambles at this very moment, and you want me to get up and leave? Can't I at least finish my work day and make some personal phone calls?"

With a bleak expression he replied, "The time is also being dictated by Lussein, and he's only giving us thirty-four hours. He said, "It's now or never.""

I ran my fingers through my hair from my forehead back, shook my head again, and sighed, "Well, I guess we had better leave."

Feeling almost as if I were being kidnaped myself, I was ushered out of my office and down to a Secret Service escorted by a convoy of limos. As I was climbing into the President's limo with him, out of the corner of my eye I noticed Michael standing on the curb watching us leave. I stopped, turned to George and said, "Give me one minute." I climbed back out of the limo and began to run toward Michael. The moment he saw me coming he turned and began to walk away. I stopped dead in my tracks, turned around and as I headed back to the limo I sadly thought, 'Goodbye, Michael.'

# CHAPTER 27

We landed in Baghdad at 5:00pm 'their time' the next afternoon, and when the doors opened; all I could see was a large military presence all around the plane. And guess what!? There was no sight of any hostages or King Lussein. As I stood there at the open door a group of forty or so armed Iraqi Soldiers approached with the staircase for the plane, and when it was in place an obviously high ranking officer came up the steps and in Arabic said, "Ms. Powers, King Lussein would like for you to accompany me to the palace."

I turned to Todd Deyo, one of the out-of-uniform lieutenants and said, "Todd, this is not what was to transpire, what should we do?"

He shrugged his shoulders, "I don't think you have any choice but to go with him, Ms. Powers."

I really became concerned, and it showed on my face when I said, "Couldn't we just take off?"

He looked very serious, "Only if we want to be shot down before we ever leave the ground."

I shook my head and said, "Oh well! I hope I'll see you later." At that, I turned and proceeded to leave with my armed Iraqi Military Escort.

When I entered Lussein's Palace, I was escorted to an extravagantly decorated dining room, and as we entered the room my escort said, "Please make yourself comfortable the King will be with you shortly."

He closed the door leaving me standing there alone. I looked around the room and noticed the table was set with flowers and candles.

It was a ready-to-go romantic dinner for two. The soft sounds of a romantic rhythm came through the sound system, and putting two and two together I thought, 'Oh God! Don't tell me Lussein has 'the hots' for me too!'

I walked over to the window to gaze out, and as I stood there, I heard the door open from thirty feet behind me. I turned around with a friendly smile and was stunned and horrified, to see Prince Fehd, dressed in all his princely attire walking right toward me. I was so taken aback by his presence I could feel my adrenalin immediately rushing through my veins. I quickly scanned my thoughts for the appropriate response to this potentially deadly situation. So with a strong, calm, smooth, motion I began to head toward him as well. With a confident seductive lifting of my eyebrows, I hid my fears behind an expression of pure surprise and said, "Mohammed! What in the world are you doing here?"

He reached me with a smile, gently took my hand, and as he lovingly gazed into my eyes he said, "I told you if you married me, I would bring an end to Lussein's occupation of Kuwait. The freeing of the hostages is just my way of showing you, what I can and will do for your love, Christina."

I was floored by his statement, and my face couldn't hide that emotion as I said, "I don't understand this! How can your father be fearing an invasion from Iraq, if you have the power to convince Lussein to withdraw his troops from Kuwait? This makes no sense to me at all, and it compels me to ask, how is this possible?"

Beginning to lead me by the hand toward the table he said, "Come with me my love, and I will explain it over dinner. I hope you're hungry. I took the liberty of having all your favorite dishes prepared."

I took my seat as he filled two glasses with white wine. When he was seated, he looked straight into my eyes and said, "It's actually not that hard to understand. Lussein and I have been faithful brothers in Islam all our lives. We respect and honor one another with such a divine love that we would do anything for one another."

Still not understanding I asked, "If there is such a great love between the two of you then why is he threatening to invade your nation?"

He was swift and to the point with his answer, "Because he despises my father and Sheik Jabir for betraying their Islamic roots and embracing the demons of the Western World."

Still confused, I shook my head in disbelief, "If you know all this, then why don't you try to mediate a peaceful solution between the three of them?"

He answered with an air of true sincerity, "I've tried to reason with both my father and the Sheik, but they refuse to listen and in doing so they've sealed their fate. Now, I can do no more to interfere with their destinies."

"But aren't you interfering now by freeing the hostages?"

"Yes I am, and for one reason only, to show you I would interfere with fate if it brought your love to me. Nothing else on this planet would make me interfere with my brother's destiny but you, and that's because you are my destiny."

At that moment the most incredibly enticing, garnished, sea food smorgasbord was brought into the room. There were lobsters, shrimps, oysters, fried flounder and squid. I mean it was all there and on separate platters ready to eat.

It smelled so good I thought, 'Well since this could be your last meal Christina, you'd better take advantage of it.' So I dug right in and as we ate I said, "You're a strangely intriguing man Mohammed, and for the life of me I can't figure you out. You tell me you're having Lussein free the hostages to prove your undying love for me, yet you nearly threw me to my death at our first meeting. Maybe I should ask you to tell me what you would think of someone with such erratic behavior?"

He smiled and said, "Forgive me for my foolish outburst at our last meeting, and let me assure you no harm would have come to you that day. My assumption you would have realized by now whom you truly are was premature."

I looked at him strangely, "Why do you speak in riddles? You compare me to someone I don't know, and then tell me I'm just like him. You tell me I should realize I'm your destiny, when I know I'm not. You tell me I'm going to bear your child and I know I can't. Mohammed, listen to yourself for a minute and you will realize I'm not the woman you think I am. Didn't you just say you hated the demons of the Western World? Well according to your Islamic beliefs, I must be the epitome of those demons. I could see it now, a woman of the world who openly flaunts despising any male dominated society, marrying the Prince of the Islamic faith. I don't think so."

He lovingly took my hand and said, "I know what you are and I don't understand myself, but I do know you were destined to be mine. Now, I will tell you how I know this to be true. It's because I am the rightful Prince of Persia, the direct descendant of Ishmael, the son of Abraham and Hagar. You are the direct descendant of Isaac, the son of Abraham and Sarah."

Struggling not to laugh, I nearly choked on my last bit of lobster as I said, "You're really in outer left field now, I know there's not a drop of Jewish blood in me."

Still gazing lovingly into my eyes, I knew he was unconvinced as he brought my hand to his lips, kissed it, and said, "If you're finished with your meal I'd like to show you something?"

I slipped my hand from his, "I'm finished."

He took my hand back as he said, "Come with me then."

He led me into a massive library, where he proceeded to go through a large old book of Islamic Prophecies. Finding what he was looking for, he handed the book to me and said, "You read Arabic, read it for yourself."

I took the book and glancing to where he was pointing began to read, "**At the time of the alignment of all celestial bodies within your solar system, the king's daughter shall rise to power and she shall be known to the world as the 'Angel of Peace'. This one is the mother of the Messiah, who is the daughter of the king and the descendants of Abraham. Her power is in her tongue of many languages, and she alone shall marry the true heir to the throne of David and bear him his first male child. The child she brings forth in the wilderness shall be the pure descendant of Adam's seed, and he represents the true returning of the Prince of Peace. He alone will finally usher in the Heavenly Millennium of paradise on earth foretold by the prophets.**"

As I finished, I closed the book and said, "I'm not usually this bad with puzzles, but I still don't get the connection."

Looking at me as if I were an imbecile he said, "You, Christina, are that woman! The one the world calls the 'Angel of Peace', and I am the rightful heir to the throne of David."

I shook my head in total disbelief and said, "You really put all this together just from a newspaper article which called me the 'Angel of Peace?'"

Taking the book from my hands, he placed it on the shelf. He turned back toward me, and taking me in his arms, he lovingly said, "That is not the only reason my love, you are rising to power in the world whether you realize it or not. The alinement of the planets spoken of in this prophecy will take place in May of the year 2000, and you are also fluent in many languages. I know everything there is to know about you. I have always known in my heart, you would one day be my bride and bear me my son. Together through peace, we shall conquer the world and give it to our son, who will lead all peoples into a millennium of peace on earth."

I had to push hard to get out of his loving embrace as I said, "Please, Mohammed, not so close, I like my space. I have got to say for someone who supposedly knows so much about me, then how come you overlooked the fact I can no longer bear children. Doesn't that put a damper on your theories as to whom you think I am?"

He was slowly coming closer to me with a very hungry look on his face as he said, "I know about your injury. If you let me, I will teach you how to heal your wounds from within. You can tap into the divine power, which is yours, and I know how it's done. Then, you will be able to bear our child. The secrets of God's power are at your disposal Christina, it lies within."

He was still slowly continuing to walk toward me as I backed away. Putting my hands up to slow his descent upon me and thinking quick I said, "You're not listening Mohammed, I just told you I can no longer bear children."

I could see in his eyes he was beginning to become upset with my resistance when he said, "You're the one not listening! You already have the power to heal yourself."

As my back reached the wall I said, "Well, I hope I can grow back a uterus, because that's what it's going to take."

His face became as white as a ghost. He took a deep breath, while hovering over me shouting, "What are you talking about!?"

That was the moment I knew I was heading for trouble and I

thought, 'Lord Jesus, please help me out of this one!' As I said, "I nearly lost my life last year in an attempt to have a child. While I was unconscious, the doctors had to perform a hysterectomy on me in order to save my life."

His eyes became red with anger. With one hand, he took my left shoulder and flung me with such force, I went flying into a book shelf sending the books toppling on top of my head. Laying under a pile of books I heard him yelling, "This can't be! I thought you were the one!"

As I looked up from under the books, I could see he was coming to give me some more, so just as he reached down to grab me, I pushed up with my legs knocking him into another book shelf. I scrambled to my feet, went running for the door and of course it was locked. I turned quickly to see where he was, and he was coming right for me. I screamed out with all my might, "Stop this, Mohammed! This is *madness*! Help! Someone help!"

Looking around quickly, I spotted two swords mounted on the wall. I grabbed for the sword which hung on the wall about four feet from me. When I had it, I swung around as fast as lightening just in time to hold its sharp point right at his throat. He stopped dead in his tracks and as I backed him into a book shelf I shouted, "Get it together or I won't hesitate to use this! I'll do it right now you crazy bastard!"

Suddenly, Lussein with twenty guards, burst into the room and shouted, "Mohammed, if we take her life now we will be destroying all our future plans. Calm down my brother and know one day, you will have your revenge on this temptress from the depths of hell. Besides, I told you she was not the one, now leave her alone and let her go back to her demon possessed nation where trash like her belong."

The thought of Lussein's prediction at that moment, nearly made me cut Mohammed's head off right on the spot. It took all my self-control not to lunge forward and plunge the blade right through him, but I thought, 'It's not worth it Christina, he's just an evil man.'

Within moments Mohammed calmed himself down and with his angelic voice said, "I'm sorry if I hurt you, but your news was devastating and it made me upset."

Still holding the sword to Mohammed's neck I looked toward Lussein and said, "You told the President you would release the hostages to me, now I'm tired of fooling around here, so please release them and let us leave at once."

With a deadly serious look in his eyes, he said, "If you give your word you will not tell anyone that Mohammed was here, you may leave now."

I smiled and reassuringly said, "You've got a deal!"

He clapped his hands, turned to his guards and shouted, "Take Ms. Powers to the airport immediately."

"Wait just a minute," I demanded. "I'm not going anywhere without the hostages."

Lussein walked right up to my face while I still held the sword and said, "You really are a gutsy broad."

Without blinking once I replied, "Thank you! I'll take that as a compliment, now please bring out the hostages."

He smiled and his smile seemed to hold a slightly detectable glimmer of admiration as he said, "It's all right to go with the guards Christina, the hostages are already boarded on your jet and waiting for you."

Looking into his eyes, I knew he was telling the truth; so, I thanked him as I handed him the sword. Confidently, I proceeded to walk out of that room holding my head held high with an air about me, as if I had total control over this insane situation and not thinking of losing my composure the entire time. But inside, I was a frightened little girl.

We arrived back at the Baghdad Airport precisely at 9:00pm, and when I boarded the jet the cheers of two-hundred and twenty-six freed hostages filled the cabin. As Lieutenant Todd Deyo locked us in, I asked, "Is everyone here?"

He nodded his head and with a pleased smile said, "Everyone Ms. Powers, thanks to you. Come on let's take our seats and get the hell out of here before he has a change of heart."

With wide eyes I answered, "You got that right!"

As I followed him to the front of the jet, I received warm hugs and kisses from everyone. I returned their greetings in kind, but the one person I really wanted to see was nowhere in sight. Finally, when I reached my seat at the front of the plane there he was. My, Jimmy! Sitting curled up like a little mouse on the seat next to mine, with Richard seated on his other side. The moment he saw me, he gazed into my eyes, with those big, sad, brown-eyes of his, and reaching his arms out to me he said, "Christina, hold me!"

I embraced him as I took my seat and said, "It's all right Jimmy, I'm taking you home." I buckled us both up, and neither one of us uttered another word. I just held him gently in my arms all the way to Germany.

We arrived at an American Military base shortly after 3:00am, and all the hostages were quickly ushered into the infirmary. Jimmy and the others had to stay in Germany a few days for physicals and debriefings. I had to leave immediately for my own debriefing with the President back in Washington, D.C.

After my short but emotional goodbyes to Jimmy, I was back in the air. I didn't get off that plane until 8:00am on December 14, 1990, and I was greeted by the largest gathering of reporters I had ever seen. They proceeded to swarm me like killer bees as I tried to walk through the airport. They were shouting questions at me, "Christina! How are the hostages? Were they harmed in any way?"

Now being joined by the Secret Service who began to lead me toward a group of waiting limos, I quickly responded to the question, "The hostages are in good spirits, and as far as I know no physical harm has come to any of them."

One of the reporters shouted, "Christina, why was your mission to Iraq kept from the public until now? And what were the terms for the release of the hostages?"

Reaching the limos with my presidential escort I answered, "I'm sorry, but I haven't given the President my debriefing yet; so, I'm afraid the answers to your questions are going to have to wait."

I climbed into the waiting limo and off we went to the White House for a six-hour debriefing. Afterwards, the President and I gave a joint forty-five minute news conference; then, it was off for a celebration dinner at the Washington Hilton with George and all of D.C.'s top brass.

With all the hoopla being in my honor, you'd think I'd be at least interested, but all I wanted to do was go home. And as much as I wanted to get up and walk out of that fancy dinner, I didn't. I wasn't able to leave for home until 11:00pm.

# CHAPTER 28

I walked into the house at 2:14am on December 15th, and headed straight for the bedroom. I started to undress as soon as I entered the room and while kicking off my shoes, I hit the message retrieval button on my answering machine. The first message **'BEEP'** was from my mother-in-law and in an obviously upset tone she said, "Christina, it's, Tess! It's now 2:00pm and I'm calling from Albany Medical Center. Michael's been in an awful car crash. He's in surgery right now, so please get here fast." **'BEEP'**

My heart was in my throat as I waited for the next message **'BEEP'**. The next two messages were from Johnny and the fourth **'BEEP'** was from Tess again, "Christina! Where are you? It's now 8:00pm, Michael is out of surgery, but he's in critical condition and unresponsive. He needs you Christina, now more than ever. He's been mumbling your name, so if you really love him please come now!" **'BEEP'** and that was her last message.

It was 2:30 in the morning when I dialed Tess's number, and as soon as she answered I shouted in a panicked voice, "Tess, it's, Christina! How is Michael?"

"Calm down Christina, he's doing fine now. He came around at 1:00am on the 13th, and thank God he's been improving remarkably since."

With a sigh of relief I said, "Thank God is right! I would have been there for him Tess, but I had to leave the country and I couldn't tell anyone."

"I know, we saw you on the evening news with the President. I'm really very proud of you for what you've done Christina, and I know Michael is too. If only you could have seen his face light up when he saw the news broadcast."

"What room is he in?" I asked anxiously.

"625 but visiting hours aren't until 10:00am"

"Thank you Tess, and Lord willing I'll see you at the hospital in the morning."

We said our goodbyes as I put my shoes back on and the minute I hung up the receiver, I dashed back out of the house, and at 2:45am, I was on my way to the Albany Medical Center.

I arrived at the hospital at 3:30am, and I had to convince a security guard that I was truly Christina Powers wherein, he insisted on escorting me up to Michael's room. I quietly opened the door so not to wake him; then, I slowly closed it behind me and tiptoed to his bedside. Tears began to flow down my cheeks, as I came closer to Michael and noticed his entire head was shaved while the top portion was wrapped in bandages. As I knelt down beside his bed, I softly started praying, "Lord, please let him be all right."

As soon as I spoke these words, I could see his eyes slowly opening. When he realized I was there he gently smiled, then began to force himself out of his sleepy fog. I took his hand in mine, kissed it and said, "Michael, my love! I'm so sorry I wasn't here for you, but I'm here now. If you will only take me back in your arms just once, I know we will never leave each other again."

He gazed down at me, stared straight into my eyes and with the most loving, tender look he had ever given me, said, "Punkie, my love for you comes from the deepest essence of my soul. And I'm truly very proud of you for what you've accomplished, and for who you are as a person. But, no matter how strong or proud my love for you is I vowed to myself I would never allow you to place me second in your life again. So for my own mental health, I am going to keep that promise to myself by asking you to leave right now."

I instantly masked the devastating pain his words brought to my heart, under an emotionless expression. I gracefully rose from my knees and just as quietly tiptoed back out of his room without uttering another peep. Somehow, I managed to hold back my tears of pain as I walked through that hospital, but there was no way I was keeping them back the moment I sat in my car. I stayed in the hospital parking lot for two hours crying before I could compose myself enough to drive away.

It was 8:00am on the 15$^{th}$, when I finally collapsed in my bed, clothes and all, and I did not get out of that bed until the same time the following morning. When I returned to my office that morning, I told Pierre not to disturb me as I started right where I left off, following up with messages. I decided it would be wiser to return all business calls first this time, then the personal ones hoping maybe this way I could accomplish something. I didn't get around to making that first personal call until 2:30 that afternoon, and it was to return the twelve messages from Johnny, each one sounding more concerned than the other. As I dialed the number, I noticed it was a local exchange and as soon as he said, "Hello!"

I said, "Hello, yourself! Where are you? This is an in-state number."

With excitement he said, "I was wondering that about you myself until I saw you on the news the other day. You sure know how to get around. One minute you drop me off at my motel, the next you're returning from a Middle East trip no one knew you were on."

I laughed, "I know how well I get around, but what about you? What are you doing back in New York?"

"I'm in Tarrytown. I've been here since Mary and I split up."

"What! What happened?" I asked with a surprised tone.

"When I arrived home the day after your birthday, Mary accused me of cheating on her. I denied it and she threw me out. I went back two hours later and persuaded her we did not sleep together. She asked me if I wanted to sleep with you and when I told her the truth, she threw me out again. So, I came to my secret hide away, my condo here in Tarrytown and like I said, I've been here ever since."

"That is ridiculous, what's wrong with her? Do you have any plans for tonight, John?"

"Not one." He answered sadly.

"Well then why don't you come over and I'll take **you** for dinner this time. Then we can talk in person." He agreed and we made a date for him to meet me at my office at 6:00 that evening.

Just as punctual as ever, Johnny entered my office right on time, and as we were leaving I stopped at Pierre's desk and said, "Pierre, I won't be in tomorrow. I'm going to be picking Jimmy up in the morning at the airport. I'll probably be in the following day."

"Christina, would you mind if I come in late tomorrow myself? I'd like to come to the airport with you and the others in the morning, if I may? Jimmy and I really hit if off well when we were in Ghana together last year, and I'd like to be there to welcome him home."

I replied with a smile, "Sure you can. I'm sure Jimmy would appreciate your being there. Why don't you come to my place at 7:00am? A few other close friends are meeting me there at that time and you're more than welcome to join us."

With a curiously delighted smile he thanked me, as I handed him a note and added, "Open this in ten minutes, and I'll see you in the morning."

I turned my full attentions toward Johnny with a seductive smile and in my best May West interpretation jokingly said, "Well big boy! Let's rock and roll; this night is on me."

We went to my place first where I changed into *Christina Powers* the sex symbol, and immediately proceeded to take Johnny out on the town. Oh yes! The note I left with Pierre read, "**Pierre, around 10:00pm tonight I will be in Albany at a gay night club called LONGHORN'S. What I want you to do is call News Channel Ten in Albany and ask for anchorwoman Angela Hamilton. Tell her I will be in town and if she meets me at Longhorn's at 10:30 tonight, I will give her an exclusive. Then, call our radio station in the area it's 'Fly 92' around 10:00pm. Tell them to announce I am at the nightclub and that I'm going to perform a surprise mini-concert for my Albany fans.**"

I had the evening planned right down to the smallest detail, and I started it out by taking Johnny for a romantic dinner, then to Longhorn's. As I parked the car, Johnny noticed two men walking into the club together holding hands. He quickly turned to me with a nervous look on his face, and in a sarcastic tone said, "Is this a gay bar?"

I gave him a strange look, "John! Don't tell me you're homophobic!"

His tone and expression quickly calmed as he answered, "No, not at all! It's just that I've never been in a gay club before. I'm telling you, I'll freak if some guy tries to hit on me."

I laughed, "Don't be an asshole, John! You're with *Christina Powers*. Do you really think any one of these guys is going to be looking at you with me here? Get real! Tonight in this place, I'm the only one who's going to be 'hit on'. So put your fears away, leave all your prehistoric views of gay men out here in the parking lot, and let's go have some fun."

"Why are we going to a gay bar anyway?" He asked like a frightened little boy.

"First, it's just a gay club and no one is going to attack you. Second, you won't have any competition. Third, I have personal reasons." I answered firmly.

He took a deep breath and said, "Ok, just don't leave me alone."

Climbing out of the car, I started to laugh again, "Stop fooling around, John! I know you're more liberal minded then that, or at least I hope so." At that, we proceeded toward the entrance.

As soon as we walked into the club, I immediately sat Johnny at a table with a drink, and proceeded to take center stage. I went up to the owner, Phil Jackowski, handed him a background tape of my music and asked him to allow me to do a few numbers for the crowd. Breathlessly, he agreed and as he readied his staff and the crowd for my performance, Angela Hamilton from News Channel Ten entered the club. I quickly walked over to her and said, "Angela, hi! Thanks for coming."

With an excited smile she replied, "Christina, it's so nice to meet you and please don't thank me. I should thank you! I can't wait to find out what this is all about."

"I'm going to be giving a small surprise performance here tonight, and I've invited you because this performance is my way of announcing to the Capital Region, my intentions to purchase properties in the City of Albany. My plans are to one day build a major new recording studio right here in your town, and I'm hoping the citizens as well as the city leaders will welcome Powers Inc. into the 'All American City' with open arms."

We went right into a live interview and just as we finished, a crew from Fly 92 entered the club. The crew began to set up a connection to their main station; so, they could start broadcasting my performance live, right on the spot. When their connection was completed, I proceeded to give the D.J. who introduced himself to me as 'Sugar Bear' a quick live on air interview.

Ten minutes later, I had that city in such an uproar that everyone and their brother knew I was in town and partying my tail off with the legendary ballplayer, John Everett. Before I knew, the club, as well as the entire city was mobbed with people and traffic. When I started to sing at 11:00pm that Thursday evening, I made sure I was loud enough for Michael to hear me six blocks away in his hospital bed.

After my mini-concert, I proceeded to dance the night away with Johnny and everyone else in the club. Of course, I orchestrated my latest public display for just one reason. I wanted to hurt Michael just as much as he hurt me, and I figured what better way than to be throwing a party right outside his hospital bedroom window with my ex-lover.

The night was so hot, and the city so busy, I didn't get Johnny to his car until 4:30 in the morning. As I waited for him to exit my car, he leaned over kissed my cheek and said, "Christina, I had a great time tonight. Thanks for taking me; I needed the change and being with you felt like old times. If I'm not being too bold, I hope you felt it too."

I smiled warmly as I replied, "I had a great time too John, it was fun. I know we really didn't get to talk about your situation with Mary very much, and I'm sorry about that. But I'll tell you what. I'm having a small welcome home dinner party for Jimmy and Richard tonight; so, if you come over around 7:00pm, I'll make it up to you by finding the time to talk privately after dinner."

He gracefully accepted my invitation, kissed my cheek once more and out he climbed. As I watched his still very muscular body climb into his car, I thought, 'My God he looks good! And if I think about it, underneath all the true reasons for this evening, I ended up really having a great time with Johnny.' As he left for Tarrytown and his bed, I took a quick shower, grabbed a cup of coffee and headed for the airport.

# CHAPTER 29

I was accompanied to the airport that morning by Pierre, James, Carman, Joe Aiello, Ann Markel, Terry Baggatta, and Theresa DiGuidia. We were met there by a large group of reporters, who were also waiting for Jimmy's arrival. We waited anxiously holding our welcome-home signs and I'll never forget the feeling of relief I felt seeing my best friend in the entire world, safely exit that plane. I became so excited I started to cry. Neither one of us holding back any longer went running toward the other like two excited little children on Christmas morning. In front of the eyes of the world, we leaped into a loving, enthusiastic, embrace.

Jumping in the air with our arms around each other Jimmy shouted, "Oh God, girlfriend I love you! Thank you, Christina! Thank you!"

My tears of joy flowed again as I replied, "I love you too, Jimmy! And I'm so glad to see you home!" In the midst of our hug, I looked behind him then added, "Where's Richard and his parents?"

Breaking from my embrace he answered, "They're coming in on a commercial flight."

I Looked at him strangely and replied with concern, "Why?"

"I'll tell you about it later," he murmured in a lower tone. "I don't want to ruin this moment."

I nodded curiously, "Okay."

At that, he turned to me with his own expression of curiosity as he asked, "Where's Michael?"

I started to laugh as we began to walk toward the others, "I'll tell you about it later, I don't want to ruin this moment either."

His face took on a shocked look as his mouth dropped open, but it was too late for him to allow anything to come out, because we had just reached the cheers and embraces of the others.

Believe it or not, that entire day turned into one big party. Friends were coming in and out of the house from the moment we pulled in at 10:00am, right up until our private dinner party at 7:00pm. That's when I told James not to allow any more visitors. I wanted to keep dinner formal so besides Johnny, I had invited only our closest friends. And for some reason, I wasn't surprised when Jimmy added Pierre to the list by inviting him to come back for dinner. But I asked no questions, figuring they could all wait until Jimmy and I finally had our time together. Still, we ended up with thirty guests for a joyful, heart-warming, dinner that evening, filled with toasts to Jimmy and me, along with lots of thanks to **God**, for Jimmy's safe return home.

Shortly after dinner as we gathered in the bar Carman entered, walked over to Jimmy and said, "There's a call for you on Christina's private line. You can take it in the den." He thanked her, excused himself and headed out.

I quickly went after Carman and asked, "Carman, who called on my line for Jimmy?"

She turned to me with a sad face, "Christina, it's Michael. He asked me not to tell you it was him."

I thanked her and headed straight for my office to do some eavesdropping. Just as I picked up the receiver I could hear Jimmy saying, "I can't believe this, Michael! Why in the world do you want a divorce if you still love her?"

"It's a long story Jimmy, and I'm sure she'll tell you all about it as soon as she can."

"Well at least let me tell her you're on the phone, I don't care what happened between the two of you, I know that girl loves you and she'll want to talk to you."

Michael's reply was harsh, "You think so, huh! Tell me one thing, is he there?"

"Is who here?" Jimmy asked with a confused tone.

"The ballplayer. That's who." Michael replied adamantly.

"Uh uh uh, uh no." Jimmy stuttered.

"You're a pisspoor liar, Jimmy."

"He can't mean anything to her, Michael. I've only known him for a few hours, but I can already tell he's a jerk just by his phoney handshake."

"It's like this Jimmy; I can't afford to care anymore, so if she wants him she can have him."

Confidently Jimmy replied, "Come on, that doesn't sound like the Michael I know. Where's the man who once told me, 'If anybody can tame her and keep her from killing herself it's me, and I'm going to succeed.' Don't you remember telling me 'that', the day Frank Salerno's murder trial ended?"

"I remember! But Jimmy, I'm telling you, there's no one who can save that girl from herself, and I just can't keep trying anymore or she **will** be the death of me. Jimmy, just take care of her for me because she needs someone looking after her more then she knows. Now, get back to your party and I'll see you when I get out of this damned hospital."

Sadly Jimmy replied, "I'll say all right for now Michael, but we're not done talking about this I promise you."

They said their goodbyes and I sat there hurting so badly, I just couldn't go back to the party. I had Carman make my excuses for me, while I headed for a hot shower.

It was 12:10am when Jimmy finally came climbing into bed with me and proceeded to prop himself up on three pillows, with a big bowl of buttered popcorn and two bottles of Catskill Mountain Cola. He began to nudge me as he said, "You better get your ass up and start talking right now, before I dump this bowl on your head."

I sat up quickly, "Don't you dare dump that bowl! I've been dying for your popcorn."

He laughed, "All right, shithead! I know you were on the phone and I know why you didn't come back down. Now, tell me what's going on with you two?"

As we munched on the best popcorn, Jimmy had ever made, I told him everything that happened. When I completed my story, Jimmy turned to me shaking his head and said, "Whoa! That's a tough call. On one hand, I can't believe Michael would be so stubborn, especially since **my**

**life** was on the line. But if I look at it from his point of view, I can totally understand. The problem here is neither one of you are right or wrong in this situation. You guys are just going to have to get through this and go on."

I chuckled, "Tell him that! He's the one who wants a divorce."

Seriously, "I'm not talking about just him, I mean you too. If you really want Michael, what are you doing with this John guy?"

"He's just a friend!" I protested.

"Just a friend! A friend who happens to be throwing Michael for a loop and his presence sure isn't helping matters any. Besides he's not just a jock, he's a jerk jock. That's the worst kind."

"I was going to bring that up to you. I don't think you are being fair to John. He really happens to be a great guy."

Sarcastically he replied, "Christina stop kidding yourself! I'll bet underneath that country boy smile lays a KKK member. I could see it the minute he looked at me."

I started to laugh then quickly changed the subject by saying, "That's enough about me. What happened with Richard?"

Sadly he replied, "Let's just say he was no Bobby, and I don't think anyone ever will be."

"Well something must of caused the breakup. After all, you spent sixteen months with him!"

"I did love him until he became a possessive, manipulative, neurotic fruitcake. He got so bad, I was afraid to go to sleep at night worried he was going to murder me in my sleep. I just couldn't take it anymore; so, I broke it off the night before we were to leave Kuwait."

I shook my head in amazement, "Wow, I guess it's true, you never really do know anyone until you live with them. Now for my next question, what's up with you and Pierre?"

Innocently he replied, "Why whatever do you mean?"

I chuckled, "You know what I mean! I can see something brewing there, I know you too well, Jimmy."

"Ha! Ha!" Jimmy replied, "I think he's a nice guy, that's all."

"You're right he is, but is he gay?" I asked with curiosity.

"Yes! You didn't know that?" He answered with a surprised look.

"No!  When did you find out?"

"The minute you first introduced him to me in Ghana."

"Well then go for it Jimmy, he's a doll."  I said approvingly.

That's when Jimmy took my hand, brought it to his heart and said, "Do you know what I would really like?"

I squeezed his hand, "No Jimmy, I don't know, but I'm sure you're going to tell me."

He smiled mischievously, "I would love to spend Christmas and New Years in 'P-town', with you and your secretary before having to face life's responsibilities again."

I smiled back, "I think I can arrange that.  Would you like me to call my secretary and inform him to be ready for a business trip in the morning, or would you like to call him for me?"

He kissed my cheek with his buttery lips, hopped up and said, "I think I'll go call him right now, and you better get some sleep girlfriend, it's starting to show around the edges."

And as he went for the door, I went flying for the mirror yelling, "Where?  I don't see anything!"

# CHAPTER 30

We arrived back home from our Cape Cod holiday on Saturday, January 6, 1991. The three of us had a wonderful time together the entire two weeks we were there; unless, I was left alone for more two minutes. That's when I would begin to think about Michael and end up crying. I would insist the two of them go have fun and they did, while I like a damned fool stayed in my oceanfront room crying my eyes out. I missed Michael so much, especially that Christmas. I called my mother-in-law, only to become more depressed when the message I received from her was, "He's out of town Christina, and unavailable to all of us."

After that message, I was able to push thoughts of Michael away, at least until New Year's Day. I was so upset Michael didn't call me back the night before, after I left him three urgent messages, that I spent the entire day blowing off steam jogging for miles on the wind frozen beaches of the Cape. So needless to say, when I did finally enter the front door of my Milton Home, I was really glad to be back. At least now I could begin to bury my pain, by diving head first back into my work.

Jimmy and I decided to take the rest of that weekend before plunging into my work, by spending it alone, just the two of us. We stayed home and talked about everything that happened to both of us while we were apart. He told me how awful it was for him to be held against his will, not to mention frightening. As for me, I told him how scared I was for him and how glad I was that at least for him the ordeal was now over. I went on to tell him all my thoughts and feelings. We talked about

Michael and our crazy love/hate relationship. Jimmy talked about his relationship with Richard and how he watched it fall apart.

At one point, I told him about my wish to someday adopt a great big family with Michael, and that's when I started to cry as I sarcastically said, "I can't believe this, Jimmy! Me! The so-called, great *Christina Powers* can't even keep her husband!" Throwing my hands up in disgust, I continued, "Look, world! The sex-queen of the twentieth century! Ha! Ha! I wouldn't know how to keep a man if my life depended on it. What the hell is my problem, Jimmy? Why can't I hold onto a man?"

He chuckled as he answered, "Christina, I love you and you're the best friend anyone could ever have, but you're also like a wild fire burning everything in your path. No man, not even Michael has been able to control your flames, and I don't think anyone ever will unless you let them."

Seriously I asked, "So what are you telling me, am I a hopeless cause in the love department?"

"No! Why don't you try thinking about what I said before you jump to conclusions?"

I thought for a moment, "You're right! I am too overbearing sometimes, but I don't mean to be. Life just seems to dictate my response to certain situations. Like you being in Ghana for instance, or the business. It's nothing I do on purpose, so what can I do about it? Stop caring and let it all fall apart just to please Michael? Well if that's what it takes, then I'd rather be alone."

"That's not what it takes," he replied. "And that's not what I meant either. What I'm trying to say is, if you let Michael know he is first in your life, he'll come back to you."

At that I kissed his forehead, "Well Jimmy, I think it's a little too late for Michael and me, but I'll keep it in mind for the future."

Our weekend went on like that until 8:00am Monday morning rolled around. It came so fast, it felt like we never had any rest at all. But all the same, when Jimmy and I entered our prearranged board meeting at 9:00am that morning, we were full of energy and ready to tackle anything. And for the next five hours, everyone in that room went through an entire review of every aspect of Powers Incorporated since the day Jimmy left.

It was 1:00pm when our review ended and without a breather, I went right into action and started giving new orders. In that entire time, we had one ten minute coffee break at 11:30am and I didn't have us break again for lunch until 3:00pm. That's when I entered my office to find a certified letter, from the Grammy Awards Committee of the National Academy of Recording Arts and Sciences.

Jimmy and Pierre were standing beside me waiting to go for lunch, as I quickly opened the letter to discover my latest soundtrack, 'One Voice, One World and Love Enough For All' had received a phenomenal total of fourteen different Grammy nominations. And the single, 'Love Grows in the Arms of Peace' had eight of those nominations all to itself. I was so excited by the letter I leaped into the air shouting, "Yes! Yes! Fourteen nominations! Can you believe it, fourteen!" I shoved the letter in Jimmy's face and continued shouting, "Look, Jimmy! Look!"

"Wow! Christina, this is great news!" He shouted back with enthusiasm then continued, "Did you read the rest of this?"

"No, I stopped at the fourteen nominations. What does it say?"

"It goes on to read, '**Ms. Powers, we the members of the Grammy Awards Committee, would like to invite you to co-host the awards ceremony this year with Barbara Goldstein, as well as perform your single, 'Love Grows in the Arms of Peace.' The ceremony will be held in L.A., on February 27, 1991. Please reply by January 20, 1991'.**" Jimmy hugged me wildly shouting, "You go, girlfriend!"

Pierre then joined the celebration by shouting, "Congratulations, Christina! And your lunch is on me! Now, may we please go eat?"

We all started to laugh as we headed for lunch and for the first time in weeks, I was feeling great.

Shortly after returning from lunch, I called to accept the Grammy Awards Committee's invitation to co-host the ceremonies. I also agreed to arrive in L.A. for rehearsals on February 15, 1991.

After that call I thought I'd better return Johnny's many calls, and as soon as I said, "Hi, John, it's I."

He said, "I swear you must be the vanishing woman, so what secret mission were you on this time?"

I laughed, "I'm sorry, John, I was on a much needed siesta with Jimmy, and we decided not to tell anyone where we were."

"Well thanks a lot! Do you realize I've been waiting three weeks to talk to you, and you've brushed me off each time?"

Remembering what Jimmy said to me about not letting any man control my so-called flames I said, "John, if you will please let me take you out for dinner tonight, I promise we'll talk."

"That sounds great shall I pick you up after work?"

"How about 7:00pm, my place?" I replied.

"I'll be there." He answered with enthusiasm, and when we said our goodbyes I sat for a moment thinking, 'I really do need to learn to be more considerate of man's feelings. The problem is I don't readily trust men unless they're gay, then I feel right at home with them. I guess it's because gay men don't look at me as a woman who must be conquered into submission.'"

Later that evening when Johnny picked me up, I wore my helpless little girl look, so as not to intimidate him. He took me to the Capri Restaurant in the town of Port Ewen for dinner and dancing. Over dinner, we talked about his break up with Mary and how much he missed his children.

As we talked, he gently took my hand in his and said, "I have to be honest with you and myself, Christina. The only reason I married Mary was because I was on the rebound from our breakup. She was my high school sweetheart and I was hurting so badly, I jumped into her arms without thinking twice. So now that I've finally admitted this to myself, I decided to file for a divorce. We go to court in March."

I was saddened and strangely pleased at the same time, but I refused to show my emotions as I replied, "Is Mary aware of your true feelings, John?"

"She is now," he answered. "I told her last week just before having my attorney file for the divorce."

"How did she take it?" I asked with sincere concern.

"Not too well, she started to cry, then said, 'I've always known your love for her was strong, but I still allowed myself to believe I could make you forget her.' I told her my decision to file for divorce had nothing to do with you. I simply said, 'We just can't keep living this lie together.'"

With a deeper sense of concern I asked, "How are your children handling this?"

"Not too well right now, but they'll get used to it. Children are like that."

Just then, the band began to play 'Johnny's Love.'

Johnny lovingly gazed into my eyes and said, "Do you think we can try dancing to my song again, I'm pretty sure Michael's not here to punch me out this time?" I smiled and gracefully accepted his invitation.

We were having such a good time we never noticed it began to snow, and by the time we were ready to leave there was already six inches on the ground and still falling steadily. Our ride home that night was slow going to say the least, and at one point the storm became so intense, we had to pull off the road to wait for it to let up. As we sat in the car watching this beautiful snow storm, I turned to Johnny and softly said, "John, you've told me so much about how you were hurting after our breakup, but you've not mentioned once why you slept with Kathy Brown. I've waited a long time to hear the answer to that question, because it was that discovery which caused me to abort our child."

With tears now filling my eyes I continued, "Would you please answer my question now? I don't know why after all these years, but I really need to know the answer."

With tears now welling in his eyes as well, he said, "It was because I was a fool. Kathy came to my home not twenty minutes before you did that night. She told me in a very persuading way if I were to sleep with her, then she would see to it Frank let you out of your contract. So foolishly I believed her and thinking I was doing something for you, I agreed."

"For me!" I replied with shock. "Didn't you think about how I might feel if I were to find out? You must have known I'd be devastated once she told me, and she would have if I hadn't discovered the two of you together myself. And when I did find the two of you together, why didn't you come after me then? You had the card from the flowers I gave you, telling you I was pregnant. Didn't you realize how devastated I was when I saw you sleeping with Kathy?"

My voice rose as I cried out the pain I hid for all those years until I was shouting with anger, "You should have known it might have caused me to have an abortion?" I opened the car door and as I began to run into a blinding snow squall, I stopped turned back and screamed, "Why didn't you come after me, Johnny? Why?"

Johnny ran after me yelling, "Christina! Wait! Come back here!"

I was so upset; he had to tackle me into a snow bank to stop me from running. Once I hit the snow, I pushed him from me crying, "Please don't, Johnny? Just leave me be."

I was freezing and covered with snow when I stood up, took a deep breath and just started to cry. And once 'again' my tears fell for all my babies. The pain I felt that moment went so deep, my body began to tremble and I knew it had nothing to do with the weather.

As I cried in the midst of that blinding, snow squall, Johnny took my hand and with his tears falling as hard as mine said, "Christy, can you ever forgive me for the hurt I caused you all those many years ago? I realized I was the reason why you had the abortion. I came to your penthouse on the night of your birthday to ask you to forgive me, but your place was empty. I looked for you for months. I even went to Barbara's home thinking you might be there, but she told me she had no idea where you were. Shortly after that I went back home, where I ran into Mary."

As he cried, I gently pulled him into my arms and we cried together like two babies. I tenderly stroked his head as I softly said, "Oh Johnny, if you had only come that morning, I would have been there and I would have forgiven you then, as I forgive you right now."

Gazing into my eyes he passionately said, "Christina, I love you. I've always loved you and I will always love you." He moved his lips to mine and softly began to kiss me as he continued to whisper, "I love you. I love you. Please tell me you still love me angel?"

Feeling lonely and vulnerable, I felt myself drifting into his loving, gentle, kisses. I allowed myself to slip deeper into his advances, as his warm tongue slid to the back of my cold neck. As his kisses grew in passion, memories of our lives together began to flood my mind. I could feel my desire rising as his hands began to caress my longing breasts. As my temperature grew, all those dull faint feelings of love I once felt for Johnny, rushed to my consciousness. So much so I wanted to cry out 'Johnny, I love you too!' But just as I opened my mouth to speak, thoughts of Michael held my tongue. It was at that moment, I abruptly put a stop to this unfolding fantasy by saying, "Johnny, please don't! Let's not rush into something we both might end up regretting, because as long as we're both still married, we can't take our relationship any further."

Still holding me in his arms, "You're right Christina, but I promise I will court you as long as it takes, if you well allow me?"

I smiled sheepishly, "I'd love to be courted by you, Johnny." And that's exactly what he did.

# CHAPTER 31

That month went by so fast that before I knew, it was 5:00pm on Sunday, February 14$^{th}$, and I was packing for my trip to L.A., the following morning. I'm sure the fact Johnny came 'a-courtin' every single night, had a lot to do with how fast the time went. He was determined to spoil me with flowers, gifts, and most of all, his full attention, and I must say, I was truly enjoying it all. And boy the tabloids enjoyed it too; they had a field-day with this one! Headlines read, **"Christina's new Love Triangle! Who will hope to win her heart this time around?"**

Thank God for Johnny and my intense work schedule, I was able to stay so busy, I hardly thought about Michael or the tabloids. And Johnny's ability to treat me like a queen, helped keep me so content and happy, I began to feel free without Michael breathing down my neck, and I thought, 'Gee! Now that I think about it, Michael was always trying to tell me what to do, wasn't he?' Shrugging my shoulders to accompany my thoughts, 'I'm probably better off without him in my life anyway. Besides, who needs a man who's always trying to control you? Not me!'

As I was convincing myself of my new found happiness, Jimmy on the other hand never ceased to remind me of how miserable I truly was, by telling me how happy Michael seemed to be living back in his Poughkeepsie Townhouse. But there was no way I would admit to Jimmy I might be unhappy. Especially since he had visited Michael several times since his discharge from the hospital, and he refused to tell me even one thing said between the two of them.

As I finished packing for my 'Grammy' trip, Jimmy entered my room, gave me a peck on my cheek and said, "You're only going to be gone for twelve days and already I miss you."

I returned his kiss, "That's sweet Jimmy, and I'm going to miss you too, but you're coming to the award ceremony aren't you?"

"I wouldn't miss it for the world!" He cheerfully replied.

He appeared too happy for some reason, so with a tone of curiosity I asked, "Where did you go anyway? I was looking for you at breakfast and Carman told me you left before 8:00 this morning."

In response to my question Jimmy looked at me strangely and said, "I told you Pierre and I were going ice fishing with Michael today."

I shook my head in a confused way as I responded, "I'm sorry it truly slipped my mind."

"Sure it did!" Jimmy laughed. "You don't really think I'm going to buy that one, now do you?"

"I really don't care what you buy, Jimmy." I snarled with indignation, "So did he ask about me?"

His smile was mischievous this time and his answer was blunt, "As a matter of fact he did. He asked when you were planning to leave for L.A."

My curiosity took hold as I suspiciously asked, "Why did he want that bit of information?"

Jimmy's smile gave me the impression he was up to something, and his cocky answer to my question confirmed my suspicions something was up, "He wants to make sure you're nowhere in sight when he comes for his stuff."

"He what!?" I shouted! I took on an air of dominance as my voice cooled, "Does he really, now? Well you tell him for me if he comes anywhere near this place without me being here, I'll have his ass thrown in jail."

Jimmy protested strongly, "That's not right Christina, they are his things!"

"I don't care, Jimmy, and don't you dare let him in here while I'm gone either, or I'll be after your hide along with his." I demanded.

He sighed sarcastically then snapped back, "Well, when can I tell him to come then, Miss Prima-Donna?"

"When I'm going to be here!" I snapped back. "I want to make sure what he takes out of here is his."

"Well since your leaving in the morning, why don't I call him and tell him to come tonight?"

"No, Jimmy! After how he hurt me you expect me to make this easy for him? Well I'm not. Besides, I have a date tonight with, Johnny."

At that, Jimmy's fangs came out as he hissed, "Oh! You're calling him, Johnny now! Wasn't that your pet name for him? What is wrong with you, girlfriend? I can't believe you could choose that phony asshole over Michael. It just doesn't make sense to me, or do you really want this Johnny?"

Losing it I shouted back, "Who the hell do you think you are passing judgment on Johnny!? And if you would open your eyes you'd be able to see Michael left me, not the other way around. He wanted this divorce because he's a stubborn, bullheaded Irishman, and now he can have it! Because I sure as hell don't want him anymore, not after he hurt and humiliated me like he did in his hospital room." That's when I started to cry and with my tears flowing off my cheeks I harshly ordered, "You may inform, Mr. Gillespie I will be returning on the 25$^{th}$, for one day, and he may come that afternoon at 1:00pm to get his things. I will be here to allow him access to his belongings. Oh yes! If he doesn't make it on the 25$^{th}$, there won't be another chance because I will have already thrown his belongings into the Goodwill box. 'Capiche!' Jimmy!"

He stood there speechless and dazed for a moment, then as meek as a kitten he replied, "I'm sorry, Christina! I don't want us to be fighting also. It's just that I can't stand to see the two of you apart like this, especially since I know you two belong together. What I don't understand is, why can't you see Michael is the best thing that's come into your life, since Tony's death?"

I wiped my eyes with a tissue as I turned toward Jimmy and replied, "I know you're right Jimmy, but I've tried to make Michael come back to me. He's refused and I've given up. So now, for the sake of my sanity, may we please drop the subject of Michael?"

With a frustrated tone he answered, "I don't like this one bit Christina, but I will honor your wishes."

I smiled, "Thank you Jimmy and I apologize for my outburst, it was uncalled for and you didn't deserve it."

"That's all right." He replied with a smile. Taking on a curious tone he continued, "The Grammy Awards Ceremony is going to be held on the 27$^{th}$ this year, so why are you coming home on the 25$^{th}$?"

"I'm only coming home for that one night. It's Johnny's birthday and I promised to spend it with him. Now would you get out of here so I can get ready."

"If I must!" He whined as he left me to get dressed.

Johnny looked like a knight in shining armor in his black tux, as he stood at my front door that evening, and that southern boy smile he wore was enchanting, to say the least. As I greeted him, his eyes lit up the night when he saw me in my low cut, black silk, evening gown, "You look absolutely gorgeous tonight, Christina." He said as he gently pulled me into his arms. "I know you said we must remain friends until our divorces are finalized, but I can't help myself. I'm so madly in love with you I want to shout it from the rooftops."

At that he kissed me with such passion I was left breathless, and as I began to return the passion in his kiss I heard, "Ahem! Ahem," from behind me, "Excuse me!"

I turned to see Jimmy standing behind me with his hands folded while tapping his left foot, "I'm sorry, Jimmy. Did you want something?" I asked with a slight touch of sarcasm.

"I just wanted to know what time you plan to be home tonight. You're leaving in the morning, remember?"

I chuckled my reply as I led Johnny by the hand, "Don't wait up 'mother-hen'." And off we went.

As we drove off I took Johnny's hand in mine and said, "You're spoiling me, and I'm going to miss this while I'm away."

"I'm glad!" He replied with a gentle squeeze to my hand.

"So where are we dining tonight?" I asked with curiosity.

With a mysterious expression he answered, "Since you're leaving in the morning I planned something extra special for tonight."

"Hmm," I replied with a smile. "This sounds like an interesting evening already."

We chatted as we drove and before I knew it, we were parked at a lover's lane over-looking the city of New Paltz, from the top of Mount

Minnewaska. Once Johnny turned off the ignition, he climbed out of the car, went to the trunk and returned with a blanket and a picnic basket. He then laid the blanket on the hood of his car and called me out into the cold, now snowy weather, for dinner on the hood of his car. I looked at him as if he were insane and said, "You want to eat dinner here?"

"Yes! Come lay on the hood and look at the stars with me."

"But there are no stars, Johnny!" I protested, "And this has got to be the coldest night in twenty-years."

"Come on, I'll keep you warm." He insisted as he rubbed his hands together.

Reluctantly, I agreed and took a seat beside Johnny on the hood of his car, and thank God at least that was warm. Johnny produced a bottle of champagne and a bucket of K.F.C. I started to laugh as I kissed his cold cheek and said, "You're too much! And this is great, Johnny. Thank you for thinking of it."

Johnny was so suave and debonair as he served dinner and drinks that night that I didn't mind the cold. After our meal, he raised his glass and said, "I'd like to make a double toast tonight. First, here's to the most incredible woman I've ever known. Second, here's to the new Assistant Coach of the New York Mets, as of 10:00 this morning."

I hugged him with excitement as I exclaimed, "Congratulations, Johnny! I didn't know you were after that position, why didn't you tell me?"

"Because I wanted to make sure I could nail the position on my own merit, not on your recommendation."

I hugged him again, "I understand completely Johnny and I'm so happy for you."

With that, somehow our hug became an embrace, then gazing into my eyes he said, "Being up here with you tonight reminds me of the night we planned our future together on the balcony of your penthouse, do you remember?"

Lovingly gazing back into his eyes I replied, "How could I forget that night Johnny, it was one of the most precious nights of my life. Just remembering it brings tears to my eyes."

"I love you, Christina!" He said as he began to gently kiss me. All at once, he pulled himself out of my embrace and reached for his neck chain. Taking off his grandmother's ring, took my hand and as he held the ring over the ring finger of my left hand he said, "Christina, will you say you will marry me as soon as our divorces are finalized, so I may place this ring back on the finger where it truly belongs?"

With tears of joy streaming down my frozen cheeks I shouted out, "Yes, Johnny! I will marry you!"

Immediately he pulled off my wedding band, and he slipped his grandmother's ring on my finger, and as tears welled up in his eyes he said, "This time this ring shall stay on your finger, and we will spend the rest of our lives together. I promise you this Christina." With that I kissed him passionately, and we just held one another in a loving embrace as we watched the snowflakes falling, until I could take the cold no longer.

It was 2:00 am when Johnny returned me to my front door. We kissed once more and promised to meet back at my home at 3:00pm on the 25th, which would be Johnny's 42nd birthday. We gave each other one last longing look, kissed and simultaneously said, "I love you."

He just smiled gently, turned and walked away. I stood at my open door watching him leave and I felt like I was floating on cloud nine. I was in love again when I closed that door and headed for my room. Unfortunately, I was intercepted by Jimmy's keen radar, and before I could close and lock my bedroom door, he had one foot in it.

I tried to push harder on the door hoping he'd pull his foot out and go away, but of course he didn't. Instead he yelled, "My foot's in the damn door you stupid ass! Now open this door so we can talk girlfriend, before I have to slap you."

I opened the door to let him in and as I started to undress I said, "Well come on in! You might as well climb in bed with me, or neither one of us is going to sleep tonight."

Looking at me strangely he said, "Aren't you going to shower first?"

I laughed as I answered, "I didn't work up an ounce of sweat tonight and I'm too tired to bother."

All at once, "Ahhh! No! No! It can't be!" Jimmy screamed. "Don't tell me that's his grandmother's ring you told me about, on your finger?"

"Calm down, Jimmy, and I'll explain."

He gasped as he softly said, "I'm calm girlfriend, now start explaining."

"Okay, now I will tell you just one time and please no questions tonight. Johnny has asked me to marry him and I've accepted. Now goodnight." And I turned off the light.

Everything was quiet just long enough for me to think I got away with it. Then all of a sudden, the light came on, "Are you, nuts!? You're not even divorced yet and you're already engaged! I can see some old patterns emerging here, that's for sure."

I interrupted, "I thought I told you no questions?"

"I'm not asking you anything smart ass! I'm telling you!" His voice calmed as he continued, "I've listened to you, now it's only fair you listen to me. Agreed?" I nodded 'yes' and he went on, "Good! First thing I want to say, if you truly love this John then I will have no choice but to accept him as a part of our family. All I ask is that you search your soul on this one, because I think it's a 'biggie' for you right now."

I looked at him with bewilderment as I sarcastically exclaimed, "I have no idea what you are talking about, Jimmy. So if you're trying to say something profound, at least have it make sense."

He hugged me gently and said, "Oh God, what did you do with this girl? She's so wise, yet so dumb." Grabbing my shoulders he continued, "Christina, just make sure you're really ready to give up on Michael before you go running off with your Johnny. I wouldn't want you regretting something you may still have the power to change."

I kissed him tenderly, "Thank you, Jimmy. I guess that's one of the reasons I love you so much. You never cease to give me something to think about." I flicked off the light, "Now go to sleep."

"I love you too, Christina."

"Shh! Goodnight."

"Goodnight."

Not four hours later, Joe Aiello along with my orchestra and me, were on our way to L.A. And thanks to Jimmy I had a lot to consider. But after arriving in L.A. and only spending ten minutes with Barbara, I forgot everything Jimmy said. As a matter of fact, I was so caught up in feelings of joy just from seeing Barbara, that as we sat on her living room sofa talking after rehearsals that night, I forgot about Jimmy completely.

That was until Barbara said, "Christina, I love you, and I want to really talk to you now from one friend to another."

"All right!" I eagerly agreed with a smile.

"I was on the phone with Jimmy last night and he told me everything that's been going on with you and your men. And I've got to tell you, we're both very concerned about you, so won't you please tell me what's really going on?"

My smile vanished as I replied, "I don't believe him! Why did he have to call you?"

"He didn't," she answered. "I called you last night and Jimmy took the call. I asked him if there was any truth to all the rumors John was back in your life. And you know Jimmy, that's all it took and he was telling me everything."

"Yes I know Jimmy," I said with a smirk. Taking on that air of confidence I present so well I continued, "Barbara, let me put your mind at ease. You know me, and I'm telling you I have it all under control."

A bright smile appeared on her face as she replied, "Enough said!"

As our conversation went on, I thought, 'Boy that was a close one! I don't have a clue as to what the hell I'm really doing!'

The two of us had our Grammy presentation roles down pat within the first week and it was 'fooling around on the set time,' from there on in. We hammed it up so much that second week, that every night another goofy story of the two of us fooling around on the set of the Grammies hit the evening news. This was the kind of news coverage I didn't mind and the public loved it. Before I knew it, the 25th of February came and I was back in my Hudson River Valley home, waiting for Michael to show up for his belongings.

I waited without Michael showing up, until the clock hit 1:05pm That's when I immediately stormed up to his closet and began packing his belongings for the Goodwill truck, as I bitched to myself, "Why you, bastard! I can't believe you could hate me so much you won't even face me to get your things." I could not hold back my tears as my thoughts continued, 'Why, Michael? Was I really so terrible?' I went for the phone, picked it up and started to dial his number. 'Ding dong! Ding dong!' went the doorbell and my heart stopped.

I just dropped the phone, quickly wiped the tears from my face, and hurried for the door knowing I gave James and Carman the day off. When I reached it, I took a deep breath as I grabbed for the doorknob, then exhaled as I opened the door to find Michael standing there, looking like the perfect Marlboro Man in his cowboy hat, blue jeans, and red plaid, flannel shirt. He nodded to me and said, "I'm sorry I'm late, I was held up crossing the bridge."

As I stood there speechless, he looked at me strangely, "Is it still all right to get my things?"

I snapped out of whatever it was holding my tongue to say, "Yes it's still all right, Michael, come on in. I was just packing some of your things myself."

He followed me up to what once was our room and went straight to work packing his belongings. I sat on the bed watching him for a few minutes before breaking the silence, "I tried not to disturb your stuff, so you should find your things where you left them."

While on his knees in the closet he glanced up at me, "Thank you, I appreciate that."

While I had eye contact I couldn't help but ask, with a flair of sincerity, "So how have you been, Michael?"

Looking back down at his packing he answered, "Well, thank you."

With a cheerier tone I added, "How's Tess doing? I've been so busy I haven't had the chance to call her."

I heard from the closet, "Fine."

I let a few more minutes pass before saying, "Is it going to kill you to talk to me Michael?"

"No, Christina, it's not going to kill me, there's just nothing to say." He abruptly answered.

"Nothing to say! Michael, I'm still your wife, how can there be nothing to say?"

Closing his last suitcase he said, "I think I have everything, so I guess I'll see you Friday morning at the courthouse to finalize our divorce."

I stood up as he began to leave the room and said, "Is that all you have to say, Michael?"

He turned to me with a tear in each eye as his strained voice cracked, "I hope your new husband can make you happy, Christina. Cause God knows I never could."

"That's not true!" I protested only to be interrupted.

"There's nothing left to say, Christina, except goodbye." Turning away from me, he headed toward the door as he continued, "Now I really have to go." With that I helplessly watched him walk out of my life and with him went part of my soul.

I just sat on the bed without moving or even thinking until I heard the slight beep of the alarm, which indicated the opening and closing of the front door. It was only then that I thought to go after him, but by the time I reached the front door, he was pulling away. I gazed longingly as his white Mercedes coup convertible, vanished into the snowy, wooded, scenery and I remembered a song I once sang to Johnny, 'The Love I Lost.' and I thought, 'I was wrong, Michael. You're the love I'll never forget.'

My thought was interrupted by the appearance of Jimmy's car coming up the driveway. He parked quickly then ran up to where I was standing with a desperate look on his face. Knowing that look all too well, I immediately became alarmed and it showed in my tone when I said, "What's wrong, Jimmy!?"

The panic in his voice confirmed my fears as he answered, "Where's John, Christina? It's an emergency!"

"He's not here yet!" I answered quickly. "Why? What happened, Jimmy?"

He nervously replied, "His son John Jr. called your office number. He said he tried to call here, but couldn't get through."

"What did he say," I asked anxiously?

"He said his mother is in the hospital on her death bed because of a suicide attempt. He went on to say he came home from school to check on her because of the deep depression she was in that morning, and he found her in the bathtub, with both wrists slit."

"Oh God, no!" I cried in horror, and putting my hands to my face I exclaimed, "What has my reckless behavior caused now!?"

"Don't you dare start that now!" Jimmy demanded. "If you try blaming yourself for this, you're only going to make this entire emotional mess worse for John when he gets here."

I looked at him strangely and snidely remarked, "Since when are you so worried about Johnny's feelings?"

"Since I heard the anguish in his son's voice." He snapped back sarcastically.

Feeling the fool I replied, "I'm sorry, Jimmy! I shouldn't have said that. I don't know why I keep jumping on you?"

"I do," he replied sadly. "It's because unconsciously you and Michael are both blaming me for your breakup."

Before I could even analyze my thoughts for a suitable reply to Jimmy's remark, Johnny pulled up the driveway and we both headed for his car. As soon as I reached him, I calmly explained what had happened. I could see the anguish taking over his expression as I told him of Mary's condition; so, I gently kissed his cheek and said, "I'll have my crew fly you to your family right now."

He looked at me with confused eyes, and with the fearful voice of a little boy who was being forced to face the unknown said, "Will you come with me?"

I gazed at him tenderly, "You will have to do this on your own, Johnny. I'm afraid my shadow over your life has caused your family enough pain, and I'm the last person any of them needs to meet right now." I held him tight for a moment, then turned to Jimmy and said, "Jimmy, would you please drive Johnny to the airport while I arrange for his flight?"

Jimmy agreed as Johnny protested, "Won't you at least come to the airport with me?"

"No, Johnny." I replied weakly, "I can't right now, but I'll be waiting to hear from you. So please call me when you know something." He looked so sad as he climbed into Jimmy's car and without either one of us saying another word; I watched as they drove down the driveway.

When they were out of sight I turned and quickly walked back into the house, where I immediately called Pierre and had him arrange for Johnny's flight to Virginia. As I hung up the phone I thought, 'God, please help Mary come through this.' Then I thought. 'What's wrong with me, Lord? Why do I destroy everyone I care about?"

As I sat there at my desk, I morbidly began to chuckle to myself as I solemnly thought, 'Oh Well! Game's over and it looks like you lose all the way around once again, Christina.' It hit me like a lightning bolt sparking an explosion in my mind and I thought, 'Not yet, you haven't! You still have one more chance to win this game lady and you better make it good!' With that thought in mind, I reached for a pen and paper and began to turn my feelings into lyrics.

I had been writing for only twenty minutes before Jimmy entered the house and yelled out, "Christina! Where are you?"

"I'm in my office!" I yelled back continuing to write.

Jimmy entered my office and as he approached me he said, "I thought you'd like to know the crew was ready when we arrived, and they took off immediately."

"Thank you, Jimmy." I replied still not breaking my concentration as I continued to write.

He leaned over my shoulder and with a curious tone asked, "What are you writing?" And all at once, came that oh-so-familiar, melodramatic screech, "Ohhh no! What on earth are you doing now?"

I turned to him calmly, "What's it look like I'm doing, Jimmy?"

I knew from his expression he immediately took offense and I thought, 'Oh God! Here we go.' As he shouted, "It looks like you're getting ready to make a damn fool out of yourself again! Don't you remember what happened the last time you sat down and wrote a song to that asshole? Don't you realize what kind of power you hold in the position you're in right now? His wife just tried to kill herself, his children are devastated, he's half out of his mind, and you're writing words like that to sing for them all to hear! Think about what you're writing, and the harm those words could do."

I fired back, "Damn it, Jimmy! You don't even know what you're screaming about! So if you're not going to at least be helpful, then please just shut up and let me finish what I'm doing!"

With indignation he snapped, "What! I don't know what I'm talking about! How could you say that? For **God sake**, wake up girlfriend, don't you remember your late husband Tony!? He died because you had to sing a song to your precious Johnny once before! What do you want to do kill a few more innocent people?"

Struggling to keep my composure I stood up, grabbed him by his shoulders and calmly said, "Jimmy, for the first time in months I know what I'm doing. So would you please just trust me? Trust me and help me, because I could sure use your help right now."

He shook his head in frustration, and gently smiled as his eyes began to radiate the kind of love that only comes when you can trust someone with your life. From those emotions he softly said, "What do you need girlfriend?"

I joyfully kissed his cheek and with excitement answered, "I need you to help me create the most beautiful symphony ever written to accompany these lyrics." Then, showing him my almost finished product with great enthusiasm, I completed my sentence with, "and we only have two hours."

Wide-eyed, he gazed at me and said, "I don't know how I let you talk me into these things, but let's do it!"

Just like the old days, we sat down together and worked the magic that made our music famous. Not twenty-four hours later we were in our L.A. studios with my personal crew, putting it all together from stage props to the color of my eye liner. I was determined even if it killed us all, to have everything perfect for the following nights live, world-wide, broadcasting of the Grammy Awards Ceremony. And after thirty six-grueling sleepless hours, we emerged with a masterpiece.

# CHAPTER 32

It was 6:00am February 27th, when we completed several, nearly perfect rehearsals. Gazing at a crew of totally exhausted, yet jubilant people I proudly said, "Great job, guys! Now let's get some sleep and meet me in the backstage setup area of the Grammies at 2:00pm We'll have to start early, we have almost as much to do setting up for the change in tonight's performance, as we did getting this song ready."

Their faces went white, and as they all gazed in shock at me, my orchestra leader Joe Aiello, came out from the speechless crowd of professional performers to say, "Christina, I mean no disrespect, but this is the Grammies your talking about. Everyone is expecting us to perform the Grammy nominated song, 'Love Grows in the Arms of Peace' tonight. What you're asking us to do is unprecedented, and I'm not sure we can go along with it."

Jimmy jumped in to add, "Not to mention the legal ramifications, or the fact that your professional credibility is on the line."

Pondering their opposition momentarily and realizing they were absolutely correct, I turned toward them all and said, "We're all friends here, so I'm going to be honest. I know what I'm asking you to do for me is historic. But I swear, this means so much to me, I'm willing to stake my reputation on it. So now, I'm asking you all as my friends to help me pull this off!"

Jimmy yelled, "I'm with you, girlfriend!" and simultaneously his sentiments were echoed throughout the room.

That evening's Grammy Awards Ceremony was incredible! Barbara and I were so captivating as the hostesses, we kept the audience filled with the excitement of each moment. With six Grammies already awarded to me for the soundtrack, 'One Voice, One World and Love Enough for All' before it was even my turn to perform my number, it certainly appeared the night belonged to me.

I became so high and confident with each triumphant, self-gratifying, moment of that night; that, I pranced on and off that stage, glowing and gloating like I was the **superstar of superstars**. That was until I received my cue to prepare for my performance. For it was at that moment, I remembered humility and fear, and I thought, 'Oh God! Please don't let this backfire on me.'

Leaving the stage to Barbara, I rushed off to get ready.

Jimmy was pacing nervously when I reached my dressing room. But as usual, in the pinch, he pulled it together and quickly helped me begin to dress in the costume we created only hours earlier. As Jimmy slid the glittering, silver, elastic straps, of the sandal woven silver ankle boots, over clear sheer stockings and attached them to a black bridal garter, I climbed into my skin tight, all lace, silver satin gown that hugged my feminine curves to just past my knees, and of course there was my famous slit up the front. Sewn to the gown were diamond studded hands, which cupped my breasts and held them in the most flattering position. While Jimmy and I did our part, Ann Markle removed the golden turban scarf I wore that evening, to reveal the hidden, one-thousand, individual, strands of diamond braids, which cascaded down the elbow length of my full bodied, dark black, hair. And when topped off with the perfect makeup, I looked like a **goddess** as I headed back to the main stage.

Three minutes later, I was taking a last minute deep breath as I listened for Barbara's cue for the curtain rise. My heart was pounding as I heard Barbara say, "Ladies and gentlemen, as you are aware, my co-host tonight is a woman of many talents, but one of them I know to her dismay is not the ability to stay out of the tabloids. Have you all read of her latest dilemma? The poor dear girl has suffered the embarrassment of having two, extremely attractive men, publicly brawling over her affections. Well, I don't know about you, but I wouldn't mind a dilemma like that for myself!" Once Barbara had them laughing, she continued, "And now, without further ado, I would like to introduce my dear friend and co-host, to perform the Grammy nominated best song of the year, 'Love Grows in the Arms of Peace.' Ladies and gentlemen, please welcome, *Christina Powers*!"

The cheers rang out as the house lights went down. While the curtains went up, the stage lights shone on me to cause my attire to flare-up like the sparks of a comet's tail soaring through the heavens.

**"Da-da-dumm-di-de-dumm!"** Began the orchestra with an unexpected thunder and as the violins rose in unison with an unfamiliar melody, so did the sudden sharp squeals of the now shocked on-lookers.

As the sounds of their displeasure echoed throughout the auditorium, flowing from my heart came the sounds that could subdue the gods, as I began to bare my soul in song to the world.

First, the tempo started smooth and soft, then slowly began to build as I sang, **"I was standing at the door, with tears in my eyes, when you walked away from me, vanishing like a ghost, into a hazy mystery. Leaving me only, lonely and lost! Did you ever care, to count the cost?**

**Now since you've been gone, like my troubled history, I'm living in shadows of solemn misery. But yet I wonder is there a way to make you see, this love of ours is destiny! Then echoes of love ring out in my mind, causing past passions to flair, burning in me everywhere, just to leave me longing and bare, with no one to care.**

**Now I've waited at home, but you wouldn't phone, you've been playing a part, which has wounded my heart. Cause like a fool, I was thoughtless and cruel, never thinking what you went through.**

**Now I know! Oh yes I know, it was our love, that was meant to grow. So I've tried everyday, in the most simple way, to say I love you and ask you to stay. But with each failed attempt, I've driven you further away. Further and further away.**

With my arms rising to accompany the heights of my vocals, **"Now I cling to the memories of passions which once was our love, for the 'thunder, the lightning', that crashed up above. For the wonders, of the heavens, your touch has revealed, and for the fires, of the love, your steps have concealed.**

**That's why I'm singing a plea, oh baby sweet baby come home to me. Darling I fear, without you my dear, this lifetime will crash and burn in despair, leaving us both so empty and bare, with nothing to spare, till neither one of us will be able to care, anymore."**

At this point the tempo slowly drops off, then begins to climb once again and so did the passion of my voice, **"Or was this just a game of love lost! Leaving broken hearts to be tossed, and memories of dreams, floating away on streams! Like shattered bits, of our past lives revealed, blown by the whims of the winds as we sailed, and it scattered our futures till we had to break free, leaving only the remnants of what was to be.**

**So baby.. sweet baby.., say once for me, now and forever, this just can't be! For where once abound love endless and true, now only dwells pain, reserved for the fool. My soul cries in despair, with each moment you're not here, 'cause I know in my heart, we must never part. For it's not destiny, for us to be free, so I'm saving my love, for what I know will be, your love in this lifetime forever with me.** Chorus: **Forever and ever with me.**

I pleaded with my body shaking as I reached for the sky with my voice,

**Oh baby... sweet baby..., bring your love home, and promise oh promise never to roam, for I'll always be here, forever to care. Forever and ever, to care.**

At that point, the symphony takes over like 'thunder and lightning' as the lights and my body movements accompany the rhythm in perfect harmony, to spin a web of passion in an attempt to hypnotize the entire audience. Dramatically everything stops.

This time I lead the tempo of the orchestra's rhythm, as it climbs to the range of my vocals, **"Now I'm lying in bed, with thoughts in my head, I'll fight for the right, to live for the light. The light that is shone, when only you're home. So baby... sweet baby..., forever and ever come home.** accompanied by chorus: **Forever and ever come home!"**

**Or we'll play these love games, time after time, forever and ever, till I make you mine.** {"Chorus: **Forever and ever! my love!"**} **'Cause you' re the spark in my heart, the flame of my soul, and I**

know the power, of the love we share, can conquer the darkness and the pain that dwells here.  So baby...., sweet baby...., won't you come home, bring your love too, take all I am, this whole lifetime through, forever and ever, never to part, forever and ever come unbreak my heart.

Although you say when it's over, one must let it die and never, ever, dare to ask why!  But I refuse to see, our love will not be, not when it's as strong, as the forces of the sea.  `Cause together there's still, mountains to climb, the source of infinity, together we'll find, and the secrets of divinity are yours and mine when we leave our bodies behind.  Then meet in the air, souring high in the sky, where two become one spirit, body and soul, on the wings of our passions, filled with dreams still to grow.   Soaring higher and higher, {"Accompanied by chorus: **Forever and ever my love!**"}

Now the tempo of the rhythm begins vibrating the auditorium, **Oh baby... sweet baby...,** **why can't you see, destiny calls your love back to me.  That's why I won't waste a breath, or shed a tear, if it won't bring your love, near my dear.  For our hearts are pure, and our souls are free, so won't you come dance, a heavenly dance with me.  Above the universe, come climb and see, beyond the hands of time with me.  Where the light we find, will help you see, this love of ours is meant to be.  That's why for your love, there is no shame, so if I must, I'll take all the blame, to bring you back to me, with feelings so free, forever and ever free for me.**  {"Accompanied by chorus: **Forever and ever my love.**"}

Now tears flow down my cheeks as I muster all my strength for the finale, **Now baby..., sweet baby... won't you come to my door, and lay with me, just once more, to taste my love, from its core.**  {"Chorus: **Forever and ever.**"}  **Then I know you'll be mine, and together we'll shine!"**  {"Accompanied by chorus: **Forever and ever my love!**"}

I know there's no way, I can force you to stay.  But I'll put it all on the line, to try and make you mine.  That's why I'm singing a plea, oh baby... sweet baby... come home to me, where we'll forgive and forget, as we soar like the angels and never regret.  {"Accompanied by chorus: **Forever and ever we'll never regret our love!**"}

**I strip away pride, as I vow to stay by your side, now and**

**forever your bride.** {"Chorus: **Forever and ever.**"}

**`Cause there's no mountain of stone, nor a tower of steel, can stand in my way, when I know what's real. Yes I am bold, I've faced bitter cold, but if life's lived without you then our stories untold. So baby..., sweet baby..., save me please save me and don't let our story grow old. Yes I'm down on one knee, where I'm singing a plea, oh baby sweet baby come home to me, and promise oh promise never to flee, forever to care and always be here, forever my love. Now I'll be waiting at home, for you all alone, preparing a place, for you in my space. Where I'll show you a life, without all the pain, where love abounds, despite the rain. For in your eyes I see visions of futures to grow, alive in the heavens forever we'll go, where the stars, in our eyes, forever will glow and the light, of our love, forever will show. Together we'll sow, the seeds of our love and together forever we'll watch from above. Forever and ever I'll give you my love. Forever and ever my love.** {"Slowing tempo. Echoed by chorus."}

**Now I'm singing a plea, where I'm begging you please, bring your love home to me.** {Now slowing to nearly a whisper} **Forever and ever! Michael, my love!**

When I finished singing, the roar of the crowd was deafening. They loved my performance so much; I was given a standing ovation through eight curtain calls. Three of them were before the broadcasts commercial break, with one still continuing when the cameras returned.

Finally, Barbara calmed the audience down enough to say, "Bravo! Christina, that was fabulous, but we wanted last year's nomination, not this year's." And the audience signaled their approval!

At that point, Barbara came back with, "Now, to present the award for best song of the year, please welcome Elizabeth Tyler and Michael Jetson."

Jointly they read the nominees, then Elizabeth opened the-envelope and announced, "And the Grammy goes to *Christina Powers,* for 'Love Grows in the Arms of Peace.'

As the cheering rang out again, I ran onto the stage from behind the curtains, took the Grammy, kissed Elizabeth, then Michael. Turning to the mike I said, "Thank you so much for this evening and your appreciation. Now I just want to say thank you to everyone who helped

make this song what it is and ask for your forgiveness for not performing
'Love Grows in the Arms of Peace' tonight.  But, this was my last chance
to touch the heart of the man I love.  So now, I'm going to take these
precious gifts that were so graciously given to me this evening, and I'm
going home with love in my heart." Looking straight into the camera I
added, "'Cause Michael, my love!  I'm praying you're going to be there."
With that, I blew kisses and waved as I said, "I love you, America!  God
Bless!  And thank you again!" I walked off the stage leaving them
cheering.

# CHAPTER 33

It was 1:00am Pacific time when our flight left L.A. for Stewart Airport, and the whole world knew I was hopefully rushing home to Michael's arms. My emotions were raw and my energies depleted from exposing my soul with such passion, it was all I could do just to get on the jet. Once seated, I placed my head on Jimmy's shoulder and stayed that way almost the entire flight home, without speaking for hours.

As I laid there with Jimmy gently stroking my head, I prayed, "Lord, please let him be home? Because if this doesn't do it, nothing will, and you know how much I love him. Lord, I miss him so desperately, I'm honestly afraid I won't be able to live with the pain, if he's not. So please let him be home when I get there."

But I found no solace, nor comfort in that prayer, because I still feared Michael's seemingly unbendable Irish pride could keep him from coming home to me. Then I decided I'd rather think of Michael being there, and the moment I did, my mind went wild with thoughts of passion.

As I envisioned my thoughts, I began to take notice of the movements of the aircraft which seemed to have been in a circling pattern for quite some time. I glanced at my watch which read 9:00am Eastern Standard time and I thought, 'We should have landed by now?'

Curiosity took over as I sat up, reached to lift the window cover so I might glance out and just as I did, my new pilot, ex-lieutenant Todd Deyo opened the cabin door and said, "Excuse me Ms. Powers, but there has been a slight change in our landing plans."

"Is everything all right with the jet?" I asked in haste, as I quickly stood to my feet.

"The jet's fine Ma'am, it's the weather." He replied calmly. "Snow has been falling heavily over the region for hours now, and the tower at Stewart has rerouted all traffic to LaGuardia. So I'm afraid your arrival home will be delayed for quite some time."

"What?" I snapped with frustration. "I'm not waiting another day to get home! Are we over the airport right now?"

He was surprised by my angered response and I could tell as he cautiously answered, "Yes, Ma'am."

Studying his eyes I asked, "Todd, are you capable of landing this craft in a blizzard?" Without blinking he boldly replied, "Yes, Ma'am!"

I smiled at him confidently, "Good! Then let's go get you clearance."

Jimmy wore a stressed expression as he followed us into the cockpit and watched in silence, as I had Todd radio the tower. Once he had the chief traffic controller on the radio, Todd handed the extra headphone to me.

I clumsily put it on and said, "Hi, this is *Christina Powers*, with whom am I speaking?"

"This is Chief Controller Colonel Jeff Roberts, Ms. Powers. How may I help you?"

"Well Jeff, you could have a runway opened for us so we may land."

A polite yet firm voice replied, "I'm sorry Ms. Powers, but it's been deemed unsafe at this time. That is why your pilot has been ordered to proceed on a new coordinates."

To that I simply replied, "Jeff, forgive me, I'm not normally this abrupt, but if you don't have a runway cleared for us in ten minutes, then I will see that the President hands me your career on a silver platter by this evening. Capiche!?"

Without a crack in his voice he replied, "Completely Ms. Powers, and you may inform your pilot to prepare for decent."

With a pleased tone I replied, "I thank you Colonel Roberts, and I will see that the President thanks you for me as well."

Todd smiled with amazement as he looked at me and said, "You might want to buckle up, this may be a slippery landing."

I studied his eyes once more, "You can handle it, can't you?"

With a confident nod he answered, "Sure thing, Ma'am."

I chuckled and said, "Great, then we'll go make ourselves comfortable, and Todd, please call me Christina. I prefer that to Ma'am, 'cause I'm sure not as old as the word implies." Then I nudged Jimmy whose mouth was on the floor and continued, "It will be fine, Jimmy. Now come on, let's go put our heads between our legs."

A nervous laugh began his come back, "Why, so we can kiss our ass's goodbye?"

"Don't panic I'm only kidding." I replied with a chuckle.

He shook his head and said, "I know you want to get home, but don't you think you might be pushing it."

I smiled devilishly and said, "When have you known me not to push it, Jimmy?" Then turning to my flight crew, I continued, "Now do a good job boy's, 'cause I need to get home."

I reassured Jimmy with a confidant rustling of his hair, as I buckled him in and said, "Lord willing we'll be down safely in ten minutes, so try not to worry."

"Thanks, that helps a lot!" He replied with a nervous look, "I should have stayed at the party with everyone else."

"What? And miss all this fun? That's not like you, Jimmy." I said with a smile as the jet began its descent.

We were doing fine, even laughing as our ears popped on the descent, that was until the tires hit the pavement and Jimmy screamed, "Oh God!" as the jet immediately began a dramatic zig zagging slide down the runway.

It wasn't two seconds before both of us were screaming out prayers as we were forcefully thrown from side to side in our seats for what seemed like an eternity, before finally slowing to a jerky stop. Realizing the danger was over I swallowed my heart, turned to Jimmy who was as white as a ghost, and started to laugh.

As soon as he caught his breath, he slapped my shoulder and shouted, "You think that was funny?"

"No, just ironic!" I answered still laughing, "That little ride made me realize I love life too much to give up on it, even if Michael doesn't come home."

Once unbuckled, I went right into the cockpit to congratulate my crew on a job well done, then I said, "Now would someone please open that door so I can go home."

The moment I saw the intensity of the blizzard we were walking into, I grabbed Jimmy's arm for strength and with a hopeless expression said, "He's not coming back, Jimmy."

"Yes he is, Christina." He answered with a big confident smile.

"No, he's not, Jimmy." I insisted with tears welling in my eyes, "Strangely, I've come to see the weather as the ultimate forecast of things to come in my life. And this storm is telling me to give it up girl, 'cause you don't have a chance in hell of him coming home!"

Jimmy squeezed my shoulder as we walked toward our warmed car and said, "Girlfriend, I know how much Michael loves you, and I know he's going to be there. So stop torturing yourself and I'll have us home in thirty minutes."

I kissed his cheek, "I hope you're right Jimmy, but the weather hasn't lied to me yet."

At that point, we reached the car and began to creep our way through the storm. As Jimmy drove, I pulled an envelope out of my purse, addressed it to Johnny, slipped his grandmother's ring in and had Jimmy stop at the first mailbox. I wrote nothing because there was nothing that needed to be said. Then, as I placed Michaels' ring back on my finger, I thought, 'Whether you come home or not Michael, I will never take this ring off again.'

Jimmy's thirty-minutes turned into an hour and thirty-minutes, before we pulled up to the house. As the large garage door began to open, my heart instantly pained. I turned to Jimmy with tears now streaming down my cheeks and cried, "His cars not here, Jimmy."

Jimmy looked at me before pulling into the garage, and said, "Well his car may not be here, but look who just stepped out onto the front porch."

I turned quickly to see my beautiful man coming toward our car. My heart filled with excitement as I screamed, "Michael!" At that I jumped out of the car without my jacket and dashed through the snow toward him.

My sad tears instantly turned into joyful ones, as I leaped into his arms still screaming, "Michael! Michael! I love you! I love you, baby! I love you! Thank God, you're home!"

"I love you too, Punkie!" He shouted back as he lifted me into his arms. Gazing deep into my eyes he gently continued, "I love you more than life itself, and I'll never leave again, not even in 'death'."

He kissed me with such passion that our souls were instantly whole again, and I knew he was home for good.

I clung to his neck as he held me like a babe in arms, and carried me toward the house. When we reached the door he opened it, and charged up the staircase leaping three steps at a time.

He didn't slow his pace until we entered the bedroom, where he kissed me deeply as he laid me on the bed and softly whispered, "Don't move, Punkie." Then he proceeded to undress.

I watched in loving awe, as this god in the flesh tossed his clothing to the floor one piece at a time. Finally he dropped his last garment, and with the look I'd die for, returned to begin gently undressing me. I couldn't help but to lavish kisses all over his chest as he slipped the gown I still wore from my Grammy performance off my shoulders to expose the now hard nipples of my firm, bare, breasts. As he leaned over to slide the gown from my hips I longingly and softly stroked the rest of his masculine body.

Slipping my last stocking off, he snuggled next to me and with a gentle air of dominance said, "Christina, you're my wife, and I'm proud to tell the world how much I love you. All I ask is that you let me be your husband, not just someone who waits at home."

"Oh, Michael!" I cried as I gazed into his eyes, "I love you, and I'm so sorry! I was blind and foolish Michael, but I'm not anymore! I want you to be my husband Michael, and I'm going to learn how to be your wife. I promise!"

Sliding his leg over mine he said, "Before we go any further, are you still on the pill?"

I lifted my head to kiss him passionately, and lovingly gazing into his eye's said, "No, Michael. I stopped taking them when we stopped making love."

He smiled peacefully and said, "I have a condom, let me get it."

I gently grabbed his hand and with loving conviction said, "Before you do, Michael, I need to say something. There is only one thing that could make my life totally complete right now, and that would be to conceive your child." Taking on an air of certainty I continued, "Please hear me, Michael? I have prayed and meditated nightly for weeks now, in an attempt to heal my body. So that if by the grace of God destiny brought us back together, then I would be able to carry our child. I know in my heart, Michael, that your seed will grow in me and I'll not only give birth, but I'll live through it as well." At that point I couldn't stop my tears as I continued, "Please, Michael plant your soul in mine so we may give birth to an angel."

He kissed me with joyful wonder and said, "I love you and I feel it too, Punkie! Deep in my soul, somehow I know you're healed! So with all my love I will give you my seed, and just like you sang, we'll watch it grow together."

From that moment on we were swept up in a whirlwind of pure passion and unconditional love. I was in heaven, as over and over we shared our love, and we didn't break our embrace until Jimmy came banging on the door shouting, "Hey guys! It's 7:00pm and you have got to get up now! It's urgent!"

**And I thought, 'Oh well, I'll figure it out tomorrow!!' ………….**

www.ingramcontent.com/pod-product-compliance
Lightning Source LLC
Chambersburg PA
CBHW030641110726
47901CB00002B/526